TRAVELER

NOLA NASH

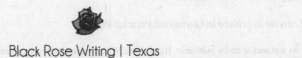

Black Rose Writing | Texas

The author grants the final approval for this literary material.

First printing

This is a work of fiction. Names, characters, businesses, places, events, and incidents are either the products of the author's imagination or used in a fictitious manner. Any resemblance to actual persons, living or dead, or actual events is purely coincidental.

ISBN: 978-1-68433-896-2
PUBLISHED BY BLACK ROSE WRITING
www.blackrosewriting.com

Printed in the United States of America
Suggested Retail Price (SRP) $19.95

Traveler is printed in Garamond Premier Pro

*As a planet-friendly publisher, Black Rose Writing does its best to eliminate unnecessary waste to reduce paper usage and energy costs, while never compromising the reading experience. As a result, the final word count vs. page count may not meet common expectations.

TRAVELER

"Travel is about the gorgeous feeling of teetering in the unknown."
—Anthony Bourdain

CHAPTER 1

There is something satisfying about slamming a snooze button, which is why Shelby Starling refused to use the alarm on her phone. The sound of the little digital clock clattering to pieces on the floor of the cabin was the *other* reason Shelby Starling refused to use the alarm on her phone. Truthfully, it wasn't until the clock hit the mismatched tile that she actually woke up. When you travel for a living, jet lag becomes a constant companion and slapping snooze buttons could be your Olympic sport. As tired as she was, Shelby knew exactly where the payoff was for the bleary eyes and aching back, but she would have to peel herself out of bed to find it.

The tattered blanket she had kicked into a wad on the end of the bed served absolutely no purpose. It couldn't even be said to be there for looks. The threadbare thing wasn't adding anything aesthetic to the place and there was no need for what little warmth the twelve threads may have offered. Had she been slightly less hungover, the wavy tile may not have seemed like a fun house floor as she made her way to the window, whose curtain must have been a very close relative of the blanket. But the squinty-eyed wobbly walk was immediately worth it when she pulled the gauzy drape aside.

"There you are, gorgeous," she whispered as if she could scare away the sight before her by saying it too loud. The bare ocean stretching out as far as she could see was modestly shrouded in the dawn mist. As the sun eased itself over the horizon, the trees exhaled under its warm touch and the mist rose to gently cover the island waking up beneath it. It was this moment that made the alarm clock not seem like such a shithead anymore.

Down the hillside, which was a careless mashup of rock and jungle, was a beach village as haphazard as the cliff that loomed above it. Huts were constructed of whatever rubbish still had some semblance of life in it as determined by whoever happened to find it and haul it to the beach. Where gaps surfaced in the hodgepodge of colorfully painted wavy sheet tin and sundry scrap metal, driftwood came to the rescue to complete the walls that were as bent as the inhabitants. It was weird and wonderful. As warm as it was wacky. The colorful walls were as vibrant as the people who would gather on the white sand in the sunset where there would be music, rum, and storytelling. Mostly rum. There is always rum in the Caribbean. Moses, her Jamaican guide and friend, had welcomed her into his bizarrely beautiful village and given her the hillside shack while she was here. The lopsided box of warped wood had become her sanctuary on an island full of clichés and tourists. Tonight, fires large and small would burn and beer and rum would flow. But today, there was work to do.

Shelby tore herself from the window and looked for something relatively clean to wear. After four days on the island, this was no easy feat. Pushing a t-shirt around with her toe, she came to the exasperating conclusion that laundry would have to be done. She pulled a Rolling Stones tank over her red sports bra, threw on a pair of cut-offs, and stepped into her flip flops once she found the rogue one under the bedside table. Having given up on appearances entirely, she wadded her dark hair into a bun, stuffed a handful of gross clothes into her backpack with her laptop, and headed into the mist.

Air hung close like an insecure boyfriend. Even at dawn, the heat of the island city was oppressive. Only in the areas where the sea breeze cut through the buildings was there any relief. Her head swam from her hangover and she knew if she didn't deal with it soon, the day was really going to suck. The only thing redeeming the stupidly early morning, now that she didn't have the staggering view, was the fact the streets were mercifully under inhabited.

Locals were opening shops in the almost lethargic way islanders do things while tourists slept off hangovers. Shelby was stuck in limbo somewhere between the two. She was up with the locals, but nursing a decidedly tourist reminder of her island overindulgence. With any luck she could get a machine at the laundromat and a cup of coffee before the idiots in Bob Marley dred hats sobered up and filled the streets again.

Luck was on her side and within half an hour Shelby was sipping a cup of Blue Mountain while her clothes washed half a block down from the cafe. She dug her laptop out of her backpack, turned it on, and chanted, "Please let there be wifi, please let there be wifi."

"There be wifi," laughed a woman's voice behind her in a beautiful Jamaican lilt. "And there be more coffee, too." The woman reached a strong ebony hand out and Shelby put her empty cup in it.

"Thanks, Hattie," she said dumping sugar and milk into the dark goodness. Sacrilege, she knew, but she didn't really care.

"I got jus' da ting for dat head, baby. Right back." Shelby opened her mouth to object, but thought better of it. One thing she learned in her time in Ocho Rios was no one talked back to Miss Hattie. All Shelby could do was pray she didn't come back from the kitchen with a plate of ackee and saltfish. There was no way she was going to keep fish and eggs down. Mercifully, Hattie returned with a bowl of curry chicken stew and a dish of johnnycakes. "Eat dat. All of it."

Shelby popped a piece of johnny cake into her mouth and logged on. Hattie was right; there was wifi. Internet connection in the islands was sketchy at best, which could be great or irritating depending on what you needed it for. One of the upsides when wifi was playing hard to get was you had digital permission to lose yourself in the island life until you stumbled upon a working connection. One of the cons was it made it increasingly difficult to meet deadlines. As Shelby was a travel writer for Pioneer Tours, this could be an issue since everything she did was online from communication with the office in the States to writing her submissions for the promotional material. Signal was better in the thick tourist areas, but she was steering clear of those until later. Until she had to go be a tourist herself.

"Can't be dat bad, girl," Moses laughed as he sat down in the booth across from her. "Hattie's not da best cook on dis island, but I never seen a face like yours over it."

Hattie popped Moses on the back of the head as she set his coffee cup on the table. "Shut ya mouth."

Shelby laughed. "You know, Moses, talking like that about your wife's cooking could be bad for you."

"Don't ya know!" Hattie snorted. "Keep it up, and don' come lookin' for any tonight!" With a grin and a wink at Shelby, Hattie went back to the kitchen to fix another bowl of stew for Moses.

He took a slow sip of his coffee and smiled at Shelby. "Well, if it's not da cookin' causing dat frown, what's got ya?"

Shelby sat back and sighed. "A hangover. Mostly." Moses raised an eyebrow but didn't push her for more. If Shelby was honest with herself, and she rarely was, there was more bothering her. Somewhere inside, hidden beneath a facade of false bravado, was an insecure child. She had a dream job, traveling the world on someone else's dime and writing about it, but she couldn't really appreciate it. No matter where she went in the world, she was lost. No matter how many places she knew inside out and backwards, she knew nothing about herself and what she wanted. She was adrift like a ship that had lost its anchor long ago and had given up searching for it. Shelby was welcome in so many places, but wasn't at home in any of them. Something was always a little off and she had no idea why. "Maybe I just need to figure out how to get my shit together better," she sighed again.

"Maybe ya need betta shit," Moses laughed.

Shelby laughed with him. Who was she kidding? She was a mess. A glorious avalanche of emotion and chaos. She had always been and would always be. Muddling through life was becoming an art form. Maybe she did just need better shit.

Her email was slowly loading as she picked at the curry stew. She had made short work of the johnny cakes, which seemed to please Hattie, but every time she passed the table Hattie tisked at her and tapped the table urging her to eat more. "Is there voodoo in this stuff?" Shelby whispered at Moses then shoved a forkful into her mouth.

He winked and answered, "There's no tellin' with dat woman. All I know is ya betta get it down. Besides, ya need ya strength t'day."

Shelby groaned. Thanks to the judgement erasing effects of her evening, she was not in peak condition for the work of the day. Ocean kayaking and climbing the Falls. Cliche Day. All that would be missing to make this the most touristy day possible on the island was one of those damned dred hats. One would be hard pressed not to find a tourist who had been to Jamaica who didn't have a picture of themselves sunburned and half submerged in one of the pools of Dunn's River Falls. Her boss, Dina, insisted the experience be part of the tour description and wanted photos of her doing it. Sure, it would have been easy to write vicarious experiences of something so typical, but Dina was a stickler for authentic travel writing so she would have to suck it up and do it. Admittedly, Dina's authenticity often meant Shelby got to do some things that were cool as hell. Climbing the Falls with a hangover wasn't one of them. The only good parts of the whole ocean kayaking and Falls climbing thing would be the cold beer waiting for her at the top and the jeep ride home. That in itself was not something for the faint of heart. The Jamaican backroads hardly qualified as actual roads and she was certain there was no driving test to be passed to drive on the island.

"What time do we leave?" she asked Moses.

"We join da cruise ship group at ten and t'irty minutes to get dere. Ya got an hour."

Shelby nodded, slung back the last swallow of coffee, and opened the email from her boss. Inside was her new itinerary. One more day in Jamaica to tie up loose ends then a mercifully late morning flight out to start writing experiences for Pioneer's new tour collection: The Magical History Tours. Punny. Very punny. Dina explained there would be more details coming, but the gist was a tour of each place focusing primarily on the historical places and legends. The name might have been stupid, but at least this new tour collection promised to be more genuine than some of the others Pioneer had done. Like this one of Jamaica.

"As soon as my laundry is done, I'm ready when you are."

Moses nodded and ate the last of the johnny cakes on her plate. Shelby left money for her breakfast and headed back to the laundromat for her clothes.

Tourists in bathing suits, sunglasses, and wide-brimmed straw hats poured down the gangplanks of the luxury cruise liner which all but filled the opening to the bay. The water was a gorgeous turquoise and the rocks a few meters below the surface looked as if you could put your hand in and touch them. Small fish darted in and out of crevices unfazed by the gargantuan boat nearby. Cameras and phones covered faces of people trying desperately to digitally preserve the majesty of the island mountains rising up in front of them. Even Shelby had to admit it was something to behold. Much of the city of Ocho Rios rimmed the beach and moon-shaped bay to make the most of the financial influx from the cruise ships. Deeper inland was where life really existed, but Shelby and Moses were here to be tourists. Groups from the ship split off as they made their way down the main pier towards the town and beach. Some stopped off at party boat docks or deep-sea fishing boats. With a nod to the shore excursion guide, she and Moses fell into step behind the group headed for the ocean kayaking launch point.

Soon, the bright yellow kayaks came into view. The Caribbean Sea was calm and clear making the boats look like bananas hovering slightly over a beach. Only the occasional ripples and shimmer gave away the fact that they were actually floating. The calm sea would make the paddling easier, and less rocking was a welcome thing for her head which was still reminding her of bad life choices with a dull throbbing behind her temples. Stretching out in front of them toward the deep blue horizon was a row of white markers guiding the boats straight out over the shallows toward the azure blue of the deeper water.

"I'll take da back so ya can see everyt'ing betta," offered Moses as they climbed carefully into their tiny craft.

"Think this thing is really seaworthy?" Shelby asked.

Moses laughed. "It'll take ya along the coast on a day like dis, but I'm not t'inkin' I'd want it in a hurricane."

"Fair enough."

As they began the slow paddle out towards deeper water, Shelby had to admit it really wasn't so bad. "I'm starting to see why this is so popular. Not bad." Moses snorted a laugh in reply and the two paddled on. Over to their right, a pair of sunscreen-slathered people were paddling in a slow circle arguing about which one of them was responsible for paddling out of sync. One of the Jamaican guides effortlessly slid his kayak up to them and began sorting things out and getting them back on track. As he headed back to his place in the group, the guide shot an eye-rolling grin to Moses. Shelby wondered how many times the poor man had to be a marital mediator as well as paddle guide. Before them was an interesting display of the human experience. Most were frantically trying to stay close to the group and missing the beautiful island vistas on one side of them and the sapphire water on the other. There were frantic shouts of "you're pushing us out to sea!" and squeals of girls who almost lost their paddles in the ocean. The people who had never been picked for the dodgeball team in PE were trying to look more athletic than they really were and not fooling anyone in their heroic efforts. Then, there were the ones who were already out of breath and silently questioning their decision or cursing their travel companion who convinced them this was a good idea. The genuinely athletic were cruising to the front of the group and settling into the scenery around them. After some time of adjustment, everyone seemed to find their own personal groove and the trip up the coastline became an ironic blend of relaxing hard work.

As Moses took over the paddling periodically, Shelby was able to get some good photos of the experience and the beauty around her. She reveled in her cynicism about tourists, but she had to admit to herself that she was wrong about this excursion. This was worth the early morning and Hattie's hangover cure. After a while, the group pulled their kayaks in for a break on an empty beach surrounded by a jungle that climbed the mountainside.

Dangling in one of the trees was a dark local. He wore a striped tank in the traditional Jamaican colors and cut-offs. His bare feet braced against branches kept him perched above the gawking newcomers. Dreds stuck out all over his head as haphazard as the person they were attached to. Casually, he asked the tourists pausing under his tree if they wanted ganga. Shelby and Moses watched the tourists' reactions ranging from outward shows of shock to sanctimonious disgust, but knew at least half were curious and a few were giving the offer serious consideration.

After twenty minutes of sunning and resting, the boats launched back out to the deep water with only slightly less cacophony than the first time. The pull of the sea was incredible. Not a physical pulling on the boat, but a pulling on her soul. Shelby could see why so many pirates and fortune-hunters were drawn to the aquamarine expanse. There was a magic in the unbroken vista stretching out to the horizon and beyond. Adventure lay out there. Not scripted tour adventure. Real adventure. Shelby could almost hear the sea whispering to her, '*Come away with me. Let me show you where you belong.*' She had almost made up her mind to run off to become a pirate when the Dunn's River Beach came into view ahead on her left.

Moses pulled the kayak in so Shelby could take more pictures of the beach and base of the Falls. The jungle drew back from the beach like lush drapes and revealed the waters of the termination of Dunn's River as it tumbled headlong down to the sand and sea below. Rather than a crashing cascade like Niagara, the many levels and pools of the Falls broke the speed and ferocity of the water to something one could actually navigate on foot. Shelby stood at the base of the river and looked from the Falls to the swath of beach and sea on the other side. "No wonder Ian Fleming fell in love with this place." Maybe if she stood there long enough, she'd find her own James Bond, but there was a climb to make.

Moses stood beside her and gazed up at the Falls and people starting to make the climb. "Pick ya poison," he said with a grin. Shelby wasn't really into close personal contact with strangers, so she opted for the solo climb over the human chain.

Before long, they made it halfway up the climb stopping along the way to indulge in some of the pools, letting their shoulders be massaged by the water rushing over the smooth rock above. If she closed her eyes, Shelby could almost tune out the squeals of the tourists and shouts of the climb guides to picture what this place would be like if she had it to herself. *I wonder what this place is like in the dead of night*, she thought trying to imagine the peace of the Falls and the sea entwined in a nighttime serenade.

By the time she and Moses made it to the craft village at the top of the Falls, Shelby had plenty of experiences and photos for her piece on the excursion as well as proof for Dina that her writing would be authentic. As she popped the lime into her Red Stripe, she determined the frosty brew was a Jamaican cliché she was happy to endorse.

CHAPTER 2

People watching is never better than at an airport, especially an international airport. Near one of the windows paced a man checking the old analog clocks ticking above the gate desk then looking out at the airport baggage team on the tarmac. With the amount of time remaining before his posted departure time, he couldn't have been worried about missing a plane. Shelby imagined the man to be trying to determine if this dingy island airport terminal was where he wanted to spend the last hour of his life before he crashed to the earth in a fireball of mangled metal and jet fuel that he was certain would be the result of this tempting of fate and gravity called air travel.

Another corner of the terminal contained a harried couple of eastern Europeans and their small children. The blonde hair of the little ones was a sharp contrast to their sunburns. As they ran circles around their parents who were trying desperately to conceal an argument, suddenly the picture of the old Coppertone kid ads popped into Shelby's mind and she barely choked back a snort of laughter. These real-life Coppertone kids were a lot more believable than the cherub on the bottle of suntan oil. They were far more entertaining, too, at least to Shelby. Most of the other passengers were already dreading the flight to Miami with the rambunctious pair of sunburned spark plugs.

As the plane took off and the blue mountains of Jamaica faded into the ocean below, Shelby settled in and rested her head on the window. Most of the conversation around her was about how hard it was to leave paradise and return to the real world, but there was no such destination for Shelby. Her reality was one trip after another with no real home to return to. The studio apartment in Queens had been given up about six months ago and her few belongings and clothes were in a storage unit waiting unenthusiastically for her return.

Even with the transient qualities of her life, under all the sarcasm and snark, she did like the work and the travel. Flying by the seat of her pants from one place to another suited her and her wanderlust. Nowhere, not even the flat in the Lower East Side where she grew up, ever felt like home. Maybe she hoped somewhere out there was a place that wouldn't feel like it belonged to someone else, anyone else than her.

Eventually she nodded off despite the noise of the engines and the intermittent squealing of one of the Coppertone kids. By the time the plane landed in Miami, she was rested and the Coppertone parents were more haggard than ever. Settling down and having kids was not winning in the life-goal contest.

She had waited until she was on the international flight to think about her next assignment and the email from Dina. Now, there was someone who knew who she was and Shelby wanted to hate her for it. She wanted to hate her for her statuesque build and striking features, but Dina was just so damned likeable. Try as she might to find something wrong with the woman, all Shelby could criticize was Dina's insistence on authentic experiences. Even that quality wasn't all bad. By day, Dina was an executive in an office on 42nd. By night, she was a bohemian in a kimono on a rooftop sipping a glass of prosecco. She had no trouble keeping her worlds apart and being genuine at the same time. It was spellbinding to Shelby who had no idea what one side of her was really about much less a multifaceted existence.

As she sipped her rum and Coke in the tiny airline cup with too much ice, she looked over the itinerary for the first of the Magical History Tours. Rome. Not having anything but tank tops, flip flops, and cut-offs, Shelby's first stop would have to be shopping. Most people would look forward to a shopping spree in Rome, but she didn't have the budget for Italian designers and would be shopping in one of the plaza markets. Those suited her more anyway. She had a feeling if she tried to walk into one of those swanky Italian boutiques she would be stepping right into a scene from *Pretty Woman*.

"Ciao, bella," Benito said with a wink. He slid into the chair across the trattoria table and held a finger up to the waiter across the room.

"Ciao, Benny." Shelby didn't return the wink even though every fiber of her being ached to encourage the flirtation. The last time she had seen Benito Moretti, he had been asleep in her bed and she was sneaking out for a flight. A week of touring with Benny and a month on the road caught up with her at the bottom of a bottle of chianti. There had been so much about the night that had been right, but so much that was very, very wrong. "Listen, Benny, about last trip..."

"Bella, I forgot already, but if you want me to remember again, you tell me, okay?" Benito laughed and winked again. He couldn't forget that night and Shelby knew it.

The waiter arrived and Benny ordered red wine with a plate of prosciutto and grilled artichokes. Shelby looked down at her pasta and knew what was coming.

"Still eating that American shit?" Benny asked eyeing her plate of spaghetti and meatballs. "They only keep it on the menu for tourists."

"I haven't been in Rome long enough to go native, yet," she replied defiantly slurping up a long noodle. "And you weren't here to tell me what was good."

"Anything but spaghetti. You learn nothing, bella."

"I learn. I just like spaghetti."

The waiter and Benny exchanged looks as his plate of authentic Roman fare was set down across from Shelby's sacrilege. Benny's plate was simple elegance. Slices of meat which put the paper-thin pieces of salted pork in the States to shame and quartered artichokes grilled to soft creamy perfection with a drizzle of rich olive oil. She had to admit his plate looked a lot better than the bane of Italian grandmas she was eating.

"So, we go to the Colosseum today? I guess you can have your tourist meal, then." Benny grinned at her over the rim of his wine glass.

Shelby half-rolled her eyes. "Yes, it's a tourist place, but it's the freaking Colosseum. Can't not go there on a Magical History Tour." She shoved a meatball into her mouth and asked, "Do you even notice it anymore?"

Benny shrugged. "It's hard to miss, but I don't stop and stare at it like 'wow, it's amazing how old that thing is!'"

"I guess if you stopped and gawked at every old thing in Rome, you'd never get anything done."

"Something like that." Benny paused. "Do *you* notice it anymore?"

It was a pointed question and Shelby knew Benny wasn't talking just about ancient Roman ruins. They had been down this road before. "It's my job to notice it all. I just don't feel it like the tourists do. They come here because they want to.

Some have saved for years to get here. It's just my job. I don't get to go where I want and do what I want. It's not my vacation. It's work. But, yes, I do look at the Colosseum and think, 'Damn, that thing's old!'"

"There's more to the world than you let inside of you," Benny said quietly.

The heat of the day was lost in the shaded alleys and streets too narrow for the cars trying to go down them much less with the bistro tables set outside every little trattoria on the block. Shelby followed Benito through a maze of buildings and plazas. She only vaguely knew where she was even though she had been to Rome only a year before. It seemed like eons ago and she had forgotten everything she knew about the city. Unlike New York, there were no skyscrapers to use as landmarks to navigate, so she was at the mercy of her knowledge of the plazas and Roman history, which was meager at best.

When the buildings finally parted and a crosswalk appeared, Shelby stepped out into the street only to be yanked immediately back again by Benny as a scooter raced past her. The woman in a skirt suit, stilettos, and a bike helmet took offense and beeped at her, shouting something less classy than her outfit over her shoulder. "What the hell was that about?" Shelby asked, her inner New Yorker raging. "It's a crosswalk!"

Benny laughed. "Shelby, bella, lines on the road are more just. suggestions."

Shelby composed herself a bit and mumbled, "You'd think I'd feel more at home here."

On the plaza outside of the Colosseum, groups of visitors gathered for their tours taking pictures and half-listening to their guides' instructions. In twenty minutes, these same people would be wandering away and getting indignant with Italian guards who would insist they stay with the group. The 2000-year-old fractured majesty beside them was mesmerizing and none of them cared about the rules of engagement at an international treasure any more than Roman scooter chicks cared about crosswalks. Shelby stared at the beautiful monstrosity and couldn't help but feel in awe of it. Which was weird. She had been here before and she thought the thrill of seeing something from her history textbooks standing hugely before her would have been lessened some. There seemed to be more to it, though. She had felt this feeling before, but it wasn't standing here. She had felt it that day on the kayak. The pull of the sea on her soul felt a lot like this.

"You ready, Shelby?" Benny asked breaking the reverie.

"As I'll ever be. Which group?" she asked surveying the choices on the plaza.

Benny laughed and took her hand. "No group. Just you this time. Time to really discover this place."

"Seriously?"

"Seriously. Come, bella, I'll show you the real Colosseum." Benny led her past the gate attendant with a nod and a smile and the chaos of the gathering tour groups faded away. The heat of the afternoon dissolved in the coolness of the travertine surrounding her. "This way." Benito turned in the opposite direction from all of the tour groups and walked down one of the corridors.

Through the arches, Shelby could see the layers of the ancient structure as they had been excavated by archaeologists. The last time she had been in the Colosseum, the exterior had been loosely covered in plastic wrap and a web of metal scaffolding. Now, the renovations were complete and the fragile shell was preserved for future generations. "It's beautiful. It must be a fortune in travertine."

Benny chuckled. "Common stuff."

"It's a fortune in the States. Everyone wants travertine floors so they can be as swanky as the ancient Romans." Shelby knew enough about the stone native to the area. It was beautiful and that's why the American designers loved it. It was Italian, so the importers could charge a pretty penny for it. It was also relatively fragile, which was not something the ancient Romans were thinking about when they built the massive structure out of it. Common and easy to quarry. That was all that mattered at the time. After thousands of years, time had taken its toll on the stone and it began crumbling away endangering the structural integrity.

Benny led Shelby on a private tour of the ruin that would have given her college history professor a hard on. While the tour groups were confined to an overview of the layers in the depths of the Colosseum, Shelby was led through the maze of dirt, stone, and ancient concrete. Benny's knowledge of the monument he barely noticed was as expansive as the building. Most of the time, Shelby had no idea where she was, but occasionally, the Roman sky would peek through and she could get her bearings from the shape of the facade rising above her. The depth of the place was immense and she was finally seeing what Benny meant at the cafe. There was much more to this place than she had let in before.

Shelby stood at the edge of the passageway and looked out at the layers of the building. Even with sections chipped away by time and wars, the walls were all-encompassing. Stone rose into the sky and enveloped her from all sides, yet it wasn't cold like the neglected shell of an English castle. There was warmth here. The Italian sun warmed the stones and created a feeling which was anything but dead and old. The place almost hummed with history and romance. There was drama in the very walls.

"There is much here to move even you, Shelby," Benny said quietly. She realized he had brought her to this remote part of the place on purpose. "Let it speak to you." Benny walked away from her to let her have a moment with the history around her.

As ridiculous as it felt, if she was going to write an authentic experience of the history of this place, this was a good way to start. Shelby drank in the smells around her. Dirt and the aromas of the street vendor food carts out front blended together in a rustic scent which was unmistakably Roman. Ostentatious oldness and humble deliciousness collided in the air itself. The sounds of the traffic. The air brakes of the busses pulling up to unload a new group. Vendors hawking their wares. Tour guides calling out to their groups. The childish beeping of scooters and Fiats.

Shelby closed her eyes to take in the sensuality of it all and put her hand on the wall to balance herself. When her palm made contact with the hard stone, an electric shock surged up her arm. A blinding white light engulfed her and she tried to yank her hand back but couldn't. It was as if she was being electrocuted and couldn't release the live wire. As her senses cleared, she began to smell things that were different than before. The dirt smell was stronger and there was something more savage in the air. Sweat. And the metallic smell of blood. The ringing in her ears subsided and she heard shouting. Not the individual voices of the street vendors and pissed off scooter drivers, but throngs of people shouting at once. The ground shook with the noise. It was as if the whole colossus pulsed with the voices and movements of the bodies inside. The building was alive. Gone was the dead ancient shell of a place. The Colosseum was spectacular and fearsome at once.

As the crowd surged forward, Shelby looked down where layers of exposed stone had been only an instant before. Now, there was an ocean of dirt and men with swords and shields. Gladiators. *Gladiators? What the hell?* Shelby thought. Frantic, she looked around for Benny. He was gone. *Where did he go? He was right there!*

She watched in horror as the men on the dirt floor circled each other. They lunged and parried, swirling away from one another and crashing back together. The morbid dance went on and grew in its terrible beauty as the crowd cheered. One stab missed its mark and the crowd turned on the fighter. Angry voices and waving arms from the fans. Coins changed hands in the stands as bets were made. Gambling with the lives of the men in the pit. For a moment, Shelby thought she saw sadness flash across the face of one of the fighters. He had the upper hand. The gladiator was going to have to strike a lethal blow and he didn't want to. If he did, he killed someone he trained with and lived with. Maybe even a friend. If he didn't, he would be killed. A life for a life. He had no choice. With his sword raised and the blade shimmering with blood in the Roman sun, the gladiator crashed into the other and struck him in the heart.

Romance novelists write moments like these as heroic and sexy. The barely clothed mass of muscle strikes a daring blow and ends the fight in glory and sweat, with one foot on the body of the fallen enemy. What Shelby witnessed was no romance novel. As the blade sank into the man's chest, blood spurted out and the fallen gladiator let out a sickening gurgle. Blood trickled out of his mouth as he stumbled backwards, then sank to his knees. His opponent watched as a man in a gold wreath crown stood in the first tier Podium. He was surrounded by fat old men and beautiful women Shelby assumed were the Vestal Virgins. The remaining fighter knew what had to be done. He pulled a dagger from the sheath on his leg and slit the throat of the man with the sword sticking in his chest. Blood gushed and Shelby fainted.

"Bella! Shelby!" Benny was kneeling over her cradling her head on his arm. He had caught her before she split her head open hitting the stone floor, but was struggling to wake her.

Shelby's eyes fluttered open and Benny smiled down at her. "My hand," she whispered.

"Your hand? You faint and worry about your hand?" Benny sat her up and held her pale face in his hands. "Bella, what happened?"

Shelby struggled to find words. She felt like she was losing her mind. Where was she? *When* was she? "My hand," was all she could get out. The palm of her hand that had touched the Colosseum wall tingled and burned. In her stupor, she was certain she had been electrocuted.

Benny turned her hand over in his. "Nothing wrong with your hand. Maybe the heat is too much for you. Drink this." Benny pulled a water bottle from her bag and made sure she drank it down.

Shelby did as he asked simply because she could think of nothing else to do. *What the hell was that?!* was all she could think. She stared up at him trying to make sense of what had just happened. "How long was I out?"

"Maybe thirty seconds. Seemed like forever."

"I saw-" She stopped. What exactly was it she saw? How could she explain it?

"What? What was it you saw?" Benny asked gently. In this moment, all flirtation and Latin heat was gone. He was worried about her.

Shelby slowly explained all she experienced from the moment her hand touched the wall. She knew he wouldn't believe her, but she needed to say it all out loud. Maybe saying it to someone would help it stay in her head. As heinous as it was, she didn't want to forget any of it. Something about the whole thing felt important and she didn't want to lose it. "When the gladiator was about to make the final strike to kill the other, I felt my heart break for him. I don't understand it," she finished.

"A man died. Anyone with a soul would feel pain for that."

Shelby shook her head. "No, there was more to it. More powerful. More personal. It was like I knew the man who had to kill him. Like I -"

"Loved him?" Benny asked finishing her thought.

Shelby nodded. Her head swam and the vast monument she was sitting in began to feel close and claustrophobic. Part of her wanted to touch the wall again just to see what would happen, but most of her was sure she couldn't bear to see it again. She rubbed her hand trying to ease the tingling, but it didn't do any good. As badly as it hurt, there was not a single mark on it. A bolt of lightning had passed through her hand and shot up her arm into her brain and there was nothing to show for it. She looked at the wall. No wires, no lightning. Nothing but cold lifeless ancient stone. No, not cold. Not lifeless. Just ancient. And somehow, very much alive.

Benny helped Shelby to her feet and held on to her hand. "Maybe we've seen enough for one day. You need rest." Shelby nodded and they slowly and silently made their way back to the street.

※

Watching the sunrise in Rome wasn't something Shelby had ever done intentionally. Once, on her last trip, she had seen the sun turn the gray dawn stone of the old town to a warm orange glow, but she had been too trashed to appreciate it. Her ears had rung with the residual noise of techno from the disco she had spent three hours and half a bottle of rum in. She didn't remember much of that night, but she did remember the look on Benny's face as she hooked her arm around his friend Antonio's waist and began the weaving stagger back to her room. Benny knew what would happen when they got there, and as much as he didn't want to say anything to her, his face spoke volumes. But Benny was wrong. Sure, Antonio got her into bed, but as soon as she hit the sheets, she was at the sickening mercy of the bed spins. Tony left that part out of the story he told Benny and it wasn't until her last night in town the story was set straight.

The sunrise on this trip was different. So much was different this time. One of the few places Shelby could get to on her own was the Piazza di Trevi. The thing was hard to miss. During the day, there was no way to get through the throngs of people with cameras held high above their heads trying to get the perfect shot of the Baroque masterpiece. At dawn, though, it was quiet. Shelby laid on the edge of the Trevi Fountain and let her hand that still tingled from the Colosseum wall dangle into the water. She looked up at Neptune standing on his seashell and watched the sun coming over the huge building start to bring his face to life. She was exhausted, confused, and perpetually lost. Sleep had been an asshole all night. Luring her in only to chew her up and spit her back out with nightmares of bleeding gladiators being burned to a crisp by rogue lightning. So, she wandered around from the hotel to the plaza and back. And then again. And she drank. Then, wandered some more. She had seen the lights go on and illuminate the final destination of the Aqua Virgo with its spectacular carvings. She had seen the lights go off again. And now, she had seen the sun rise.

Over and over, Shelby had placed her palm flat on the side of the fountain but there was no electrocution and weird visions. She wasn't yanked back in time. Just a cold wet palm. She had gone over the experience at the Colosseum time and again. Was it some freak of heat exhaustion? Dehydration? Jet lag? No. None of that seemed right. It was...a memory.

As the thought slowly dawned on her, she opened her eyes and saw Benny standing over her with a cappuccino in his outstretched hand. She smiled sleepily up at him. A sexy silhouette against the rising sun. The more time she spent with Benny, the more she understood how that night happened. "Morning."

"It is," he answered handing her the cup as she pulled herself up and swung her legs down. "Sleep well, bella? You look like hell."

"Spent the night with Neptune. He knows how to show a girl a good time."

"He's Roman, so..." Benny laughed, but his eyes kept their cautious observation of her.

Shelby and Benny sat on the edge of the fountain sipping their coffee until the crowds began to press into the piazza. More tour groups and guides began to descend on what had been a quiet sanctuary moments before. Empty and dark, the piazza had felt open and free. It didn't take long for Shelby to become jealous of Agrippa and his commanding view from the top of the monument far from the crush of the crowds.

Benny again led Shelby through the narrow streets stopping in at a local bakery to get something to soak up what was left of Shelby's midnight tour of the Roman bar scene. Shop owners were cranking open awnings and sweeping front stoops. Small handcart wagons of fresh produce were parked in corners where the streets turned. Women shouted what sounded like insults at each other across the alleys from upstairs windows. Benny shouted back up at one of them and sent them into peals of laughter. One of them threw a dishrag down at him and playfully slammed the window shut. It was his world and Shelby was carried along in his wake. By the time they reached the Pantheon, she had let some of the night terrors fade and was at least able to appear more under control than she felt.

The Fountain of the Pantheon always seemed oddly comical to Shelby. There were dolphins on either side of Romulus' head with an obelisk of Ramses II rising above. As a tribute to the founding place of Rome by Romulus, that part made sense. Although, it seemed the Egyptians were given unbalanced credit for the columns gracing the front porch of the ancient dome. Of course, the really amusing part was the dolphins. Not really something Shelby ever associated with Rome. "Hello, boys," she said patting the sea creatures on the heads as she passed.

"So, no electric fountains today?" Benny asked.

"Nope. Must be something wrong with your fountains. I figured if anything was going to electrocute me, it would be something full of water." Sarcasm only barely veiled the seriousness she was struggling against. It was ludicrous to think what she experienced the day before was real and even crazier to think it would happen again.

"Makes sense," Benny shrugged.

Benny sat on the edge of the fountain to give Shelby time to take some pictures of the exterior before leading her through the tour groups and wandering tourists. Navigating was tricky since tourists spent most of their time looking up with their mouths half-open. They were so immersed in the ancients they seemed to forget all about the living breathing people around them trying to get past.

Shelby tentatively stepped over the Pantheon threshold. Something here put her on edge, but not in an anxious way. It felt more like anticipation, like standing on a street corner waiting for a parade to pass, but she had no idea why. So much history filled the building that it almost pulsed with it like the Colosseum had yesterday, and she wasn't sure it was a sensation she wanted to feel again. Benny put a hand on her shoulder. "Bella, you okay?"

Shelby nodded. "Yes." No.

"No more tour groups this trip. Just us. I'll show you *my* Roma." Benny smiled.

Shelby wasn't stupid. She knew there was no romantic notion about her falling madly in love with him or his city. Benny was worried about another episode and didn't want her to have one in the middle of a crowd. She almost loved him for it.

The Pantheon dome swept up over her head completely unsupported. This ancient feat of engineering was awe-inspiring even to jaded travel writers. Standing in the center of the original ancient marble floor, she began to feel very small. "It really is incredible that it hasn't come crashing down," she said quietly.

"It is well designed. Perfect proportions."

"Like a Roman goddess," Shelby laughed.

Benny nodded. "Or a god. The ancients weren't as particular."

The monument created to honor all gods began by the Emperor Hadrian was indeed a monument to religion. Being in continuous use since its completion gave it a tremendous sense of purpose. It also helped to preserve the spectacular temple. Originally built to honor pagan gods, it was given to the Christians in 609 AD, which also helped keep the place from being looted for building material like the Colosseum had been. "Hadrian outdid himself on this one."

"Come, bella, there's more to the Pantheon than standing in the middle of the floor." Shelby pulled her gaze away from the massive dome and followed Benny to the edge of the room. Standing against the columns, she began to feel small and insignificant again. Anticipation washed over her in a sickening wave this time. The walls and columns seemed to sway like drunks trying to pretend to their wives they haven't been out drinking with the boys. Almost steady, but just a little too loose. But these things were made of stone that had stood for almost 2000 years. They weren't going anywhere. Shelby was. She sank against a massive stone column as the room closed in around her. Without thinking, she put her hand against the stone behind her.

White light blinded her again and a surge shot up her arm. *God damn it! Not again!* She tried to yank her hand away from the stone, but it didn't budge. Soon, like before, the white light began to dissipate into a mist and finally vanish. She blinked hard and looked around but hardly recognized the room she was standing in. The floor was the same, but the walls were richly gilded with intricate bronze work. Gold glinted off of some of the gilded panels and columns that drew her eyes upwards to the center of the dome. Blue sky shone through the oculus in the center and sunlight pierced through the perfectly round hole shining in a blinding burst against the polished metal on the walls. Dust danced like fairies along the sunbeam and down to the floor. Gone were the church furnishings. Gone were the gaping tourists. In their place were somber looking men murmuring prayers standing in a circle around someone at the center of the marble floor. In the distance, outside, there was a crowd shouting again, but different than the bloodthirsty rage of the Colosseum. There was music playing and singing among the shouts. It sounded a lot like a parade. There was an energy out there that was bordering on frenzied. Inside, there was a more serious atmosphere. Something big was brewing.

As the sunbeam sank lower on the wall nearing the tops of the huge bronze doors, the praying of the priests around the man in the center of the room intensified. Impassioned Latin chants rose and echoed inside the dome. Singing in rich harmony soared through the gleaming oculus to the gods themselves. Religious power seemed to surge out of the men as the song and chanting crescendoed. As if it was a well-rehearsed movement, the priests broke formation and opened into a horseshoe to allow the figure in the center to have a clear path to the doors. Shelby stared at the man from the shadow of the column she was being held to. It was the same man who had ordered the death of the gladiator in the Colosseum.

As the man strode slowly to the door, he looked up at the sunbeam, studying it and adjusting his steps. The beam sank even lower on the doors and the rim of the golden circle was almost to the bottom of the bronze panels. The emperor slowed his steps and came to a stop in front of the closed doors as the bottom edge of the light brushed the marble. As it did, the doors were flung open and he stepped onto the threshold with his arms open wide.

Again, the frenzied crowd surged forward and Shelby could see the glint of metal flash in the open doorway as a bodyguard drew his sword against the advancing horde. The wave of flesh fell back and the emperor was left to stand alone in the doorway. From Shelby's perspective, he was silhouetted in the brilliant sunlight and could easily have been taken as a god himself. The sunlight shifted slightly and the gold on the doors flashed a blinding light into her eyes. She sank against the column, catching a glimpse of her own sandaled feet before the white light engulfed her vision.

CHAPTER 3

After many reassurances to the people around Shelby that she would be fine, Benny helped her back out onto the piazza and into a cab.

"Where are we going?" she asked, rubbing her tingling palm. She was groggy as if she had been yanked out of sleeping off a night of hard partying.

"Tuscolano," Benny answered and gave an address to the driver.

"Why?"

"Answers."

Shelby wasn't sure what Benny hoped to find in Tuscolano and she didn't give a shit at this moment. Her night of hanging out with Neptune and Agrippa coupled with the Emperor's ceremony was taking a toll on her body and her sanity. She laid her head back on the cab seat and Benny let her drift for a few minutes. Again, sleep was a jerk and decided she needed a high-speed mash-up of everything she had seen in her visions. Giving up on the idea of ever sleeping again and resigning herself to being the founding member of the zombie apocalypse, she sat up to face Benny.

He smiled wanly. His worry was showing. "What was it this time?" he asked softly.

"It was a ceremony for the emperor. Same guy." Benny looked at her expectantly. "I have no idea what was happening. The Pantheon was shining. There was metal and gilding all over the place. Not the marble on the walls. The floor was the same marble, but the rest was flashier somehow." She told him about the priests, the singing, and the fervor of the crowd outside. It wasn't until she mentioned the light on the bronze doors that some hint of recognition crossed his face.

"April 21st. It was April 21st," Benny said as if it was supposed to mean something to her.

"Look, Benny, I may as well tell you I barely passed my history class and I feel like dog shit. You're going to have to help me out here." It was harsh, she knew, but she couldn't think that hard right now. She needed Benny to just spit it out.

Benny sighed. "Sorry, bella, I forget this isn't your history. April 21st is the day that celebrates the founding of Rome. From ancient times, there is told of a ceremony on April 21st when the sun shines through the oculus and through the front doors of the Pantheon. The Emperor Hadrian designed it that way so when he stood in the doors, it illuminated him like a god."

Shelby stared at Benny. "That's exactly what I thought then. He could have been taken for a god in that moment."

"Well, now we have things to work with. We know when you were. Or close anyway." Shelby raised her eyebrows. He was making her think again. "When we get to Tuscolano, we will be sure, but I think the man you saw was the Emperor Hadrian. He could have been in both places. Interesting guy. Gave so much to Rome, but lost his mind and became a tyrant. Executed the architect of the Pantheon over the design."

"Sounds like a real charmer. How will we know for sure in Tuscolano?" All of this was giving Shelby a headache.

"A friend may be able to explain, but she needs to meet you first."

"Benny-"

"Please, bella, trust me."

Benny was tight-lipped and Shelby quickly tired of pumping him for more information, so she laid her head back on the seat and watched Rome fade from a beautiful ancient city to a modern suburb. Modern was a relative term. The buildings looked like something from *Welcome Back, Kotter* and she half expected men in fluffy mustaches and bell-bottom corduroys to be strolling the streets. Actually, there were a few of those, but for the most part, the people looked like her great-aunt's bridge group from Jersey. Stuck in a time warp with fashion sense that would be all the rage on the Jersey shore. Men in gold necklaces and women with long fake nails, and both in clothes two sizes too small.

The cab driver pulled up to the curb of a small pink building with white iron balcony rails. It looked more like something from a Florida retirement community than the other sedate brick structures around it. It was unassuming but hideously obtrusive at the same time. So were the residents. As they got out of the cab, Shelby surveyed the place and realized she was being gawked at through the curtains of several windows. Most were trying to be furtive about it, but others seemed to be openly irritated about a stranger in their midst.

Benny led her through the breezeway in the center of the building and up the concrete and metal steps to the third floor. By the time they reached the top, Shelby had come to a firm decision about this place not making it on the Magical History Tour. One of the brass numbers on the door was missing and only a shadow of dirt in the shape of a number let her know this was apartment 6B. A small plate of tuna with an advancing horde of ants gave away the occupant's affinity for cats but probably didn't actually own the one the snack was for. Other than that, the door looked no different than all of the other grimy white doors in the building.

Benny knocked on the door and the 6 of 6B became a little fainter as dirt dropped away. Another few visitors and it would disappear entirely. As the locks in the door were turned and slid back, Shelby was giving serious second thought to her tendency to follow Benny wherever he led. Any sense of fear she had evaporated when the door opened and revealed a tiny woman with gray hair piled high on her head and a bubblegum pink pant suit which clashed hideously with the powder pink building. Her lips were slathered in a daring red Shelby was sure had been purchased in the 1940s, and her eyelids were a sparkly ice blue with fake eyelashes and lined with heavy 60s cat-eye wings. Whoever this woman was, she was definitely someone Shelby wanted to know. This was who Dina would be if she was Italian and old.

As soon as she laid her eyes on Benny, her mouth spread into a wide grin only to have it run immediately away. She said something to him in Italian which didn't sound much like sweet old lady and smacked him on the cheek. Then, the smile returned and she planted her candy apple lips on each cheek leaving Benny looking very much like a little kid whose grandma had just come through the door. Benny's face turned almost as red as the lip prints, then he recovered slightly and introduced Shelby.

"Shelby Starling, meet Carmelita Esposito. She was my Nonna's best friend. I grew up on her raviolis."

Carmelita scoffed. "Because your Nonna was terrible cook. Her ravioli-" She spat at the very idea of Nonna's ravioli as if having terrible ravioli was a capital offense. Of course, in Italy, it very well could have been. She surveyed Shelby and elbowed Benny in the ribs. "Now I see why you no come to see me this week, eh?" She winked a blue flash of eyelid at him and looped her arm through his. "Come, we go sit and you tell me about this American beauty you show up with." Looping her other arm through Shelby's, Carmelita led them into the living room.

The room was everything Shelby had hoped for. It was the epitome of Italian grandmother. Frames of every shape and size on any flat surface contained pictures in various shades of fade. Across from the creamsicle chenille sofa was a portrait of the Sacred Heart. Odd ceramics and wooden tchotchkes filled in the spaces between the frames. The curtains had been drawn against the heat of the day and candles in rock crystal holders were lit to keep the shadows at bay. Not cut-glass crystal, but actual clumps of stones with spaces hollowed out for the candles to rest. White quartz, rose quartz, and amethyst sparkled in the dancing glow of the flames. In the corners on either side of the windows were macramé plant hangers that had likely hung there since the 1970s birth of the building itself.

"Sit, sit," Carmelita insisted. Shelby and Benny did as they were told. "Now, tell me, Benito, what brings you to Tuscolano?"

Shelby looked at Benny and raised an eyebrow. She damn sure didn't know, so this ought to be good.

Benny looked side-eyed at Shelby likely knowing that what he was about to say was probably going to get a sarcastic comment at best, and walking out on him at worst. "We need a psychic and you're the best I know."

Shelby opened her mouth to make the expected sarcastic comment, but decided that after all she had been through, what the hell? Adding a psychic grandma to the mix didn't seem so weird anymore.

Carmelita shook her silver beehive. "Benny, you know I don't do readings no more." She paused and looked at Benny, then Shelby. "But maybe I make an exception this time. You want to know if she's the one, eh?" Her dark eyes twinkled.

Benny blushed hard again, and shook his head. "No, it's not like that. Shelby has...visions. We need to know what's happening. The last one took a lot out of her."

Dark eyes settled on Shelby's face. Carmelita seemed to be looking through her rather than at her, as if she was searching Shelby's soul and wasn't overly impressed with what she found there. "Tell me what you see," Carmelita said finally.

Shelby took a deep breath as Carmelita settled back into her chair. Slowly, she went through the events of the last two days feeling more and more like a lunatic as she talked. It seemed so real as she went over it in her mind deep in the heart of old Rome surrounded by the history and mystery of the city. Here, in the burbs, it just seemed ludicrous. Once in a while, Benny would chime in with what he saw when she had the episodes, which wasn't much. Her long minutes in the past were only seconds in the present. All the while, Carmelita was quiet and unphased by it all.

After a long moment of contemplative silence, she pushed herself up from her chair. "Come with me." Carmelita led them into another room down a cramped dark hallway. This room was sparse in comparison to the living room clutter, but still cozy. In the center of the room was a small table draped with an ornate scarf in reds and golds. Lining the walls were shelves loaded with books that were covered in a thin layer of time and neglect. One case held vials and canisters with odd things in them Shelby could only assume were herbs or spices of some sort. Plants struggled for survival in small pots on top of the cases, reaching for the little light that streamed through the dingy window pane. Above the table hung a lamp draped in a blue scarf giving the room a soft watery glow. Laying in the center of the table was a small bundle wrapped in fabric and a large white candle on a short pedestal candlestick.

Shelby scanned the room taking it all in. "Now this is what I would expect of a good psychic."

"Grazie, bella." Carmelita smiled. "Sit down. There's something you need to see."

Shelby sat at the table expecting her to get out tarot cards or a crystal ball, but she returned to the table with a book. Carmelita set the tattered volume on the table and carefully opened the pages. The leather cover seemed to groan as the cover settled on the cloth underneath it. Inside, pages were yellowed and brittle. No typed chapters graced the fragile sheets. This book was ancient. The writing inside was flawless hand-printed calligraphy centuries old. Large first letters on each page were illuminated. Something deep inside her started to surge as if she were somehow connected to the book. Not the weird electricity that seemed to herald time warps. It was a wave of relief which flooded over her and she didn't even know why. "I'm sorry, I don't understand," she whispered. For some reason she felt like she should be reverent around something so old.

"Of course not. Unless you read Latin." Carmelita smiled. "This belong to my grandmother. She would not tell me where she get it, but she pass it to me." The old psychic ran her wrinkled hand and long crimson nails over the intricate page. "The ancient writers knew more than people today like to think. The church once believed in more than they tell the people today. This book comes from that time."

Shelby shook her head. "I don't follow."

"This is book of legends. Legends that are not so much fiction as they sound. Each legend is true, but unbelievable to one who thinks too much. To know the truth is to forget what you think you know." Carmelita turned a page and pointed to the word *viatorem*. "Traveler. You, bella."

"Sure, I'm a traveler. It's my job."

"No, it's not what you do. It's what you *are*. The story speaks of those who wander lost in the world. Never quite settled. Never fitting in. Never home, really home." Again, her dark eyes searched Shelby for comprehension. "Sound familiar?"

Shelby nodded slowly. "Sure, but that's got to apply to half of this generation."

Carmelita shook her head. "So does cynicism. Let go of it for now. Half the generation doesn't go leaping back in time when they touch a wall."

The old witch had her there. "What happens to the Travelers in the legend?"

Carmelita smiled. "They use their visions to lead them home. Not to a place. A time. To their destiny."

"Destiny?"

Carmelita nodded. "Destiny. What you were destined to do."

Shelby didn't really want to offend Benny's surrogate grandma, but she knew this was not her gig. There was no way she was meant for more than drinking her way around the world as long as someone would pay her to do it. Destiny was a word that sounded like it came with responsibilities and she was not down with that.

Benny had been reading the legend over her shoulder as best he could. "My Latin is a little rusty. Does this say 'memories'?"

Carmelita nodded. "Visions is not a good word. Really, what Travelers see, they have seen before. Memories." Comprehension finally settled on Shelby even if acceptance hadn't. "But you knew that."

Shelby nodded. "It felt like I was really in that place. Seeing it through my own eyes. Not like a dream. I could feel everything. Sense everything. Like I had been there before. Like a memory."

"You tell me of watching great things happening, yes?"

"I should hardly call the public murder of an innocent man a great thing," Shelby snorted.

Carmelita shook her head. "No, but when it happened, it was. Hadrian's ceremony was great. Yet, both things you watch from the shadows. Lifetime after lifetime, you have watched great things happen. The legend tell us here," she said pointing further down the page, "all Travelers have the same. Watching others do the great things. When you find your way home, to your true time, only then you will *make* great things happen."

Benny broke off from his stilted translation of the ancient Latin text to ask, "How does she know when her time is, and how to get there?"

Carmelita sighed and sat back in her chair. "That, I cannot tell you. The legend doesn't tell us and I don't know. Each Traveler finds their way, but the path is not known. You must follow where you are led."

Useless information. Shelby followed where she was led for a living. Guide after guide, city after city, but she had never before felt anything of a destiny. "Why now? Why is this happening to me now? I've been to Rome before. I've traveled the world before. Never has this happened." All of this was becoming too much to wrap her head around, much less believe. Sure, there were electric shocks and visions which left her confused on the ground, but being some life-hopping destiny seeker couldn't be the explanation. It was crazy. Or maybe she was. That would make a lot more sense than some old Latin legend written by priests in the middle-ages who had clearly spent too much time alone with sacramental wine.

"Why now?" Carmelita shrugged. "That, bella, is between you and the universe. I wish I knew."

Some psychic she was.

Carmelita had little more to offer Shelby except if she kept her eyes open and listened to her gut, the information she needed would find her.

✳

Shelby returned to Rome proper more confused than ever. Not wanting to risk another episode, Benny suggested sites she was not likely to actually touch, like the Spanish Steps. She even managed to get around the Forum without touching anything. She felt rather like a child who had been told to keep their hands in their pockets so as not to wreak toddler havoc on a china shop. Much of the day was spent in a heroic effort to avoid talking to Benny about the insanity of Carmelita's theory while simultaneously avoiding offending the one person who Shelby needed to believe she was telling the truth. By the end of the day, she had more photos and writing fodder for Dina, but mercifully no bending of space and time.

As the Italian sun sank over the tops of the buildings into an early twilight, Shelby found herself wandering alone through a maze of streets and piazzas. Benny had plans with friends in Ostia. The last night she went with him to the Roman beachside suburb ended with her waking up next to him, so she decided to decline his invitation to join him and spend the night with the shadows of the city. She felt both deeply connected to the city and oddly out of place at the same time.

Turning over and over in her head what Carmelita had told her, Shelby wandered aimlessly past trattorias, shops, and churches. The buildings faded one into the other with little distinction, like visual white noise as she walked deep in thought. Much of her musings revolved around her own mental stability and the mental stability of the fabulously odd little Italian woman who believed every word she said.

Ahead of her, yet another piazza opened up revealing one of the seemingly infinite number of churches in the deep city. Sant'Agostino. The early Renaissance church tugged at her and she knew it wasn't because of the pull of a higher deity calling her to her purpose. No, the facade of the place had been constructed, like so many Renaissance structures, from travertine taken straight off the Colosseum. There was no way in hell she was going near the church.

Instead, she stopped at an unassuming metal gate in a concrete wall. On one side of it was an old Opel with an aftermarket teal paint job next to a red and white scooter probably belonging to an ill-tempered woman in stilettos. Through the gate was another unassuming entrance framed in a peachy yellow stucco. Over the unassuming door were carved the words 'Biblioteca Angelica.' A library. More old books. Great.

Something brought her here and she had promised Carmelita to listen and follow where she was led, so she tried the door. As late as it was, it was still open so she made her way inside. An older man at a counter nodded at her, but looked at his watch. Closing time must be soon. As she walked into the main chamber of the library, the room opened up like the main hall of a medieval castle. The place smelled of old paper and worn leather with just a hint of mineral oil. Books, whose once colorful spines had aged into a wash of dullness, soared in rich wood tiers up to the vaulted stone ceiling. Rolling ladders rested against the shelves while rows of heavy wooden desks flanked a center aisle through the vast room. Shelby stood in the middle of the aisle and took in the austere place. It was a veritable cathedral of knowledge.

At the back of room was a door with a warm glow spilling from it onto the cold floor of the main hall. Shelby made her way past the desks and stares of the locals as old and worn as the books they were pouring over. Just for shits and giggles, she winked at the most shriveled of the old men as she went by him towards the doorway.

The cozy room had no windows and the twilight was lost to the glow of old globe lamps. Above her head were intricately carved plaster reliefs meeting in points and arches. Below them were two rows of wooden and glass cases holding exquisite illuminated works and rare books, one of which was the Divine Comedy. "Holy shit," Shelby whispered letting her hand hover just over the glass.

Wondering what other literary masterpieces might be hidden among the aging volumes, she walked slowly along the walls scanning the shelves. Most were huge volumes of little to no interest, but one small book wedged in the middle of a row of matching spines caught her eye. It was bound in worn brown leather with gold gilding which had been worn off in most places as if it had been well-loved and well-read. The surrounding tomes were bound in white linen with red trim. The little book was definitely out of place. Her hands tingled uncomfortably then the familiar burn returned as Shelby squatted down to the bottom shelf and gently removed the book. She pushed the pain out of her mind and focused on the book in her hand. Unlike its neighbors, this one had no library markings on it. No title. No catalogue numbers stamped on the outside of the pages. Shelby opened the soft leather cover and revealed a hand-written name. Not a title. A name. *Elijah Faircloth*. She turned the page. So far, every volume she had looked at was in Italian or Latin, but this was different. It was in English. It was also no reference book or illuminated manuscript. This was a journal.

Before she could turn the page to see what the journal said, a soft throat clearing at the doorway broke the magic of the moment. "Mi scusi, signora. La biblioteca sta chiudendo."

"Sorry, I don't understand," Shelby answered sheepishly.

The old man who had been at the counter when she came in smiled and tapped his watch. "Library closing." With another smile and nod, he walked back out again. Clearly, she was meant to follow.

Shelby quickly looked at the back of the journal in her stinging hand. There was no check out card or bar code. Nothing to say this was a library book at all. This book wasn't supposed to be here. "Or is it?" she whispered. With a quick glance back at the door, she shoved the journal into her bag and headed out through the vast main hall to the main entrance.

The little old man was waiting by the door for her holding it open. The cuff of his pressed white shirt had moved slightly above his wrist revealing a small tattoo.

A compass rose, but where cardinal directions should have been were the numbers from a clock face. He saw her taking notice of the tattoo, and pulled the cuff back down to cover it up. With a wink and yet another smile, he said in fragmented English, "I wish you find what you look for."

"Grazi." Shelby smiled and could have sworn the man glanced down at her bag as he closed the door behind her. Perhaps it was the guilt of her book thievery messing with her mind.

It wasn't until she was settled at a table under the trattoria lights in the Piazza Navona that his words really sank in. At the time, she thought it was only an attempt at idle pleasantries. She took it as a simple 'hope you found what you needed.' As she sipped her chianti, the true meaning behind his words slowly dawned on her. He could have meant he hoped she found her destiny, which would have been truly bizarre. Or maybe she was getting drunk and making things up. Either way, she was certain by the bottom of the second glass that the old man meant for her to find and take the book. With her guilt assuaged through the magic of Italian vintage, Shelby was finally able to dig the journal out of her bag and see what Elijah Faircloth was writing about.

She ran her fingers slowly over the outside cover of the book. Her hand, which had been continuously tingling since the Colosseum, began to almost surge and spark under her skin as her palm brushed the leather. It was a simply bound book but sturdy. The pages had been sewn together, not glued, making the spine more flexible and the pages more able to withstand the constant opening, closing, and shoving into bags the journal would have been subjected to. The pages were aged yellow and the black ink faded to a deep brown. Filling the pages were varying types of penmanship, from careful and even, to hurried and scrawled. Illustrations and maps were interspersed throughout the entries. At the top of the first page was a date. August 22, 1871.

I have chosen this journal as a place to record some occurrences that I don't dare share with anyone, certainly no one at home in the strait-laced London society. The pages herein are blessedly silent and won't judge the soundness of my mental faculties, which are giving even me some pause. Some would be quick to proclaim senility, except my thirty years would barely qualify me as a doddering old fool. A fool, though, yes. Perhaps it is madness that is causing these strange experiences, yet, I don't feel mad at other times. But, then, mad people rarely do.

Shelby had to admit that Elijah, in his professional stodginess, had a point about madness. Crazy people never think they're the crazy ones. He seemed to be introducing his writing as though he were trying to convince himself, or anyone who may one day read it, he had it all together. Anyone who had to try this hard to sound sane probably had something a tad off. Still, she was intrigued by his opening and purpose to his writing, even if it wasn't the steamy love story she had been hoping for. Something in it was all too familiar. Then, things got really weird.

Over the last several days of my travels, I have had strange experiences at some, yet not all, historic sites I have visited. The other day, as I stood on a parapet on China's Great Wall, I looked out over the expanse of empty wilderness before me. There was nothing but scattered stones and grasses along the rolling hills as far as the eye could see. As the wind picked up, I braced myself against the cold by placing my hand on the fortification. As I did so, I felt a surge of pain through my arm as if I had been struck by a lightning bolt-

"Holy crap!" Shelby slammed the book shut and barely caught the wine glass that rocked perilously on the table. This was too strange. Too much for her frazzled nerves and drunken brain to take in. She shoved the book back into her bag. Whatever was happening here was more than she could handle right now. Visions, memories, suburban psychics, elderly librarians, and Victorian diarists. It was enough to make her head swim even without the chianti.

Never being one to make good decisions under pressure, she opted for more wine rather than less. Nothing was going to make anything make more sense, so she might as well drown it all out. With a wave of her hand, the waiter refilled her glass and she put her plan of purposeful inebriation into action.

Shelby sat in front of her laptop at a shaded bistro table up the block from her hotel. In her hand was her second cappuccino, which was a weak hangover cure. Benny pulled out the chair across from her and ordered a pastry and another cappuccino. "Well?" he asked after a bit.

"Well, what?" Shelby asked looking around the corner of her screen.

"You should have a good story to look like shit again this morning. Beautiful, but shit."

"Thanks. Good to see you, too." Shelby rolled her eyes, but it hurt, so she decided to fess up. "There's a great trattoria with a very good chianti in the Piazza Navona."

Benny laughed. "I'm disappointed, bella. No midnight wandering? No sleeping with Neptune?"

"If you must know, I spent the night with Elijah Faircloth."

Benny's laugh ran away from his face and a twinge of jealousy crept in. "You met at the trattoria?"

The bitch in Shelby was enjoying torturing Benny. "No, at the library. He's a writer."

"Oh? Anything I would know?"

"No, I don't believe so. He's British. Or, at least, he was."

"I'm sorry?"

If she was going to feel like crap, she may as well have a little fun. "He's dead."

Benny's mouth dropped open. "Dead? What do you mean? How? What happened? How can you just sit there like it's nothing?"

"Because it *is* nothing. Here." Shelby finally released her sadistic grip on Benny's emotions and handed him the diary.

"Where did you get this?"

"I told you. The library. I did go for a walk and wandered around a bit. Then, somehow I ended up at the Biblioteca Angelica." Shelby explained how she happened to find the diary that had no library markings and how the little old man with the odd tattoo who worked there almost seemed to know she had taken it and wanted her to have it. "Maybe it was the wine. Maybe not. Who knows?"

Benny flipped through the diary like she had done the night before. "You read it?"

"Only the first page. It- it hit a little close to home."

As Shelby checked emails, Benny read the first page. At the bottom of it, he slowly looked up and met her eyes. "I see."

Shelby nodded. "Yeah." Shelby shut her laptop and stuffed the journal into her bag. "So, where to first?" She wasn't ready to face Elijah Faircloth and historical weirdness with her head pounding. This was her last day in Rome and she needed to focus.

❖

Shelby and Benny did the obligatory tours of the Vatican and the Sistine Chapel with no mind-bending episodes. Not for lack of trying, however. Somewhere near the middle of her third glass of wine, Shelby had formulated a drunken theory which didn't seem any more ludicrous in the sobriety of daylight. Nothing happened at Trevi, which was a baroque structure. She had been careful about the Spanish Steps and Forum so she didn't know about those. Both the Colosseum and Pantheon were memories of moments during the reign of Emperor Hadrian. If the only things that triggered visions were related to Hadrian's time, she would know her time in Rome had been sometime between 117-138 AD.

So far, the Vatican was a bust. Sure, there was plenty for her travel writing, except for the annoying bit about not being allowed to take pictures inside the Sistine Chapel. As far as time warping went, nothing. Since there wasn't time in the day to make it back to the Steps and the Forum, she would have to test her theory on the Circus later.

In the piazza outside of St. Peter's cathedral, tourists looked up at the balcony where the pope would bless the faithful, and at the apartments where future popes would be debated and decided. Others strolled through the columns of the Colonnade of Bernini. A sense of reverence was lost on many of the children who mimicked the poses of the statues high atop the columns as their parents spoke of saints who were only names from stories to the children. Standing serenely in their ludicrously vibrant blue and yellow striped pajama uniforms were the less-than-intimidating Swiss Guards. All Shelby could figure was they were either for atmosphere, or were secretly bad-asses to pull off being dressed like the palace joker. Out of the shadow of the massive cathedral, the growing heat of the day radiated off of the expansive stone piazza making the massive obelisk in the center seem to waver. Shelby could relate. Her faith was a bit shaky at this point, too.

"So far, so good?" Benny asked as they climbed into the cab bound for the Circus Maximus.

"I guess. At least I know when I wasn't here. I mean, assuming Carmelita's theory is right and these are memories. The history of the Circus Maximus is so long there's no telling when I will end up if this works."

"What about other places? You think Rome is the only one, only life, for you?"

Shelby shrugged. "God only knows."

"Not God. Elijah."

She didn't want to think about the diary. Something about it gave her the creeps because of how she found it, or how it found her. She could barely handle holding it to read it, not for very long anyway. Every time Shelby touched the thing, her tingling hand buzzed harder. "Maybe he does know. Maybe he's a crackpot."

"Bella, you don't believe that."

No, she didn't. Elijah Faircloth was a Traveler. In only a few words, she knew. She was slowly coming to grips with the fact that she was a Traveler, too, even if she didn't want to admit it to herself or anyone else. What she was really struggling with had nothing to do with time jerking and lightning bolts up her arm. She was struggling with something Carmelita had said. Until she found her destiny, she would only be watching great things happen instead of making great things happen. Who the hell was she to make anything great happen? She was a complete mess of a human with no drive to do anything but find lucrative escapes from her own reality. Her job with Pioneer was the best one she had found for that and now it had brought her to chaos and purpose she had been so happy to avoid thus far. Reading more of the diary and finding her way to her destiny scared the hell out of her. "Fine, you're right."

"There, was that so hard?" Benny asked with a laugh.

Shelby smiled. "Yes, actually, it was. Thank you for your concern." She shoved his shoulder and tried to laugh with him. She knew he was trying to take some of the weight of things off of her and she was grateful.

Passing through the city, she began to look at the buildings differently. When she arrived in Rome, she saw them as a mass of pinkish stone with little definitive personality. The tight alleys and a maze of shops, restaurants, and homes bled into each other in a haze she didn't understand. Now, though, the city seemed almost alive to her. Each facade and doorway had a personality. Each window was an opening to the souls of the people who lived within. Each piazza had a community of its own that enveloped it. She watched the people going about their business and saw relationships and a passion for their city and the lives they had built here. They were stunning. Apparently, you had to be a contender for a career as a supermodel to be a young Roman. The older people were softer and more comfortable in the olive skin they were in. There was a richness in the culture that ran through their veins. All of this had been lost on her before, but it seemed to almost be part of her own fabric now. The connection to the city was powerful. Somehow, sometime, it was her city, too.

The cab pulled up in front of the Circus Maximus as the sun reached its full height above the valley between the Aventine and Palatine hills. The ruins soared above in ragged heights revealing the ravages of time and scavenging on the ancient structure. Shelby stood outside of the walls, closed her eyes, and took a deep breath.

"Ready, bella?" Benito asked quietly.

Shelby nodded and followed him through the opening and looked out at the oblong expanse in front of her. She pulled her camera out of her bag and began taking photographs for Dina, but for some reason, these photos were beginning to mean more to her. Her hand had begun to tingle more the closer she got to the Circus and she knew this place meant something to her once. But what? And when?

"This part is newer. Well, newer than Hadrian," Benny explained. "And what you see there," he said pointing to the oval indentation in the park grass in the center, "is not the original track. This place floods so the track has been long buried below the earth."

"Is there anything here of Hadrian's time?"

Benny nodded. "Over there. On the far end is older. You sure about this?"

Shelby knew Benny was concerned. Whenever she was jerked backwards in time, he was left with her in a strange state of paralysis which was terrifying for him. To make matters worse, to keep from raising the fears of surrounding tourists, he had to do whatever he could to make the whole thing seem completely normal. A difficult task since there was little normal about a beautiful girl standing frozen against a stone with her eyes lolling back in her head. The best he could hope for was to find an area that was relatively deserted. Of course, since tourists were notoriously self-absorbed in their own experiences, it probably was a non-issue anyway.

The far end of the Circus was a hodgepodge of construction over the centuries. The whole place seemed a bit like a child's Lego set in shades of tan and pink. Bits were added to suit the fancy of whatever emperor happened to have his ass on the throne at the time. Some wanted to be on display for the games leading the controlled chaos that was the chariot races. Others wanted to distance themselves from the plebeian masses who packed the stands. Some spectator seats for the high and mighty were right out in the open while others were concealed behind turns of walls, arches, and colonnades of concrete and travertine.

Shelby and Benny wove through clumps of tourists in cargo shorts and knee socks to a section of the structure that seemed far less impressive than the surrounding parts. Shelby could only hope this meant the section was one of the older parts that would connect her to her own history. Because of the section's dowdiness, the crowd was sparser here, which meant less to worry about if she did go paralytic.

"Well?" Shelby asked. "What do you think?"

Benny shrugged. "It's a start."

Shelby's hand felt like there were sparks under her skin. The tingling was almost unbearable. She was starting to understand the nuances of the sensation, and that the changes she felt heralded part of her own story. The only problem was she knew she was tied to the Colosseum and half the city proper was faced in scavenged travertine from the place. The other half was faced with bits of the Circus Maximus. Since she was now standing at the source of some of the materials, her hand surged like a live wire.

With a glance over her shoulder at the tour group engrossed in some tale of glamorous races, she stole into a shadowed corner of aged stone. Even though she could sense what was coming and understood it better now, her hand still trembled as she reached out for the wall in front of her. She could almost see sparks jump from her fingertips as they hovered a hair's width from the smooth surface. Benny put his hand on the small of her back to steady her and she felt a shivering up her spine. In the back of her mind, she wanted him to keep his hand there. Or anywhere else he chose to put it.

Pushing thoughts of Benny out of her mind as much as she could, she placed her hand flat on the wall. As expected, the bolt of energy raced through Shelby's veins holding her fast to the spot. The serenity of the park and murmurs of the tourists gave way to the rush of crowd noise even rowdier than the gladiator fight. There was a thundering sound along with the screams and roar of the crowd making the whole place sound more like a NASCAR race than something out of antiquity. A crowd was on their feet in front of her blocking whatever was happening on the main track, but the only logical conclusion was that a race was on. She tried to pull her hand from the wall to get a better view around the fat togaed men and the women with their hair piled in intricate braids on top of their heads, but it was no use. As with the Pantheon and the Colosseum, she was rooted to the spot.

With a final surge from the spectators, the race ended and the crowd broke up just enough for her to see more of where she was. Servants brought baskets of fruits and breads around for the elite gathered in the shade of the portico. Looking out at the people, Shelby noticed something different from the crowd at the Colosseum. This crowd was not only more crass, but it was also more co-ed than the other one. At the Colosseum, men and women were divided and slaves weren't allowed in the building at all. Here, there seemed to be no lines of decency that weren't being crossed publicly and with enthusiasm. Hawkers cursed at patrons who argued about the price of their wares. Couples seemed to forget, or not care, they were in full view of their neighbors and engaged in whatever lustiness overcame them at the moment. In awe of it all, Shelby barely noticed the man standing across from her silhouetted against the afternoon sun. It wasn't until he stepped toward her and into the shadows that she focused on him. The man carried himself with the confidence the gold laurel crowning his head entitled him to as he slowly walked toward her. Hadrian. She had seen him twice already and knew his face well. Neither time had she been close enough to see him as truly human. He had seemed distant, like a portrait in a textbook. This time, she was really seeing him. And he saw her.

In the memories of the Pantheon and the Colosseum, she had felt like she was a part of it all, and yet a ghost watching others going through the motions of the moment. This time, she was real. She was here.

Hadrian raised an eyebrow as he came closer to her. Every cell in her body wanted to let go of the wall and vanish back into her own time zone, but her hand was held fast. The emperor reached out and brushed the back of his fingers on her cheek. "Tonight, you are mine," was all he said, then walked away with a consort. She stood staring after him and heard the starting gates slam open and the surge of horseflesh and chariot wheels. As the crack of a whip rang overhead, white light flooded over her and she slid down the wall to the warm stone floor.

When she came to, Benny was once again crouched over her cradling her throbbing head. "Bella, are you ok?"

"Yes," she answered weakly. Benny helped her sit up and leaned her against the wall. Shelby laid her head back on it and closed her eyes. "And I've learned something. Carmelita was right. I was only watching the great things happening around me. The only thing I did was give Hadrian an erection."

"Sounds great to me," Benny replied with the look that made Shelby do stupid things.

CHAPTER 4

Shelby's last trip to Rome ended in pretty much the same way as her first. Sneaking out of Benny's bed to catch a plane. Only this time, instead of guilt washing over her, it was longing. He was the only one who knew what was happening to her and he didn't flinch about it. Heading to Egypt filled her with a sense of dread and loss. Tarek was a great tour guide, but what would he say if she was suddenly thrust into Cleopatra's court? How the hell was she going to explain these episodes to him? And she would have to. That much she knew.

As she slid out from under the covers, Benny caught her hand and whispered, "Do great things, bella." His words hit her with the full force of the good-bye that this was. She would talk to him again, but if she did find a way to end her travels through time and space, she was unlikely to ever see him again.

There didn't seem to be any rhyme or reason to the itinerary for Egypt Dina had sent her. It seemed erratic and loosely planned leaving much of it for her to figure out on her own. Shelby failed to see the logic in even sending her there when so much history was closer to Italy. Greece or France would have made more sense than sending her all the way to Cairo only to surely send her back up to the other side of the Mediterranean again. Of course, Dina did little that made logical sense. How she could run a successful company while giving in to her bohemian whims was beyond Shelby's comprehension.

The flight to Egypt gave her plenty of time for Elijah Faircloth and his journal, but she was still reluctant to read it. Shelby tried everything from crossword puzzles to the shopping magazines in the seat pocket of the plane to stall reading the diary. After seriously considering ordering the magic wand remote control and finding a few fairly legitimate reasons for wanting a wall-mounted half-squirrel, she finally shoved the shopping magazine where it belonged, in the seat back next to the barf bag. Reasons for putting off the diary were starting to verge on the ridiculous. Shelby needed to suck it up and read the damn thing. It was bad enough it gave her the creeps, but it hurt to hold. She would have to get over that, though. There were answers in there she needed and only reading the ramblings of a semi-sane dead Victorian was going to give them to her.

She steeled herself against the pain with a rum and Coke first, then pulled the worn book from her backpack. Her hand sizzled, but she pushed the feeling to the back of her mind and focused on the writing inside. To ease into the weirdness, she reread the first page. It still seemed surreal. As she read on, the link between her and this random Brit became even more pronounced.

-and as the pain found its way up my arm, a blinding white light enveloped me. Sounds from around me changed to unfamiliar ones. At once, the quiet countryside sprang to life with the thundering of horse hooves and shouts of men. As the light faded and the world came back into focus, an arrow raced past my face and struck the soldier behind me. The Wall was under siege and I was standing in the middle of it! The Chinese soldiers in their armor sprang to the parapets firing arrows down on the advancing horde below. Archers stood ready in the openings, being fed arrows from men crouched below the wall, raining a shower of death down on the invaders. Men on the ground fell as arrows found their targets in the vital organs of the poorly protected advancers. Most of those below were on horseback wielding spears against the onslaught of arrows. This wasn't going to go well for them. As I watched, hundreds were taken off their horses spurting blood from chest wounds. Many were shot in the head, their fur hats being better protection against cold than weapons. Ladders were being carried toward the wall, but they were woefully short. Realizing this, the men fell back to lash them together to make them taller. Precious time would be lost in this effort and the Chinese soldiers were using the delay to pick off more of the attackers quickly reducing their numbers.

Watching from my corner of the fortification, I began to feel a panic for my life that felt very real. I could smell the sweat and blood around me. Dust rising from the horse hooves below stung my eyes. And yet, no one seemed to notice me. No one shoved a crossbow in my hands or pushed me out of the way. They seemed to look around me and through me, but the sensations I felt were very real indeed.

As soon as the ladders were being hoisted again by the barbarians, the Chinese archers stood in a silent row along the expanse of wall to my left. I watched as a flame ripped through them along the tips of their arrows, the flame being passed with remarkable speed from archer to archer. As the tip of the arrow was lit, it was held in the bow and launched forth in a burning rain onto the men and horses below. The archers could cover a staggering area with their shots, but still invaders broke through and made it to the front line. In horror, I watched as one of the ladders crashed against the wall and men began to climb with daggers in their teeth and swords swinging wildly at their waists. I pulled back in fear as the head of one of the barbarians topped the ladder and he swung a leg over the ledge. Before he could launch himself over, a Chinese soldier lunged from behind me with his saber drawn, and, in one swift motion, slit the man's throat. Hot blood surged from his gaping wound and showered me in crimson. My stomach turned as his eyes rolled back in his head. I sank to the ground when my hand was mercifully released from the wall where I had been held fast, and the white light flooded me once more.

As things returned to focus, I found myself in a heap on the stone ground of the parapet where I had been moments before. The quiet of the wilderness returned and the only sounds were the concerned murmurs of the travelers gathered around me. Gone were the soldiers and advancing horde. Gone were the horses and shouts. Gone was the chaos of battle. Only the serenity of long-dead history remained. Silence and a tingling in the palm of my hand. Nothing more.

Shelby was captivated by the eloquence of Elijah's description of the battle. Who *was* this guy? A scholar? Explorer? Some rich guy spending daddy's money on a lavish world tour? A writer like her?

She reread one part of it as she sorted through similarities in their experience: *And yet, no one seemed to notice me. No one shoved a crossbow in my hands or pushed me out of the way. They seemed to look around me and through me, but the sensations I felt were very real indeed.* Her first experiences had seemed to be more like being on the outside looking in as Elijah's had. No one seemed to notice her at the Colosseum or the Pantheon. But, why, then, had Hadrian seen her? He touched her and spoke to her. She was as real to him as he was to her.

Before she had a chance to read more, the captain came over the crackling airplane speakers to tell the passengers to prepare for landing in Cairo. Shelby closed the journal and put it back in her bag, much to the relief of her hand. As the book was tucked away, the sensation of needles being thrust into her palm ebbed some. With a jolt and a bounce, the plane wheels found the tarmac. Shelby braced herself for whatever life awaited her in the ruins of ancient Egypt, a country with a history as storied as Italy's and eons older.

Just a block from her hotel sipping a glass of chianti, Shelby sat by a window in a touristy street cafe that seemed to be a relic of the Victorian fascination with ancient Egypt. The heavy wooden bar framed in wood columns seemed strangely out of place in the middle of old town Cairo. The wooden plank ceiling made the room seem tight and dark. The only thing that made the cafe look like Egypt was the rich Persian rug covering the floor under the small tables and chairs. Other than that, the place was decidedly and strangely European, which suited her just fine. Shelby wasn't willing to let go of Rome just yet. The warmth of the wine and the veil of cigarette smoke hanging in the air was somehow comforting, even if it was nothing like the trattoria she had been sitting in waiting on Benny a week ago. She liked the anonymity of the place. No one knew the train wreck that was Shelby Starling. It was in the heart of the city at the edge of the chaos of the market, so it wasn't somewhere full of locals who knew each other's names and business. Here, she could vanish into the crowd and watch the people around her. But first, wine. Always first wine.

She ran a finger around the top of her glass. The warm yellow glow of the setting desert sun illuminated the wine making it look rich and crimson. Shelby picked up the glass and slowly swirled the deep red liquid inside. Her mind took her back to the Colosseum and the gladiator who stood holding his blood-soaked sword high in the air for Hadrian to see before he struck the final sickening blow. She had loved the young gladiator once, whoever he was. Blood had flowed from his opponent like wine from a tapped keg. Shelby could never forget that sight. Elijah had seen blood flow from the throat of a man in his first vision, too. History was damn bloody and she was immersed in it now.

Tarek wasn't going to meet her until morning at the Cairo Museum, so tonight Shelby was on her own to get lost in the city. There was something mystical and modern about this place. The ancient slammed unmercifully into the present day. Ruins were unapologetic as they loomed in the distance reminding the people of times and crimes gone by. Relics freshly made yesterday were being sold to tourists who publicly doubted their authenticity but secretly hoped they were doing something sexy like buying ancient contraband. Even from the edge of the market, the smell of oils and spices in the air was overpowering, which was good since there were plenty of things that didn't smell sweetly earthy like a hookah bar. Maybe it was the press of sweating humans with a wide variety of grooming habits, and maybe it was the animals roaming underfoot that were the source of the stench. Probably, it was both. And more.

Above her head, a shadowed web of wires was spun between the dilapidated modern buildings which lacked the permanency of the ancient architecture. It seemed the brilliant architectural minds of the ancients hadn't been passed down to the modern builders of the city. The only structures that seemed like they would survive the inevitable sandstorm were, ironically, the ruins. Crumbling bland facades were pressed together huddling close against the onslaught of sand, noise, and weird smells. In the distance, horns from sand weathered cars and trucks belted the general chaos of the streets. "Well, at least that's relatively Roman," Shelby said to no one in particular as she emerged from the bar.

Her words grabbed the attention of the nearby shop stall owner who began insisting in very broken English that the 'pretty lady need pretty scarf.' He was older and dressed like all of the other shopkeepers in a long plain loose shirt and pants. The leather on his sandals was cracked from a decade of dry desert heat and sand. Behind his pushiness was a kind smile and Shelby was just buzzed enough to tolerate the fawning over her from the old man. From the dozens of colorful scarves hanging at the opening of his stall, he began pulling them down one by one and holding them against her dark hair. When she declined the scarves, he began to go through the list of other items crammed into every possible inch of his broom closet sized shop. As she tried to explain she wasn't interested, her American words sparked a ripple effect through the stalls that were so desperately starved for tourists after some recent attacks in other nearby cities. Nothing about the experience was the fading into the background she was looking for. To escape the sales pitch onslaught, Shelby headed for her hotel.

Turning the corner from the edge of the market, the setting sun dazzled her eyes. She blinked hard against the black spots in the middle of her sight line. "Jesus," she bitched.

"There are others here who may be more help to you," a voice said and faded into a gentle chuckle.

Shelby put on her mental armor and turned to face the owner of the chuckle. The weathered gray man shrugged an apology for startling her and nodded as he opened a door to a hookah shop. Smoke poured out into the street in a heady earthy cloud. Tendrils curled around her chin caressing her face. *There are others here who may be more help to you* he had said. But why? Her palms burned and, without understanding why, she put her stinging hand on the door and went inside.

Stepping inside onto the mosaic floor was stepping back in time, but this time without the blinding flash of light and minor electrocution. It was more like time had stood still in this place. Golden paint peeked through spaces between mirrors framed with dark ornately carved wood in a seemingly haphazard collection of shapes and sizes. Above them hung small stained-glass lamps and a few exposed light bulbs. Once in a while, there would be a metal fan that looked like it came straight out of a World War II film where it had been hanging in the tent of some grizzled old commander planning to sack a small village in the name of democracy and the queen. Small tray stands with brass tops and simple metal bases sat next to equally small wooden tables. Shelby was sure she had seen the chairs before at Vito's Italian Pie and Pasta in Queens. The seats were streaked and worn thin from decades of backsides sitting and smoking for hours. A wooden lattice arch gave some grace to a yawning opening in the back which led to a palm-filled patio dotted with more small trays and seats along the back walls of the courtyard. In the back corner of the long narrow room near the patio opening, was the man who had spoken to her outside. He sat facing the door with an empty chair across from him. The man's eyes looked straight into Shelby's. He was waiting for her.

He nodded again and she made her way past the clouds and smoke rings, past mothers bouncing babies on their knees talking to old women, past the old men gesturing wildly with their hands and hookah hoses in the heat of debate, to the man who sat still and silent at the back of the room.

"Have a seat," he said gesturing to the perilously thin chair in front of him.

"I half expected you to greet me with 'Whooo are youuuuu?' I feel a bit like Alice in Wonderland talking to the caterpillar. Somehow I feel you know more about me and why I'm here than I do."

The man chuckled the rich sonorous laugh again. There was warmth in it, even though Shelby had steeled herself for danger. "You may be right about that. I've been expecting you."

"Have you? Why?" Shelby was starting to feel as stupid as she probably looked sitting in this exotic local hangout.

"We have something in common, you and I. Can you not guess what it is?"

"I can't imagine. There could be so many things and so few things." Shelby was starting to engage the game of vagaries, not because she enjoyed mental acrobatics, but because if she didn't answer a question, she couldn't be wrong and as idiotic as she felt.

"You have arrived from Rome, yes?"

"Yes, but how did you know?"

The man smiled his rich warm smile again. "Don't be afraid. We have a friend in common."

"Benny?"

The man shrugged. "Carmelita."

Shelby stared at him. How could a man in the streets of Cairo know a half-crazy Roman psychic? She put her palms on her face and rubbed them back into her hair. "Ok, I'll bite. How?"

"Anyone who seeks the spirits will long to seek them in Egypt. Carmelita made a trip here many years ago. She was hungry for knowledge about the gods of the ancients and I was her guide to the ruins. She asked questions most tourists would be afraid to ask. Questions of faith and ritual more than history. Fascinating woman and gifted in her craft. There was more to the old ways than I could teach her in the time she had here, so we often wrote to one another as she thought of more things she was curious about. Over time, we became good friends."

Shelby could see Carmelita in her red lipstick and pant suit with her beehive wrapped in Egyptian scarves traipsing around the ruins. There was something both comical and fitting in the picture. "Then, you are at an advantage, Mr.-?"

"Forgive me, Shelby. My name is Rafeeq Said," he answered with a slight bow of his head. "Rafeeq, please."

"Rafeeq." Shelby nodded. "I only just met Carmelita. My connection to her comes from Benito Moretti. I guess she told you about the weirdness?"

"She didn't call it that, but yes."

"What did she call it?"

"Destiny."

Somehow, coming from Rafeeq, it didn't sound as ridiculous as it had when Shelby thought it on the cab ride back from the burbs of Rome. "So, you actually believe all that stuff. I'm having a hard time wrapping my head around that word, myself. Weirdness seems a whole lot easier to take. Destiny sounds too big for me. I'm not a destiny kind of girl."

Rafeeq leaned back in his chair and rested his head on the back wall. He looked down his crooked nose at her just long enough to make her squirm a bit on the paper-thin seat. The hum of the hookah bar faded into the background in the moment that passed between them. Shelby felt like she was being sized up and coming up short remembering a similar moment in Carmelita's flat. The stare-down was broken when a waitress set a glass of chianti and a fresh bowl of shisha on the table in front of Shelby. "Perhaps," Rafeeq began, "you don't know yourself very well."

She lifted the glass to her lips and drank a rather unladylike swig of the rich Italian wine. She didn't care that it showed up without her ordering it. It felt warm going down and reminded her of Benny. The only sane person in this whole mess, which in itself was bizarre.

Rafeeq sat forward with a groaning creak of the pathetic wooden chair under his small frame. "There is time for all of this heavy talk later. For now, let Egypt surround you. There is much to experience here. Starting with this," he said with a wink as he peeled the foil halfway back on the small cup on the top of the tall elegant contraption beside him, pushing the small hot lumps of coal on the foil over to one side. He then filled the cup with shisha from the bowl the waitress brought. The small piece of foil was replaced over the cup with his masterful touch which kept him from the scalding Shelby would surely have gotten had she tried. Tiny holes had been punctured the tin foil so the heat of the small lumps sitting on the tin could heat the shisha beneath them. Once everything was prepared, Rafeeq handed the hose to Shelby.

Before Shelby knew it, minutes had melted into an hour before the final pull on the pipe was had. Rafeeq was true to his word. None of the heaviness of destiny and weirdness permeated the smoke or conversation for the rest of the evening. Instead, he lightened the atmosphere with tales of Carmelita in her pant suit scrambling up and down the ruins of Giza and Luxor.

As they parted ways in the lobby of her hotel, Rafeeq promised with a bow he would accompany her and Tarek on their tours of the ruins. "Tarek is a good guide with plenty to teach about the history, but he doesn't put much store in the spiritual. For that, you need me."

"And Carmelita would have it no other way, I'm sure."

The deep chuckle followed him into the night.

CHAPTER 5

Shelby stood on the dingy platform waiting on the evening train that would take them south to the Valley of the Kings overnight. Giza would be her last stop rather than the first since Tarek thought it would make a more impressive end to her visit. It didn't make any difference to her, so she went along with it. The Great Pyramid leg of the trip meant a camel ride and Shelby was all for putting off the ridiculous spectacle as long as she could. Since the Egyptians were trying to do everything possible to protect the Americans and their dollars, she and her companions had been assigned one of the small train cars to themselves.

The station resembled the train stations back home in the city. God, that seemed like lifetimes ago. In a way, it was, she thought as the train thundered into the station and sighed with the exhaustion of the old and weary as it came to a stop. The Crayola green paint was chipped and cracked from the many forays through the blowing desert sand. Chrome art deco trim made it look like a tired relic from a more fashionable era of wealthy youth on the Grand Tour. She wondered if Agatha Christie's Orient Express was inspired by this old desert rail serpent. Questioning her life choices when it came to trusting her tour guides, she joined the crowd preparing to board the geriatric train taking her into the wilds of Egypt.

Tarek took her small bags and boarded first. Rafeeq handed her up into the car and followed behind the young people. Since picking her up, Tarek relished his part of guide and protector with Oscar-worthy gusto.

Rafeeq chuckled. "Look at him. You would think he was valet for the Queen of Sheba." Tarek was shooing common passengers out of the aisles for Shelby to pass. "Better go on, your majesty," Rafeeq said with a wink. "The natives will not stand for his attitude for long."

Shelby pushed through the crowd in Tarek's wake murmuring apologies no one understood. Soon, they were outside of her berth in their private car.

"Tarek, would you order dinner for the three of us to eat here? I don't think Shelby needs to be on display in the dining car."

Tarek nodded with the wisdom of a sage. "My thought as well," he said to Rafeeq who looked at him with grace only the patience of true wisdom can bring. Then to Shelby, "Is there anything else you require?"

She resisted the urge to play the royal regent and opted instead for, "No, I'm good. Thanks." Tarek bowed and slipped out of the door. Shelby sat on the narrow vinyl bench seat and leaned her head back closing her eyes. The train wheels spun then caught the tracks as it pulled out of the station and began its journey to the Valley of the Kings.

"Perhaps you would like to rest before dinner?" Rafeeq asked with his hand on the door preparing to make a polite exit.

"No, please stay," Shelby insisted. She rubbed her stinging palms on the cool plastic upholstery, not that it actually helped anything. The pain in her hands kept Elijah Faircloth and his journal constantly in the back of her mind. She was drawn to the thing, but hated it at the same time. As she tried to find cool spots of the 1970s for her hands to rest, a thought slowly dawned on her. Carmelita didn't know about the book, which meant Rafeeq didn't know everything. If he was supposed to be Carmelita's eyes and ears on this strange adventure, he was going to have to go all in. Damn it. She was going to have to get the thing out. She hated touching it when she wasn't buzzed to dull the pain. "There's something you need to see."

Rafeeq raised a gray eyebrow. "Oh?"

Shelby pushed herself up and peeled the backs of her thighs off the bench. As she reached for her backpack and unzipped the pocket, the sparks under her skin danced wildly. When she touched it in the darkness of the pocket, a blue flash leaped from her fingertip to the journal. "Shit and daffodils!" she cursed dropping the book on the floor.

Rafeeq's dark eyes widened. "Are you alright?"

Shelby poked at the book with her toe and rubbed her fingers. "I'm fine, but that was new."

"New?"

"Yeah, it usually hurts to touch it, but the blue spark was a fun twist," she said rolling her eyes. "This tiny torture chamber is what I wanted to show you." She pushed it across the floor to him with her foot.

Rafeeq hesitated as if wondering whether he would be in for a similar shock when he reached for it, but was too intrigued to resist the temptation. His palm hovered just above the cover for an instant before he lowered his hand and picked it up without incident. "Nothing. Perhaps it is just some static from the rails?"

Shelby shrugged. "Maybe, but I doubt it. Hurts me to hold it. Didn't hurt Benny. Open it and read the first pages, then tell me if you still think it's static."

Rafeeq opened the cracked leather cover of the book and began to read. Every few lines, he would glance up at Shelby. As he read, his expression began to change from passive interest to genuine concern. Once in a while, he would slam it shut and open it right back up again.

"I only managed to get through the Great Wall," Shelby explained. "It freaks me out."

Rafeeq closed the book and let it rest on his lap. "I can see why. Where did you get this?"

"From a library in Rome. I was wandering and thinking and just ended up there." Shelby explained how she came across the book and how the little old man with the odd tattoo there seemed to want her to find it.

"He's a Watcher," Rafeeq answered plainly.

"A what?"

"Watcher."

Shelby stared at Rafeeq. Either she was losing her mind or there was more to the old guy sitting across from her. "What the hell is a Watcher? And how the hell do you know about them?" Her hands sizzled harder as he handed the book across to her. She didn't want to take it back, but did anyway. A spark danced along her fingers as they wrapped around the cover. As she watched the blue light jump from finger to finger, she realized it didn't hurt any more than usual. "What the fuck is happening to me?"

"You're getting closer."

Shelby leveled her gaze at Rafeeq. "I think you better start talking, old man."

A quick knock on the door broke the stare between Shelby and Rafeeq. She tossed the book into her bag as Tarek opened the door. Behind him stood a man in a uniform carrying a tray with food. "Dinner is served," Tarek proclaimed proudly.

Rafeeq and the Watcher would have to wait. There was no way in hell she was dragging this simple soul into her madness.

Over dinner, Tarek babbled on about the wonders of the ancient ruins Shelby would see in the morning. Rafeeq said little. Shelby desperately tried to make polite conversation as she picked at the allegedly authentic cuisine. She'd eaten her fair share of delicious Egyptian food, but this reminded her more of airline food with an ethnic twist. The spices were odd and the colors were dull and monochromatic. The vibrancy of the food in Cairo was glaringly absent. She choked down something beige and pasty as Tarek explained the most recent excavations in the Valley of the Kings and the archaeological reconstruction of sections of Karnak. Rafeeq pushed something grayish around on this tray with a piece of bread. The dinner babble seemed interminable, but finally Tarek took a breath and went to find the man who would clear dinner and bring coffee.

"I'm not sure coffee is what I need this late, but what the hell? It got him to stop talking," Shelby sighed and leaned back into the vinyl.

"He means well."

Shelby opened her eyes and fixed them on Rafeeq. "He does, doesn't he? He's not the one I'm worried about right now."

Rafeeq smiled slightly. The spark his eyes had the night before at the hookah bar was gone. "It was not my intention to concern you, Shelby. I said too much."

Shelby leaned forward and rested her arms on her knees. "I'd say you haven't said quite enough."

"There will be time for that later. Tarek returns."

As if on cue, the clinking of cups on a tray heralded the arrival of Tarek with the coffee. Rafeeq held the door for the young man and the train steward, casting almost furtive glances over their head towards Shelby. Once the dinner plates were taken by the steward who made a valiant attempt to conceal his irritation at her guide's holier-than-thou attitude, Tarek placed the coffee service on the small table and resumed his stream-of-consciousness history lesson. Shelby smiled and nodded in all the right places, but kept stealing looks over the chipped rim of her cup at her companion on the other side of the compartment. She wanted to trust him, and she had last night in the haze of the hookah bar. But there was something she doubted now and he knew it. Why didn't he just answer her?

Soon enough, Tarek decided the time had come for his American guest to rest for the adventures of the next day. He gathered the coffee cups and made his way out into the corridor to find the steward again so Shelby's berth could be made up for the night.

As her young guide hurried off, Rafeeq stood to leave. Shelby held up a hand to stop him. "Wait. You still have explaining to do."

Rafeeq paused at the door. "There is one who can explain better than me. Tomorrow at Karnak." With a slight bow of his silver head, he slipped into the corridor and was gone. More goddamn riddles.

A moment later, the steward was back to make down her bed for the night, even though Shelby was fairly certain it wasn't really part of his job. He pulled the bench out so it went from a sofa shape to a flat bed. Then, he got sheets and pillows down from the chrome rack near the ceiling and made the bed for her. An avocado green velour blanket was placed at the foot, though she wasn't likely to use it. The stuffiness of the train was closing in on her enough without the added weight of a blanket. She thanked the steward as he left, then sat cross-legged in the middle of the bed. "How in the hell am I supposed to sleep?" she muttered. "Coffee, itchy starched sheets, and an old weirdo who speaks in riddles. Yeah, that makes for a great night." Her eyes settled on her backpack in the corner of the floor. Elijah Faircloth's journal. And a couple of tiny bottles of liquor from the hotel minibar. "Well, Eli. Let's you and me spend the night together."

She pulled out a little bottle of Jager and shot it, wincing hard as it burned its way down her throat. "Ugh. No wonder people drink that shit cold," she grumbled tossing a few little bottles of vodka and a bottle of what she assumed to be whiskey on the bed. Blue sparks danced along her fingertips as she pulled the book from her bag. The electricity in her hands was only slightly dulled by the alcohol, so she threw back one of the bottles of vodka and settled onto the bed.

The strangeness of my experience at The Great Wall has left me shaken, but curious. I am the picture of health so I cannot contribute the episode on the wall to any medical concern. Yet, I feel as though my mental faculties could fall into question. I can tell no one about what I saw—

Elijah's entry left off and a map was below the words on the page. No words were included to help her figure out what it was supposed to be. There was a rectangle in the center that was slightly cock-eyed in relation to the rest of the drawing. Above that was a semi-circle that radiated outward. Scattered around them both were small squares and dots. She stared at it for several minutes trying to make heads or tails of what Eli was trying to create. Giving up, she turned the page and the narrative picked back up again.

I don't know what the map is, but it was so clear in my dreams and lingered with me as I awoke. So much so that to get the image to leave my head, I decided to draw what I saw.

"Well, shit, Eli. All that time staring at it and you didn't know what the damn thing was either," Shelby griped at the dead Victorian.

It has been an arduous journey through the ancient lands of China. The vastness of this place staggers the imagination. I was able to get passage on a boat traveling from the Wall down the Yellow River. Nothing glamorous, but comfortable enough. As we sailed, once in a while, I could see the Wall from the deck, looming like an ancient specter that knew my troubled spirit well. It almost called to me and once, just once, did I consider going back. But for what reason? Would there be answers or more terror? There is safety on this boat. Nothing like the experience at the Wall has happened here. I wonder if I imagined the whole thing.

"Nope," Shelby said as though Elijah Faircloth was sitting at the foot of the bed telling her his story. For a moment, she almost imagined him to be there looking at her.

It had been too real to be imagined. One doesn't imagine all of those sensations, or those feelings of such intense emotion. No, it was not imagined, but I can't think of what it could mean.

His journal entries became shorter and related only the steps in his journey through China and into the Middle East for several pages. Nothing useful there. As she read them, she could feel a need from him for a sense of normalcy. It was like he was focusing on the mundane to keep the memories of his experience at the Wall out of his mind.

My pilgrimage along the Silk Road has been uneventful. There was a moment of very real fear when the train was robbed in a remote Persian town, but the criminals were quickly apprehended and tossed quite literally off the train. Otherwise, the trip has been a swirling tapestry of people and places that has lived up to every expectation I had about this adventure.

Elijah Faircloth's script handwriting was relaxed and clear in this section of the journal. Quite a change from the hurried scrawl of the first few pages. No sense of urgency. Then the handwriting changed again. As Shelby's eyes came to the place on the page where the writing became erratic, her hands began to buzz hard with electricity. She shot back one of the vodka bottles to numb them, but it would take a few minutes before the pain subsided. Blue sparks shot from her fingers to the pages they held. Energy, but no heat to ignite the aged paper. She wanted desperately to put the book down, but it was held fast in her hand like a massive magnet.

It has happened again. Just as I was comfortable in my freedom from the horrific events on the Wall, it has happened again. I fear I am losing my mind, yet feel completely sane. No sane person would write the things I am recording here. I cannot be in my right mind. But what I have seen and felt is so real. It cannot be madness. There must be a normal explanation. There must be.

Our caravan through Persia arrived at the Great Colonnade in Palmyra without incident. We had been warned about bandits lurking in the Arabian desert, but there were none seen. All was going well as we explored the vast structures. The sun shimmered above the sands and glinted off of the ancient columns adding to the splendor of the place and highlighting the magnificent carvings. Our guide spoke broken English, but enough to enlighten us on the history of the place and its importance to the prosperity of the Silk Road. Columns soared above our heads as we walked along towards the center of the ancient town. Ahmed, our guide, stopped to speak to one of the locals, and our group spread out to look on our own. The sun was high and I paused under a sliver of shade from the Monumental Arch. Being so far from past memories of China and taking such interest in the Roman architecture in the Middle East, I thought nothing of placing my hand on the wall to steady myself as I rested.

The jolt of electricity raced up my arm with more force than before and the white light enveloped me again, blinding me to my surroundings. As my senses came back to me, I found myself in the midst of another battle. However, this time, it was tearing through a marketplace being overrun by soldiers. Wooden shop stalls lined the colonnade filled with all the treasures of the East spilling out of toppled shelves and shattered pots. Fabrics, spices, and trinkets once admired, now trodden over. A mixture of an Arabic language and Latin filled my ears as soldiers raced by shouting orders. On a horse, leading the charge, was a woman. Armor and the sword in her hand was a stark contrast to the feminine braids in her long dark hair. She was fearless as she rode in front of her troops against the Roman regiments. The Palmerian troops were rougher and less organized than the disciplined Romans who marched with swords and shields locked and protecting them against the Arab onslaught. All around me, the battle raged and the fear in me mounted, though I wasn't sure why.

As I stood watching my surroundings, people passed by without seeming to notice me at all. Soldiers marching, women and children screaming. Like the Wall, I seemed to be there and not be there at the same time. Yet, somehow, it felt familiar. The more I took in my surroundings the more familiar they felt. It was as though I was standing in a -

"Memory," Shelby whispered as she read the word. The moment she realized the same thing came flooding back to her. One more bottle of vodka.

As this thought began to take shape, I felt a hand slap my face. Startled, I looked to see who had struck me and came face to face with the woman I had been watching from a distance moments before. "Slave!" she said, and I realized she was talking to me. Actually speaking to me as though I was really there.

"What?" I stammered in shock.

A man standing beside the woman raised his hand to strike me, but the woman stayed his hand. "No, let him be. Poor fool is frightened. Come, slave. We're riding out of the city. I won't be a Roman trophy."

"You're leaving the battle? The people? But, you're the—"

She stood tall and proud and she spoke firmly. "I'm Queen Zenobia and I will not be questioned by a slave! Bring him," she ordered the man who almost hit me. He grabbed my clothes and pulled me. When he did, he yanked me away from the column.

Again, the white light surrounded me and I found myself back in the ruins of the Grand Colonnade. A woman was fanning my face and an older man was holding a flask to my lips. They assumed it was the heat that had gotten the best of my English constitution and bade me rest where I was a few moments longer. I knew it was not the heat, but did as they suggested so as not to raise suspicion that anything else was the cause of my collapse. After a few moments' rest, I insisted I felt well enough to continue.

As I walked, I pondered the experience from the Arch. At first, no one responded to my presence. People were all around me, but no one acknowledged anything. Then, suddenly the queen spoke to me. She called me "Slave." Slave! Then, it suddenly came to me. The others could see me all along, but I was only a slave. Not worth their attention! So much confusion has settled in my mind. Once the realization occurred to me, I walked through the rest of the Colonnade as if I were in a trance. I made polite excuses to those who were concerned about my health and did my best to distract myself from my own thoughts.

Once aboard the train and in the security of my compartment, I was finally able to let my mind think through the experiences. There were so many thoughts, reasons, and possibilities for what could be going on, but I continued to return to the idea of madness. It was the only thing that made any sense.

"I've got news for you, Eli. Nothing is going to make sense to you for a long time," Shelby sighed. Between the rhythm of the train and the booze, sleep was starting to look like a better and better idea. Closing the book, she slid between the sandpaper sheets and slept.

CHAPTER 6

Tarek had spent the better part of the morning being overly attentive to Shelby giving her no time to corner Rafeeq about what he said the night before. Over and over, it played in her head, but she couldn't figure out how he knew what the odd little Italian in the library was. A Watcher. The man seemed to know she would be there and what she needed to find. So, she figured he was a Watcher of her. What she didn't understand was why.

The bus to Luxor was a microcosm of Egyptian tourism. People from all over the world had collected in what passed as a bus but looked like something that had driven out of a Norman Rockwell painting and didn't fare well in the harsh Egyptian climate. British tourists tried to maintain their aloofness, but it just made them look like assholes as they made cold vague remarks in attempts to discourage the boisterous intrusion of their space by the Americans who were thrilled to have someone who understood them. The Brits looked snappy in their khaki trousers and pressed white shirts, while the Americans looked comfortable but ridiculous in their cargo shorts and mid-calf athletic socks. Both looked insanely out of place next to the Egyptians in their loose trousers and tunics. In the back of the bus were hipster college kids who were trying to look cool, but were failing miserably as the ruins came into view through the filthy film on the bus window. Shelby, in her cut-offs and Rolling Stones tank - which had been more of a pun than she intended among the scattered remnants of temple pieces- was decidedly more touristy than she cared to admit.

One by one the group clambered out of the creaking old bus and did the same thing. Their eyes scanned the temple complex and mouths dropped open. Massive stone structures loomed in front of them. "I had no idea-" Shelby stammered. Usually when it came to ancient ruins, she was hard to impress, but there was no denying the majesty of what stood in front of her. Even the pyramids of Giza standing sentinel in the desert seemed less impressive. The sheer size of the place was staggering, even if the exterior walls were less ornate than she expected.

Tarek began his narrations of the comprehensive history of the Valley of the Kings. Over her shoulder, she heard the quiet voice of Rafeeq. "Can you feel it?"

Shelby stopped and looked at him. "Feel what?"

"There is an energy here different from anywhere else. The tourists felt it but didn't know what it was. They mistook it for amazement. What they felt is power."

"Power?" Shelby raised a skeptical eyebrow at her spiritual tour guide.

"You feel it. You know you do."

She nodded slowly. The electricity in her hands had become almost unbearable.

Tarek urged her forward through the avenue of ram-headed sphinxes to the towering First Pylons that formed the entrance to the temple complex. "This is the newest part of the temple built by the Ethiopian king Nectanebo I. Many kings and pharaohs added parts to the temple and tore down the work of others over 2,000 years. Of course, the famous Ramses II constructed a portion of the complex, and altered some of it, as well."

"Altered?" Shelby asked.

Tarek nodded. "His father, Seti I, constructed the Hypostyle Hall, here." Tarek led them over to the rows of massive columns and prattled on. "There were once one-hundred thirty-four of them under a stone slab roof. Ramses, of course, wanted his own legacy to surpass that of his father, as well as any of the kings of the past. He changed many of the hieroglyphs to erase the names of predecessors he didn't like, including some belonging to Seti. A king is as good as the eternity of his name, and if he has no name, then he is no king. See, here." Tarek pointed high above them on one of the huge columns of the great Hypostyle Hall. "See the one set deeper than the others? The original one was chiseled off and Ramses' name is carved in its place."

"What an asshole thing to do," Shelby said louder than she intended. An older couple turned their noses up at her then stuck them back into their camera viewfinders.

"Great rulers can afford to be that way," Rafeeq replied. "Come, meet the great asshole." The three of them wound their way through the crowds and ruins as

Tarek stopped to show Shelby obelisks and statues that were essential parts of any good tour of the Amun temple. As impressive as the sheer size of the ruins was, it began to fade into a swirl of reddish stone and camera flashes overwhelming her senses to the point where it lost its majesty. Dust floated in the air adding a pinkish haze to the mix. Finally, they entered an open court with a gargantuan statue that could only belong to the equally gargantuan ego of Ramses II.

"Ramses was one of the great warrior kings, and some say too great. When he ran out of enemies, he risked losing his power," Tarek explained like any good walking talking textbook.

"So, naturally, he decided to gain his glory by making himself a god," Rafeeq finished.

"Naturally. I mean, that's my plan as soon as we're finished here," Shelby said flatly. She wasn't one to go all googly-eyed over the male tendency to oversell themselves.

Rafeeq sent Tarek on an errand for bottled water insisting they would not continue the tour of the temple until his return. Shelby raised an eyebrow and waited for an explanation. "There's someone you need to meet," he said simply. With a glance around him, he stepped over the ropes marking public boundaries around the stones and slipped into the shadows of the colossal statue. He held one arm out in a gesture for her to follow. Wondering how she was going to explain being tossed out of an ancient ruin to Dina, Shelby shrugged and hopped over the rope. They had been standing at the feet of the mighty pharaoh and he now led her to the back of the throne the ego's ass had rested on for eons. "Here."

"Here. And?" The buzzing in her hands had become insane. Her teeth were set on edge trying not to let on how much power this place had over her. She was drawn to it and completely terrified by it.

Rafeeq tilted his head expectantly. After coming to the realization Shelby had no idea what he was getting at, he finally spoke. "How do your memories find you? Like Elijah? You touch things?"

"So, that's why you sent Tarek away," she said pulling a water bottle out of her backpack. "Clearly it wasn't because we needed water."

Rafeeq shook his head. "No, we don't need water."

"Answers?"

"Answers."

"Shit." She was going to have to touch the damn thing. Knowing what was coming made nothing any easier. If anything, it was worse. No one willingly electrocutes themselves. No sane person, anyway. "Memories don't happen to me just anywhere, you know. We could get ourselves tossed out for nothing."

Rafeeq chuckled the same laugh she heard in the Cairo street. The laugh of one who knows something you don't. "Go on. I'm here and will deal with the tourists if anyone sees us. You know what you have to do."

Shelby wanted to take a deep breath to prepare herself for the pain that would come, but knew it would mean inhaling half a lung of desert dust. As she raised her hand slowly to the throne and the electricity in her body thrummed, she ached for Benny. Insane as all of this was, there was a comfort in knowing Benny was there when she opened her eyes. This time, she would come to looking up at a silver-headed Egyptian she hardly knew, not the bronzed smile trying to hide the concern in those rich Roman eyes.

Her own eyes closed, Shelby placed her palm flat on the warm stone. Electricity shot through her arm and surged through her entire body. White light engulfed her once again. As the shock abated and the light faded, the temple plaza burst into a carnival of color. The reddish-brown stone was a bland backdrop for vibrant illustrations covering the massive stone columns. Gone were the tourists. In fact, everything was gone. No sound, no sand dust in the air. Just a staggering technicolor temple.

Out of the shadows between the massive papyrus columns, a figure emerged. Not wanting to let go of the throne and risk losing her chance for answers, Shelby stood rooted to the spot letting whoever it was come to her. As the light illuminated the approaching shape, she realized it was a woman. Shelby had half expected another pompous ruler like Hadrian, or even the Great Ego himself.

The woman held herself with the regal grace of a queen as she stood in front of Shelby. Her dress was made of leopard skin with a crescent collar beaded with turquoise and precious stones. Thick black hair was arranged in what must have been a hundred tiny glossy braids held back from her bronzed face by a red silk cord around her forehead and simply tied in the back. Her feet were bare, but there were delicate blue beaded bands around her ankles and wrists. Red lips and charcoal eyeliner made her exotic features strikingly beautiful. The woman stood for a moment with her head cocked to the side examining Shelby before she spoke. "My name is Seshat, Goddess of Wisdom and Keeper of the Book of Knowledge."

Shelby stared in disbelief. "I know I should kneel or something, but I'm afraid if I take my hand off the stone-"

"No need to bow, child. You may release your hand. Here I decide who stays and goes, not you or the stone."

There was something comforting and terrifying in the goddess' words. Beauty, grace and power combined inside Seshat like a sports car on a starting line. Shelby knew this woman was no one to be trifled with, but was somehow drawn to her. Letting go of the throne, Shelby rubbed her hands out of habit, but quickly noticed they weren't stinging now. "Where am I? This doesn't feel like-"

"A memory? No. You were never here. In fact, you were never in Egypt. There are no memories for you to chase here. Only knowledge."

"What is this place? I mean, I know it's the temple Amun, but-" Shelby found herself with a startling lack of words to finish sentences. For someone with snark always on the tip of her tongue, it was a weird feeling to be so intimidated.

"Between the plane of the living and the realm of the spirit. Here, the gods walk with the living and the dead."

"Holy shit," Shelby whispered.

Seshat smiled and her regal carriage relaxed with a chuckle. "In a manner of speaking. Come." The goddess led Shelby to the base of one of the towering columns and motioned for her to sit on the wide base. Seshat sat beside her and took Shelby's hands in her own and turned them over in her palms. The goddess' hands were soft and warm. Almost human. "What have you learned about your hands, child?"

"They hurt like hell around certain things. It was worse around the places connected to Hadrian. Then, there's the book."

Seshat nodded. "Elijah's journal."

"How do you know about that?"

"Goddess of Knowledge."

"Right," Shelby said sheepishly. "The blue sparks have been a fun addition lately."

"They won't hurt you, but notice when you see them. They're trying to get your attention."

"The sparks are alive?"

Seshat chuckled again. It was almost musical when the goddess laughed. "No, child, but the energy around you is connected to things beyond your comprehension, and the universe can use that energy to guide you. However, it only works if you pay attention," the goddess added as she released Shelby's hands.

"So, is Carmelita right? Am I a Traveler?"

Seshat nodded, her rich black hair shimmering with the movement. "You are."

"Really? She told me I would travel until I found my destiny to make great things happen. That I would only watch great things happen until then."

"And she's right."

"Come on, you're the Goddess of Knowledge. Surely you know what a fuck up - sorry- I am as a general rule. There's no greatness here."

The goddess smiled and stood. "Come. Walk with me, Shelby." Doing as she was told because you damn sure don't argue with goddesses, she followed Seshat across the plaza. "Do you see these carvings?" the goddess asked. "Each has a story behind them."

"Yes, Tarek was quite enthusiastic about those."

"And he did a good job. However, he only knows the history on the surface."

Shelby's mind flashed back to what Rafeeq had said about her needing a spiritual guide along with the history. "There are some pretty big egos on these stones," Shelby mused running her hands over some of the carvings she could reach.

"True. And there are some that may not be what the history books would have you believe. You see, every one of these names belongs to a man, and occasionally a woman. Each of them were born into a destiny they did not choose and had to learn to navigate in their reality. Some, admittedly, did that better than others. But all had to come to the realization at some point or another that greatness chose them, and there was nothing they could do about it but rise to the occasion."

"You can't possibly be comparing me to these giants of the ancient world!"

"They *became* giants. No one is born a giant," Seshat said plainly. Clearly, this was no big deal to a goddess. Hell, she was a goddess. What could possibly be a big deal to her?

"I'm just some chick from Manhattan who can't get her shit together," Shelby insisted.

"Apparently one who needs better shit," Seshat replied with a twinkle in her black eyes.

Shelby couldn't stop it. Laughter spilled out of her like the Nile over the banks after the rains. The sheer ridiculousness of the whole thing was hysterical and then adding an Egyptian goddess quoting a Jamaican tour guide was just too much. Even Seshat began to laugh. The music of the goddess' laugh echoed off the temple walls. As they finally caught their breath, Shelby looked up at Seshat and said, "This is just not who I am."

"You're right. It's not. Not yet. It's who you are supposed to be, though. You see, if you had been born in the time you were destined for, you would have had a similar experience to the kings on these walls. Your destiny would have played out in front of you. But that's not what happened."

"What *did* happen?"

Seshat paused a moment, considering how to explain. "Energy doesn't always play nicely. Occasionally things get out of balance and, despite our best efforts, there are shifts we can't control. You see the results of our efforts to control it on your plane in the forms of comets, solar flares, and anomalies science tries to explain away. All those things are really our ways of redirecting rogue energy safely. Sometimes, that redirection has effects we can't do anything about."

"Like tossing people out of their destinies," Shelby said.

"Exactly," Seshat conceded. "All life is energy. Sometimes, that energy ends up in the wrong life."

"But why the constant life hopping? Why can't the universe just put the energy back when it realizes there's been a misfire?"

Seshat sighed and leaned back against the temple wall. "Imagine every decision you make and every decision of every person you cross paths with has a string tied to it. Now, picture those strings over time. What happens?"

"I'd imagine something that looks roughly like a knitting basket in a herd of kittens."

"On a cosmic scale."

Shelby sighed. "So, it's up to me to unravel my own life yarn?"

"Right. We keep the universe spinning and you untangle your string. With a little help from us, of course."

"Watchers."

"Watchers. They work for us to keep you on track."

"Library guy?" Shelby asked. Seshat nodded. "Rafeeq?"

"No, he's not one of ours officially."

Shelby knew there was something Seshat wasn't telling her, and apparently, she'd have to figure Rafeeq out on her own. Like how the hell he knew she'd find a goddess to answer her questions at Luxor. Rather than press a goddess to answer questions she didn't want to, Shelby opted for a new questioning path. "So, Eli has done all of this?"

"Every Traveler forges their own path. But, yes."

Shelby thought for a minute, and Seshat gave her the time and silence to come to the question which was bubbling to the surface. "Can you tell me how to find the way back to my destiny?" she asked at length.

Seshat shook her head slowly. "I can, but, no. That's yours to discover. The answers will find you, but you have to allow yourself to see them. And there is much to be learned in the process."

The vibrant stones began to shimmer and Shelby could sense her time with the Goddess was coming to an end. "But what if I can't see them?" Shelby asked feeling panic setting in.

Seshat took Shelby's hands in hers again as the tingle began to slowly return. "Follow what you sense and you'll find your way." The goddess smiled and walked Shelby back to the throne of Ramses II. "And if you don't, there's an eternity in front of you to get there."

Seshat stood behind Shelby holding Shelby's palm against the stone then placed her own hand on Shelby's back as a blessing. White light blazed around them as Seshat faded away and the colors began to run down the stones like melted crayons. The tingling in her hands became a steady burn as the temple came back into focus. In a blur of semi-consciousness, just above her hand she saw a carving of the goddess. Blinking the world into focus, she looked up at Rafeeq who was decidedly not a hot Italian.

✳

The sun began to set in the Egyptian desert leaving the avenue of the sphinxes in shadow. In a few months, the avenue would be packed with tourists and locals to watch the ball of fire drop between the First Pylon at Winter Solstice. It must have been spectacular when the temple was in its heyday. Parades, chanting, and incense as men were made into gods. As it was, there was just a quiet shift from golden to gray. Once the sun sank below the horizon and the sky blackened, the temple lit up in a low warm yellow glow of incandescent lights. Silhouettes of palms gave the imposing old stones a sense of softness and life. The occasional breeze danced through the fronds that waved and beckoned the ancient deities to come rest for the night.

Shelby sat on the rooftop of a cafe overlooking the great gates of Karnak sipping a glass of wine and picking at a plate of beef moussaka. The food was delicious and the view of the temple illuminated in the night was breathtaking, but

Shelby's mind was somewhere between reality and eternity. Rafeeq and Tarek had been gracious enough to allow her a table to herself under the pretense she needed to get thoughts and notes together about her tour for Dina. She was pretty sure Rafeeq knew it was bullshit, but he went along with it anyway.

When she came to from her time with Seshat, Rafeeq had looked at her expectantly, but her only response was a nod. There was no way she was bringing him into everything she had been told, no matter how much he seemed to want to help. Seshat's words rang in her head: "He's not one of ours officially." What the hell had that meant? Was she supposed to trust him or not? At the moment, she was going with not.

The day had gone on with an extensive tour of the temple, more photos for the Magical History Tours, and Tarek's constant babbling narration. Shelby pretended to be interested to keep him talking enough to not allow Rafeeq a moment to question her. She needed time to process everything before she was ready to pull out some snippet she could tell him without telling him much. More than anything, she missed being able to talk to Benny.

"More wine?" a voice asked over her shoulder. Shelby half-nodded not really hearing or caring what was said. The waiter refilled her glass and she absently tapped her pencil on the edge of it. "Seshat?"

Shelby snapped into focus. "What did you say?"

The waiter pointed at the paper in front of her. "Seshat? There."

On the paper she had been faking making notes, was a drawing of the carving on the back of Ramses' throne. In her reverie, she had sketched the goddess. "Oh. I suppose it is."

"She who scribes."

"Sorry?"

"Seshat. It means 'she who scribes.' Goddess of Knowledge, Wisdom, and Writing," the waiter explained. Across the rooftop, the noisy table of hipsters was waving him over. With a smile, the waiter bowed and walked away.

"Well, well, your grace," Shelby said to the image on the paper. "It seems you and I have something in common. You, me, and Eli." Shelby downed the wine and signaled for her check.

CHAPTER 7

Winding northward in a slow dance with the Nile, the train rattled through the desert silence as its passengers slept. Most of them missed the dawn that resurrected the dead gray waters of the river into the life-giving elixir flowing to the heart of Egypt. Shelby had managed to get a few hours of sleep thanks to some American dollars and a bartender willing to sacrifice a bottle of rum. As the Great Pyramid came into view across the river banks, she began to regret the decision to drink her way to sleep. "Yeah, I'm destined for great things," she grumbled to her reflection above the wash basin in the carriage bathroom. Shelby's eyes wore deep shadows from lack of sleep and a raging hangover. Her stomach rolled with every sway of the train which wasn't boding well for her camel ride. Where was Hattie's hangover cure when she needed it?

By the time she staggered back to her berth, Tarek had set up breakfast and coffee for the three travelers. Thankfully, it was comprised of various breads and fruits next to a pot of black coffee. Had it been more gray mush, Shelby would have seen a good portion of that rum again. She took the cup Tarek handed her and blew across the top. "Thank you, Tarek. Just what I need."

"Rough night sleeping?" Rafeeq asked quietly as he spread butter on a pastry.

"Does it show that much?" she asked swallowing the bitter brew. Rafeeq nodded. Shelby leaned back on the cool vinyl and sighed. Her hands were buzzing almost as much as she was. "I guess you could say that."

He nodded his silver head. "Understandable."

Tarek passed her a plate of fruit and a piece of bread. "If you would prefer to put the pyramids off today, we could go tomorrow."

Rafeeq nodded. "They aren't going anywhere."

Shelby forced a smile at him. "Thank you, both. No, let's do it today. Although, I may need some time before I'm ready for a camel ride."

Tarek took the opportunity to walk her through possible changes to the itinerary that could push the camel excursion later in the day. By the time the plans had been laid and the breakfast cleared, the train was arriving at the Cairo station and the bread had soaked up enough alcohol to make the lurching to a stop slightly less nauseating. As Rafeeq bowed and stood in the doorway of her compartment to go, he said, "You won't find your destiny at the bottom of a bottle, Shelby."

"That all depends on the bottle."

Even Shelby in the state she was in could appreciate the magnitude of Giza. As usual, Tarek managed to narrate every history lesson she ever had on the pyramids, plus a few she hadn't. Rafeeq said little, but watched her closely, especially when she touched anything as if waiting on something to happen. Once she realized what was going on, Shelby couldn't resist entertaining herself. She hadn't told Rafeeq there were no memories for her in Egypt and he was expecting her to get electrocuted at any second. As Tarek shooed the local scammers and pointed things out, Shelby touched everything she could. For a while, it was amusing to watch Rafeeq tense up every time she put her hand out, but even that got old after a while. She wasn't sure whose side he was on, but it seemed cruel to torture him any longer.

"There are no memories here, so you can relax," she finally hissed in his ear as they stood in the claustrophobic line to experience the burial chamber.

"Having a little fun with me, were you?"

Shelby shrugged. "A little. I'm usually the one in the dark about things lately, so it felt good knowing something for a change."

"Is that all she told you? 'Feel free to touch Egypt. Have a nice day'?" Rafeeq said as sardonic as the night they met in the Cairo street.

"And Ramses was compensating for something."

Rafeeq chuckled. "So, nothing new, then. All that electrocution for nothing."

"I wouldn't say that." Or anything else as the line moved through the chamber and back out into the blazing Egyptian sun.

After the obligatory camel ride, which resulted in some of the best photos of the pyramids along with sore thighs Shelby could think of better ways to get, they took a cab back to Cairo. There are certain romantic notions commonly held about the ancient ruins based largely on carefully framed photos. The reality of the pyramids is they reside in their glory perilously close to the urban sprawl of the city. Slums and high-rise buildings encroach upon the Wonders of the World spoiling the majesty of the moment under a haze of smog. Shelby wondered how long it would take for the city to completely surround the monuments like the Luxor in Vegas, just without the neon and drag shows.

⚜

Shelby had taken a lot of showers in her life, but few held a candle to the one she took after her days in the Egyptian desert. The sponge bath on the train had scraped a layer of dust and sand off, but that was about it. Her dark hair was coarse from the sun and sand and her scalp gritty. Several washings later, she emerged feeling cleaner than she had in ages.

Her room was tiny, but neater than she expected of a Cairo hotel. Paper thin walls were the only real downside. Although, if she spoke whatever language was drifting through the paneling, it could have been an upside. Those people were either about to get busy or break up. For the sake of a good night's sleep, she was pulling for a break up. At this point though, all that really mattered were decent water pressure and creepy-crawly-free sheets and she had both. And wifi.

Shelby curled up on the bed and turned on her laptop. While she was waiting for the wifi that made dial up look like greased lightning, she towel-dried her hair and thought back over what Seshat said. There was so much she needed to talk through and no one to listen. Rafeeq didn't count. Something kept her from taking him into her confidence, but she couldn't quite figure out why. If Seshat had said he was one of her Watchers, she would have had no trouble opening up to him, but she didn't. Nothing negative was mentioned, but there was no glowing endorsement either. She needed Benny.

Elijah Faircloth keeping a journal to record things he knew no one else would believe was making more sense. Writing it down must have kept the thoughts from spinning out of control in his head. The rooftop waiter's words drifted into the mix of thoughts roaming free in her mind. "Seshat. Goddess of Writing," Shelby muttered. "Well, Eli, hope you won't mind if I take your idea into the 21st century a little." A quick text to Tarek with her flight information from Dina, then she began typing everything she wanted to remember from her time with Seshat, pausing only to toss back the occasional tiny bottle from the minibar.

Shelby's hands stung and blue sparks danced along her fingertips as she worked, but getting everything out of her head felt too good to be distracted by it. By the time she was current, the moon was high and the minibar was sparse. It was a poor substitute for a night with Benny, but it would have to do. With thoughts purged onto a computer screen, she slept.

✳

By the time she made it down to the restaurant in the lobby, Tarek and Rafeeq were finishing their breakfast and sipping coffee. The older man motioned to the empty seat next to him as her young guide put on the role of step-and-fetch-it once again ordering breakfast as though she was Cleopatra. "Sleep well?" Rafeeq asked as she poured a cup of coffee for herself.

"Except for a few hours where Seshat and Hadrian had a lover's quarrel over which gods were better dressers."

"Who won?"

"Seshat. Hard to argue with a woman in a leopard dress when you're a dude wrapped in a bed sheet," Shelby replied flatly.

Rafeeq shrugged in agreement and dropped a sugar cube into his coffee. "Tarek has arranged for a tour of the Cairo Museum, then some time in the markets before your flight this evening. Is there anything in particular you want to see at the museum?"

It was his way of fishing for information and Shelby wasn't biting. "I'm sure Tarek will make sure I see all of the best things. I'll let him take the lead," she said with a wink to her young guide who blushed and beamed.

Her breakfast arrived as Tarek excitedly told her of the plans he had made for her to have special access to some of the places where antiquities not on display were stored. Rafeeq watched and waited for some sign of particular interest from Shelby. He wasn't buying that there was nothing for her here and she knew it. Carmelita may have told him everything she experienced at Luxor, but Shelby was being tight-lipped. If she had Carmelita's gifts, she may have been able to see into his soul to know whether or not to trust him, but she didn't. The New Yorker in her was going with her gut and keeping on her guard.

Tarek paid the bill and called for a cab to take them to the museum. Much like Karnak, Tarek was full of information that meant little to nothing to her. Sure, it was interesting to see the real versions of the forgeries being sold in the market, but she liked the colorful sales pitches of the street vendors better than the dry history lessons of the museum. She obediently followed Tarek through the labyrinth of exhibits and was appropriately enthusiastic and awed at the museum's off-display items, but her mind was in Luxor. Even as genuine as the articles were, they seemed to lose much of their impressiveness after seeing the full glory of Karnak with Seshat.

The marketplace was far more Shelby's speed, even if the vendors swarmed her like vultures, albeit good-tempered ones. "Welcome to Khan Al-Khalili," Tarek said as they stepped out of the cab and began his unceasing history of the marketplace.

The smells and energy of Cairo's massive bazaar enveloped her like an exotic fog. Death and life danced together through the bustling shop stalls tucked into the old mausoleum arches. In every opening something glittered enticing shoppers with lanterns, jewelry, and figurines of everything from ancient gods to new ones. Clothing hung from wherever the stall owners could find crevices in the stone walls to put a hook and stacked in precariously teetering piles beneath them. Crowds were gathered in shaded shops to escape the heat of the day whether they were interested in the knock-offs sold there or not, and a sea of ethnicities flowed through the narrow passages between shop stalls.

Baskets and plastic tubs overflowed with spices in colors which shamed the gray mush of the train food and reminded Shelby of Elijah Faircloth's Silk Road journey. She hadn't wanted to read more of the journal because it hurt and freaked her out, if she was completely honest, but began to wonder if she should have looked for references to Egypt while she was in Cairo. In the wash of color and shimmering metal of a stall next to the spice seller, something caught her eye. The shop vendor immediately noticed her attention and pounced.

"Something special for pretty lady?" he asked with a wide smile.

"I'm just looking, thanks," Shelby answered knowing full-well it wasn't going to stop his onslaught of sales pitching.

"Only the best for the pretty lady. Best jewelry and trinkets in whole market. Whole Egypt!"

Shelby couldn't help but smile. "Oh? In all of Egypt?"

"Yes! Yes!" he insisted pulling out one thing after another as proof.

"I'm not one for flashy things," Shelby said in another attempt to quell the enthusiasm of the shop owner.

"Not flashy. Ok, ok. Let me see," he answered and set off searching for something Shelby may be interested in.

As he searched and pulled things out for her to see and she shook her head at all of them, her hands began to sizzle. Blue sparks danced along her fingertips like they had with the journal on the train. *'They are trying to get your attention.'* Testing the goddess' words, Shelby began to move her hands and watch the sparks to see if they changed at all. The stinging under her skin began to heat up as she moved her hand toward the item that had first caught her attention. It was tucked behind a pile of gilded jewelry and only a small part of blue peeked out. The turquoise reminded her of something and the sparks seemed to leap to the piece as she reached for it. Sliding it out from under the others, she was finally able to get a good look at it.

"It seems it is meant for you," Rafeeq said over her shoulder. He could see the sparks jumping from her fingertips to the bracelet in her hand.

Shelby stared at the bracelet. It was delicately beaded turquoise and was familiar somehow. Gently, she turned it over in her hand watching the sparks whose dark blue color contrasted with the greenish blue turquoise. The little bit of gold glittered as she turned it, but it wasn't like the other gold in the shop. This was darker, older. Not the blazing yellow shine of the fake pieces. As she looked at it, she realized where she had seen it before.

"How much are the bracelets?" she heard Rafeeq ask. They had agreed in the cab he would bargain for her so she wouldn't be cheated in the market. The shop owner gave a price without looking at what was in her hand, basing the cost on the pile she had removed it from. Shelby handed the money to Rafeeq.

The shopkeeper was beaming at having something to interest his pretty lady customer. "Wrap it up for you?" he asked.

"No, no. Thank you," Shelby answered. "I'd like to wear it." The shop owner's wide smile nearly split his face in half with pride as he thanked her and reminded her of his shop name so she could tell admirers.

As they walked away from the shop into the noise of the street, Rafeeq spoke. "Why that one?"

"It spoke to me," Shelby answered.

"Oh?" Rafeeq raised an eyebrow at her. "It isn't like the others. But you knew that, didn't you?"

Shelby nodded as she turned the bracelet around her wrist.

Rafeeq went on. "You seemed to recognize it. And I'd bet the shopkeeper had never seen it before if he had looked at what was in your hand."

"I did recognize it," she said at last, "and I wouldn't bet against you. What does this say?" she asked showing him a small hieroglyph carved into one of the turquoise stones.

"Destiny."

CHAPTER 8

Airports, like street cafes in crowded markets, are great places to hide in plain sight. The frazzled passengers focused on luggage and departure times were blessedly oblivious to anything else and Shelby was grateful for it. The tapestry of travelers woven through the concourse was rich in ethnicity and culture, but paled under a wash of fluorescent light and stained ceiling tiles. Women in headscarves sat and chatted alongside women with hot pink hair. Men in turbans discussed local news with the hipsters. Everyone had a destination. Everyone had a story to tell. If she cared to join the utopia of the airline waiting area, she could have had plenty for her travel writing, but the only story she was interested in was Eli's.

By the time she had finished her second rum and Coke at the bar a few gates away from hers, she had resolved herself to reading more of the journal. It wasn't without some coercion from the bracelet she wore and the damned hieroglyph goading her on. Seshat knew exactly what she was doing when she tucked that thing among the junk in the jewelry stall. The goddess had some answers for her, Eli had others, and still more were hers to find on her own. If the creeps got in her way of reading the journal, she'd be oblivious to information she may need. Seshat knew she would require something else to go with her liquid courage. The bracelet and the hieroglyph were the nudge she needed.

Sitting in a corner of the gate area, Shelby pulled the worn book from her backpack. As usual, the sparks danced along her fingers and the electricity in her hands sizzled. "Alright, Eli. Let's do this." She opened the book to where she had left off on the train to Luxor.

There is nothing like the comfort of one's berth on a train through magnificent countryside to put spirits to right again. As we traveled on the great Silk Road, I began to relax from the experiences at the Wall and the Colonnade. What had seemed like madness began to be excused more and more as a trick of the Arabian heat. Part of my mind still believed in what I had experienced, but the logical part pushed nonsensical notions out of my head in favor of the more rational ones. Perhaps that is what mad people do to justify their delusions.

We arrived in Constantinople mid-morning, which afforded me some time to explore before dinner. I had been properly cautioned against pickpockets and merchants who may be tempted to take advantage of the lone foreigner, but I wasn't concerned about either as I roamed through the narrow, cobbled streets of the city. Without hesitation, I made my way directly to the Galata Tower. There was no difficulty in finding it as the conical roof could be seen from almost any open space in the city. Parts of the old town still bore scars from the fire which recently ripped through many of the homes there, but repairs were coming along. There were places in which the buildings, set one on top of another and closely against the cobbles, seemed almost British in design. Once in a while, a minaret would rise up out of the buildings reminding me this was a truly Ottoman city.

Being a port, there was a constant influx of foreigners, so I was able to explore relatively unnoticed. Or, if I was noticed, it was with little interest. Soon, I came upon the tower itself rising up through the center of the buildings on either side of the street that led to the massive structure. For something so simple in design, it was both imposing and elegant as it loomed above me.

I had been told by a fellow traveler the most breathtaking views of the city and harbor were to be gained by climbing the steps to the top deck of the tower. While the climb was only mildly arduous, it seemed more so to someone who had not been inclined to physical activity from weeks on a train. It was certainly close and confined on the wooden steps spiraling tightly up one side of the stone tower with doors to the various levels on the way up. None of those doors interested me more than the view I was after, so I didn't stop to even see what was behind them. Rather, I pressed on to the top deck becoming embarrassingly breathless and conscious of an uncomfortable tingling in my hands. I had noticed the stinging sensation many times, but not often with such severity.

As the stairs reached their pinnacle, suddenly the space opened before me revealing a spectacular stone room with great arches framing the city on all sides. The sun glinted off the water in the distance drawing me out onto the viewing deck facing the harbor and the Bosporus. Breathtaking had indeed been the proper word for what unfolded before me. In the distance, across the water, rose islands whose mountaintops disappeared in a mist settling over them in the coolness of the coming evening. Sunlight shimmered on the water around ships in the harbor and shadows danced along the minarets rising like spindles up the hills.

Above it all, I stood like a giant drinking it all in. Fatigue from the climb began to catch up with me. Not willing to part with the sight before me, I leaned forward on one of the rounded tops of the carved stone posts dotted along the iron railing. As soon as my hand touched the stone, the all-too-familiar feeling of lightning shot through my hand and up my arm. White light blocked the beauty of the port and blinded me. As the whiteness began to fade, so did the serenity of the place atop the tower. Instead, there was screaming from below me. Smoke rose in eerie gray tendrils from different places in the old town becoming more intense closer to the water and the great sea walls. The minarets were nowhere to be seen. In the harbor sat huge warships waging battle with smaller ships which were raining fire onto them with little effect and sustaining more damage from cannon fire than they inflicted. It was only a matter of time before the ships would go down. From my post atop the tower, I could see Byzantine soldiers firing crossbows and guns from the sea walls at the invaders, but the numbers were sadly lopsided. In the village below me, buildings were closed tightly, except for once in a while when someone would emerge in hysteria and attempt to flee the city. Distance could be seen better than details concealed in the narrow streets between the buildings, so I have no idea if the attempts to flee were successful. I would be given no time to find out, either. As I stood staring into the distance, a small whimpering sound came from behind me. Turning to see what had made the noise, I saw in the haze the frightened dirty face of a child huddled against the cold stone wall. He was frail, almost sickly, and seemed to plead with me without saying a word. Clearly, he had come to the tower to hide from the horde. My heart broke for him and his plight, knowing that his fate was not likely to be good if he stayed in the city during the fighting. I didn't know what I could do for him, but I had to try. No human with a heart would leave the frightened child there like that. I knelt down to his level. At first, he drew back in fear, but seemed to slowly trust me as I smiled. Hoping to encourage him further, I leaned forward extending my hand to him. As I did, my other hand came away from the post and the blinding light once more covered me.

As I came back into reality, I caught myself swaying close to the rails. A woman beside me gasped thinking I was going to fall, but I murmured some excuse about not being fond of heights and leaned against the strong wall of the tower. That face. It continues to haunt me. The waif seemed to see me there, but since he never spoke, I cannot say for certain. No, I am certain. Those eyes bore into me, silently pleading. He saw me.

There are many memories from my travels I knew I would remember forever which have already begun to fade, but these visions, or memories, or whatever madness they may be never fade. I can remember each one as vividly as when I experienced them. Nothing changes. No blurring of sights, sounds, smells. No. It is all there. The face of the man sliced open on the Wall. The face of the child on the Tower. All of it is clear. All of it haunts me. But why? Why do I have these visions? What madness has taken hold of my mind? Even now, as I write these words with stinging hands, I must once more question my sanity.

"Now boarding Flight 722 to Madrid." The hollow voice repeated the instruction in three different languages pulling Shelby out of the journal and Eli's self-diagnosis of psychosis. As she put the book into her backpack, she thought through her own experiences. Shelby remembered every word Seshat had spoken. Everything she had seen in Rome. Every feeling she had from the revulsion at Hadrian's touch to the heartbreak watching the gladiator she loved once. She had written everything down in case she needed to tell someone. But Shelby had forgotten nothing. Slowly, as she found her seat, she knew why she had done it. Somehow, somewhere in her mind, she was telling it all to Benny.

Part of her ached to pick up the damn phone and tell him, but that would mean putting herself out there in a place she wasn't sure she was ready to be. Shelby wanted Benny and needed him in so many ways, but stepping outside of the unspoken boundaries of her times in Rome was something she didn't know if she could even handle. She'd put him through enough crap last week. Shelby screwed up everything she touched and couldn't bring herself to drag Benny into her trail of debris. Pushing the thought out of her mind, she wadded her pitiful airline excuse for a blanket against the fuselage and stared out the window until the pyramids vanished into the blur of earth below. Only then, with Seshat, Ramses, and Rafeeq behind her did she drift into a mercifully dreamless sleep.

⁜

Madrid. A city of art, culture, and gastric orgasms. One benefit of a late flight and a long nap was having the energy and appetite for the bar crawl that was the Spanish nightlife. Wine, beer, and exquisitely simple tapas practically flowed out of the old city restaurants and into the streets. In some places, this was more literal than figurative where tables and chairs were set outside for anyone wanting fresh air with their drinks instead of the crush of people inside. Cafe lights were warm and inviting while the smells of chorizo and bread wafted into the stone streets promising to soak up the alcohol locals and tourists drank with gusto. The Spaniards did everything wrong by American health standards. They ate long lunches then took naps for hours. Dinner was closer to midnight and preceded by hours of drinking and eating appetizers. Yet, Madrid, like Rome, was full of beautiful people. None of it made sense, but it was a mystery no Spaniard was going to question. It worked for them. And it worked for Shelby.

Naomi, Shelby's guide for the weekend, was one of those beautiful people. Olive skin and long dark hair set off her espresso eyes and full lips. Curves squeezed into a pair of jeans and a low-cut red top were only slightly concealed by her jacket. Peeking out from the scoop of her shirt was the edge of a tattoo revealing enough to be seductive, and not enough to give away what it was. As funny as she was sexy, Naomi was fabulous company for a night of eating and drinking around the old city. And Shelby wasn't likely to end up drunkenly in the bed of her guide this time. Not as likely, anyway.

"Come, this one." Naomi nudged Shelby into the crowded doorway of one of the tapas bars lining the street.

"There's so many of them. How do you decide where to go first?" Shelby asked scanning the other side of the street. Doorway after doorway was open and lit up with golden light glinting off of shelves of liquor bottles and beer taps. There were more bars than shops lining the bottom floors of the ornate buildings which seemed to fade from one into the other with only slight variations in color giving their individuality away.

"We all have favorites after a while," Naomi answered with a shrug. "But we like to try new things, too. Best to start with something new and end with something familiar."

"So that when you're drunk at the end of the night, you know how to find your way home?" Shelby asked.

Naomi smiled wickedly. "Something like that."

"Or when you wake up in someone else's bed, you aren't far from your own," Shelby said returning the grin.

"Maybe." Naomi winked and found them a table in the back amid a crush of locals.

In the air hung the tang of wine and the yeasty smell of bread with the sharp punch of spice from the chorizo. It was intoxicating before the booze ever made it to the table. Naomi ordered something Shelby only caught pieces of from the little bit of Spanish she knew. She was awesome at ordering Mexican food, but that was about it.

Soon, there was a flat round loaf of hot bread and a plate of fried calamari rings. No sauce, just a lemon wedge. Simplicity. Chunks of grilled chorizo and discs of fried potato came alongside a pint of beer for Naomi. The waiter set a glass of red wine down in front of Shelby and smiled. Picking it up and swirling it like she knew what she was doing, Shelby took a sip. "Chianti. How'd you know?"

Naomi shrugged. "You've been to so many places in so few days, but as you talked, the only one you seemed sad to leave was Rome. So, I thought Rome should come to you."

"You know me too well," Shelby said taking a deep drink. Idle chit-chat from the airport had paid off.

"And, Dina told me you liked chianti."

"She's a good woman. Nuts, but good." A vision of her boss in her kimono, throwing darts at a map popped into Shelby's mind. Somewhere on a New York patio was a woman who may play throw-and-go with her life, but always managed to come through on the important things. Like wine.

By the second glass of wine, Shelby was beginning to relax and talk more about her recent trips. Naomi was easy to talk to because she liked to ask questions. There were no awkward silences and it felt good to be at ease with someone again. Rafeeq had put her on edge with his mysterious comments and popping up out of nowhere in the streets of Cairo. Naomi was familiar and comfortable. She had been Shelby's guide a few times on different trips to Madrid and Andalucia, which helped loosen her tongue. That and the wine. So much wine.

Every couple of glasses, they would go out into the street in search of a new place to try. The cool night air felt good after the pressing heat of the bars and helped sober them up a little for the next round. Naomi was oblivious to the eyes watching her everywhere they went. She was gorgeous and, as the city slipped more and more into its evening buzz, she was almost irresistible to men young and old. Having an American with her gave the men an excuse to come and talk to them. The pretense was wanting to meet Shelby, but she wasn't an idiot. Drunk, but not an idiot. The men were using Shelby to get to Naomi, who was either innocently clueless to their intentions or masterfully polite.

Madrid was intoxicating. Not just the free-flow of alcohol, either. The city itself seemed to buzz with energy that made Shelby forget about the familiar buzzing in her hands. Maybe, just maybe, she would get through Madrid without anything going all time-warpy.

Settling into a corner table in the front window of yet another bar with fresh wine and a plate of cheese, Naomi asked, "So what made Rome so special this time? What magic does it hold for you?"

Shelby almost choked on her drink. "Magic?"

"Well, there has to be something about it. The ruins are impressive, but nothing has ever captivated you like this."

For the first time the entire night, there was an awkward silence at the table as Shelby waged war against her sanity and lost. "Magic isn't the right word, but you're onto something." Why she decided to spill everything to Naomi, she had no idea, but there it was. Maybe it was because she desperately needed to tell someone. Maybe it was to distract her from the fact she was finding Naomi more attractive than she was comfortable with. Whatever the reason, over a glass of wine and a plate of cheese, she told Naomi everything.

Naomi sat serenely sipping wine as Shelby talked. Once in a while her dark eyes would widen or a half-grin when she mentioned waking up with Benny, but nothing more. When Shelby finished, Naomi stared at her for a moment. *Great, now the hot chick thinks I'm a maniac*, Shelby thought.

Naomi narrowed her eyes in thought. "So," she began, "if I hadn't asked you about Rome, and there were memories here that made you go limp, you were just going to let me freak out?"

Shelby stared at her across the tiny table. "That's what you have to say? After all the weirdness I just spewed out, *that's* what you latched on to?"

Naomi shrugged. "Well, it was my first thought." She took another sip of her drink and set the glass gently on the table. "I mean, I can see why you wouldn't want to tell people crazy shit like that."

Shelby sighed. The room spun a little as she realized how drunk she was getting and how insane she must have sounded. "I should've- It's the wine, I guess-" she muttered.

Naomi put her finger under Shelby's chin and lifted it to look her in the eye. "I believe you, Shelby."

"Why? I mean, you do?"

"I do. It's just crazy enough to be true." She picked up her glass and laughed. "And, now I don't have to freak out, so that's good, eh?"

"That's very good." Shelby downed the rest of her wine and signaled for another.

True to her nature, Naomi peppered Shelby with more questions once she had the gist of what was going on. Shelby talked more freely about everything she had seen and been told. She wasn't sure if Naomi really believed her or not. Something in the wine was telling her the more she babbled, the more likely it would sound like truth. Of course, Naomi could just be humoring her drunk friend by going along with the crazy talk. Either way, Shelby kept answering questions leaving the job of believing it or not to her Spanish guide. The serious bits seemed to go with little comment, but the kinkier ones had her undivided attention.

Naomi got a particular kick out of her would-be tryst with Hadrian and teased her that she should have hung onto the wall a little longer. "Not many people can say they screwed a Roman emperor. Especially one that was more into men." Finally, she got around to asking Shelby about Rafeeq. "What was it about him that made you not trust him? I mean, you told me everything after a few drinks."

"Few? I'm not sure I would call this a 'few.'"

"Maybe not, but still."

Shelby thought for a moment. It wasn't easy to put her New York-ness into words. "Other than appearing out of thin air in the street and knowing who I was when I didn't know him?"

Naomi laughed. "There's that. But you said you spent an hour smoking a hookah with him anyway. Why didn't you tell him what Seshat told you? By then, he knew so much."

"That's just it," Shelby began, "he knew so much. Yet, he said so little. He knew things he wouldn't explain, but wanted me to tell him everything I knew. I don't know."

"Do you think he would have told you more if you told him what she said?"

"Honestly, no, I don't think he would," Shelby answered toying with the rim of her glass. "Rafeeq had his chance, but was going to leave that to the goddess. It wasn't until after I saw her that he wanted to get chatty with me. Something didn't seem right about it."

"Maybe he was afraid to tell you things Seshat wanted you to find out on your own."

Shelby fell silent. Could she have been wrong about him? Could he have simply been guarded so he didn't offend Seshat by spilling more than he was supposed to? Maybe he would have told Shelby more once he knew what the goddess had told her. Maybe that's all he was after. Permission to speak freely. "Fuck," she whispered.

Naomi shrugged and fiddled with the neckline of her shirt. For a moment, her tattoo peeked out then vanished behind the cotton. "Who cares about the old guy? Tell me more about Benny," she grinned.

"Fuck," Shelby said quietly as her own stupidity dawned on her.

"I know that much," Naomi laughed.

CHAPTER 9

Plaza Mayor was bustling with people by the time Shelby peeled herself out of the bed in her hostel and managed to find Naomi. As usual, she entered the massive building-ensconced square through the wrong arch which meant wandering almost around the entire structure before she found the right place. Since the shops and signs were all under the covered walkway behind a million arched openings, she couldn't look across to see where she was supposed to be. So, she was stuck walking all the way around.

"Wrong arch?" Naomi asked when Shelby finally found her.

"Yeah. You'd think I'd get it right by now."

"Seeing as how there are only four of them."

Shelby shrugged. "The damn place is a square. One corner or another. It's all the same."

Naomi found a table on the outside of the cafe so they could watch the street performers while they had breakfast. She knew Shelby could have cared less about them, but the pictures would be good for her travel piece. Jugglers in carnival harlequin tossed bowling pins around while Shelby swan dived into a cup of coffee. With any luck, it would take some of the haze of her tapas tour down with it.

"Look, about last night," Shelby began.

Naomi waved off the coming comment. "No need. Your story is safe with me, and for what it's worth, you're a hell of a kisser when you're drunk."

Shelby snorted and coffee almost choked her. "What?"

Naomi laughed. "Well, the first part anyway. Pretty sure the second part is true, too, but I wouldn't know myself."

Shelby's laugh ended in a sharp pain in her head. Hangovers were becoming common place, but no less unpleasant. "Thanks, and thanks." Naomi went over the plan for the day as Shelby soaked up her night with pastry and coffee. A week or so before, she had done the same thing with Benny. She wanted so much to have him across the table. The first time she left Rome and snuck out of Benny's bed, all she wanted to do was forget the whole thing. It wasn't that she didn't like Benny, but she wasn't one to make a habit of getting into relationships. It had been one hell of a night, but not something she planned to repeat. This time, she couldn't get their last night out of her head. More than that, she wanted every moment in Rome with him again. He had wanted Rome to get under her skin, and in a way it had. Just not in the way either of them expected.

"Shelby?" Naomi asked.

"Hmm?"

"You seemed far away. Anything wrong?"

Shelby shook her head. "No, I'm sorry. You were saying?"

"Do you want to take a tour of the Plaza before we head to the Palace? A lot of history here. Not as old as Rome, though."

"You mean, do I want to try touching it?"

Naomi smiled. "I suppose so. Maybe you'll end up in a bullfight, or the Spanish Inquisition."

Shelby half-laughed, again coming to the shaky feeling Naomi was only humoring her and her story. "Is there nothing less violent that happened here in the Plaza?"

"Not here. Well, maybe a procession, but that's not exciting."

"Then," Shelby said, "I guess I'll take my chances and hope for a sexy bullfighter over a murderous priest."

"Well, then, let's go roll the dice." Naomi insisted on paying for breakfast despite Shelby's protests. Once the check was paid, the pair made their way into the growing throng of tourists who didn't seem to know what to do with themselves. Most just wandered in vague circles looking up at the stately buildings. Bored kids tried juggling whatever they had in their hands or chased each other around the oblivious adults. The Plaza Mayor was a huge open square of stone tiles completely surrounded by ornate buildings that framed it. The bottom of the buildings was a lace of stone arch porticoes that peeked in at shops and tiny eateries under the covered walkway. People standing in the middle of the square had only architecture to look at and wonder what might have been there in the past. Other than a huge statue of King Ferdinand III on a steed, there was nothing to tell anyone what the plaza meant.

Naomi explained the open space had once been home to bullfighting and even the auto-da-fé, or 'act of faith,' of the Spanish Inquisition. Here, hundreds had been condemned to torture and death at the hands of the Church. "Madrid's history is not as ancient as some places, but the architecture is beautiful. Which helps to take the focus off the killing people for over three hundred years thing."

Shelby looked around at the stately square. "It is beautiful, but sedate for a place with so much history. Violent history at that."

Naomi nodded. "Which actually was the point. King Philip II wanted to bring order to the chaos of the area, so he commissioned this. It has changed some because of fires and war. When it was used for events, they could transform the space however they wanted inside. The square was just a backdrop."

The two had made it to a shaded corner under one of the porticoes which was less inhabited than other areas. "Well, place your bets. Bullfight, Inquisition, or nada," Shelby said as her hand hovered just off the wall.

"What do you choose?" Naomi asked.

Shelby's hands tingled, but there was no surge of pain or sparks like other sites. If she was learning anything from all of this, it was to read the signs of her hands. "I vote nada."

Naomi furrowed her brow. "I'll agree with you, but I'm going to pull for a bullfight. Not much sexier than a bullfighter."

"Tight silk pants on a Spanish ass. Yep. I'll pull for that one, too." Shelby gently placed her hand on the wall and braced for electrocution. As her hand made contact, she felt the cool smooth stone and nothing else. Like Giza, there was nothing for her here. "Damn. Nothing, and I was really hoping for the bullfighter."

Naomi's eyes narrowed as she looked at Shelby. "How did you know?"

"My hands. Apparently, they know things I don't."

The rest of the day passed with Naomi giving all the details and photo ops she could think of for the most historic places in Madrid. Shelby had been to most of them before, and, like most places she went to, it had little effect on her. Even a cynic the likes of Shelby Starling couldn't help but appreciate the place to some degree. Sure, it was a beautiful city where modern and old collided routinely, but no wow factor. Nothing that drew her in. Ever wandering, ever lost. Never home anywhere. However, she had a job to do and testing the waters of her own history made things more interesting. By the end of the afternoon, she had seen more gorgeous buildings than any human has a right to see and no time warping whatsoever.

The two took a break at a local spot for chocolate and churros to get off their feet for a while. Shelby sat back and sighed. "You must think I'm full of shit and I wouldn't blame you."

Naomi dunked her churro in the cup of molten chocolate and said, "Not really. All it means is you weren't in Madrid any more than you were in Giza or Luxor. I don't need to see you electrocuted to believe you, Shelby."

"I guess," Shelby said halfheartedly. If she had been able to prove to Naomi she wasn't making stuff up, she would have felt better about telling her. Now, she felt like a fraud. She was beginning to see why Eli only told the pages of his journal. He didn't have to worry about anyone thinking he was crazy or a liar. "What's on the schedule for tomorrow?"

"A day trip. Toledo."

Shelby sat forward in her chair. "Toledo? That seems an odd choice."

Naomi shook her head. "No," she answered. "It's full of history. Much of the history of Castile lies outside of Madrid. Avila, Toledo, Segovia. For a proper history tour, we go outside the city."

"So, that would be why Dina gave me a few days here. Day trips."

"Now you see," Naomi said with a grin. "So, time for a siesta, then we meet up again later, eh?"

The Spanish tradition of the afternoon siesta was something Shelby had been positive was a cliché until she came to Spain a couple of years ago. Like the tapas and wine, it was a tradition she was more than happy to partake in. "Sounds good to me."

The hostel was only a few blocks away from the land of liquid chocolate and fried dough, and Shelby easily found her way there using the graffiti on the walls as landmarks as much as the street signs. Madrid wasn't dirty like New York, but there seemed to be a lot of graffiti for such a clean place. Some of it was pretty good. Of course, she had no idea what any of it said since it was all in Spanish. Maybe it was terrible profanity. Maybe it was answers to the great questions of life. Who knew and who really cared?

Back at the hostel, Shelby waved at the clerk behind the polished desk before heading upstairs to her room. Outside, the hostel looked like any other building in old Madrid. Ornate and elegant. Inside, it looked more like an Ikea showroom. Clean lines of simple Scandinavian furniture made good use of the small spaces in the lobby and tiny bedrooms giving the illusion of space and airiness. Pulling back the white duvet, Shelby sank into the bed. She set an alarm on the tiny travel clock to get her up in time for tapas and dinner, then plugged her phone in, hoping silently there would be a message from Benny when she woke up. "Jesus, Shelby. Get a grip on yourself and go the hell to sleep."

The alarm went off a few hours later and narrowly escaped being smashed to bits by a reluctant wakee. By then, Shelby had spent a considerable time betting with Seshat over whether or not Benny would live through the bullfight across the Plaza Mayor from the Inquisition officials coming off like tiny assholes threatening to draw and quarter the infidel goddess. Vivid dream mash-ups were becoming as common as tapas bars in old Madrid. And like those bars, they left her with a headache.

As she got ready to go out and properly earn her headache, she reached into her backpack for her Chapstick. Shelby had almost forgotten Elijah Faircloth and his creepy diary until her hand brushed it in the dark of the pocket and blue sparks popped again. "Damnit, Eli. Not now." She zipped the pocket, shoved the backpack into a drawer, and slipped out into the Spanish nightlife.

⁎

"I have a little surprise for you this morning," Naomi announced as they walked through the old town.

"If it's a day trip to Toledo, you've already let the cat out of the bag," Shelby answered dryly. Her well-earned headache was only slightly better from the aspirin she had chased with some very strong coffee.

Naomi laughed. "No, no surprise there. Just wait. You'll see."

As Naomi led her through the maze of buildings, Shelby wondered why Naomi didn't seem to feel the nights of bar hopping like she did. Maybe it was years of tolerance built up. Maybe it was just part of Spanish DNA.

Finally, the tight alley opened up to a small plaza. "I can see why you brought me here. Staggering," Shelby quipped. There was nothing at all remarkable about the plaza. Three buildings met in the haphazard ways most small plazas came together in the old town. A few anemic balconies with ornamental iron railings and straggly potted plants gave some charm to the stone and brick walls that would otherwise have been less than inviting.

"This way," Naomi instructed. She walked to the far end of the plaza toward a set of large wooden doors with smaller doors set inside them. The doors were typical of Spanish churches.

"So, you thought I needed some confession? Or maybe an exorcism?" Shelby asked reading the sign for the Monastery of Corpus Christi.

Naomi laughed. "If I was taking you to confession, I'd have to go first. No, something far more delicious."

Shelby wrinkled her nose. "I'm all for some bread and wine, but I'd prefer mine to come from a bar with a side of chorizo."

With a laugh, Naomi pressed the buzzer by the wooden doors. A voice answered and Naomi replied in Spanish which left Shelby still in the dark about what they were doing there. After a brief exchange, the lock clicked. Naomi opened the small door inside the larger ones and led Shelby through a corridor smelling of old dust, floor polish, and candle wax. The bustle of the city outside vanished with the closing of the carved wooden door. Inside, the place seemed to demand silence in a quiet and unassuming way. Like the look a cranky librarian gives you when you laugh too loudly about the scintillating words in the dictionary.

At the end of the hallway about halfway up the white tile wall, there was a small version of the wooden doors on the outside. It was propped open and inside was a small torno, a lazy susan. Unlike the small plastic disc her mother had kept spices on, this one was large and had three partitions which blocked out anything behind it. The dark brown panels maintained the cloister of the nuns within. Next to it, mounted on the wall, was a menu of some sort.

Shelby raised her eyebrow hoping for some sort of explanation. Naomi just winked and pressed the small buzzer. From somewhere in the recesses beyond the torno, footsteps approached. "Si?" asked a voice through the buzzer speaker.

Naomi spoke a few words which included the word 'dulce.' Shelby's eyes widened and she mouthed the words, "Sweets?" Naomi nodded and pulled out a five Euro note. She laid it on the torno as it slowly turned around. A moment later, it turned again and revealed a small white box. Then, turning once more, one Euro appeared. Change.

"Gracias," Naomi said to the lazy susan, then something Shelby couldn't understand, except for what sounded like her own name. Slowly, the torno revolved again and a piece of old paper, neatly folded, appeared. Naomi didn't touch it, and instead gestured to Shelby. "This is for you, not me."

As Shelby reached for the paper, the electricity in her hands surged and blue sparks jumped from her fingertips to the paper. Naomi's eyes widened then softened into a smile. Shelby's hands almost sizzled as she picked up the yellowed old paper. Part of her was intensely afraid the page would ignite before she could see what it was. She almost drew her hand back, but a glance at the bracelet reminded her the sparks only meant to get her attention. Wrapping her hand around the note, Shelby managed to whisper, "Gracias."

With a short exchange Shelby didn't understand, Naomi and the nun ended their cookie deal. Following her guide back down the corridor and out into the Spanish sun, Shelby held the note in the palm of her hand fighting hard against the pain of it. Sparks danced gaily from her fingers to the paper, then all but vanished from sight in the sunlight.

"Cookie?" Naomi asked as if everything about secret nun cookie deals and weird spark notes were completely normal things.

"Sure," Shelby answered as if everything about secret nun cookie deals and weird spark notes were completely normal things.

As Naomi opened the small white box labeled Montecadoes de Yema and opened the clear cellophane, the sweetness of the powdered sugar and shortbread wafted through the air. Shelby reached into the box and pulled out a small sugar-coated square of shortbread. With one finger, she tapped off some of the loose powder, vaguely remembering inhaling and choking on the powdered sugar from beignets in New Orleans once. The cookies were simple, but delicious. Of all the things Shelby expected of her time in Madrid, eating clandestine cloistered cookies in a plaza was not on that list.

Shelby dusted the remnants of sugar and crumbs on her jeans and turned the small folded square of paper over in her hands.

"Well?" Naomi prodded.

"Might as well." Shelby gently unfolded the paper, realizing it wasn't as fragile as it appeared. Rather than being normal aged paper, it felt more like a dollar bill. Thin, but strong. She opened the small folded square into a larger square. On it was written a single word: perdón. Below that was a small drawing of a compass with the hands and Roman numerals of a clock. Shelby's confused eyes met Naomi's grinning ones. "Great. Now another one of my guides has some explaining to do."

"The word means 'forgiveness.' I can't tell you why, not because I don't want to. I don't know why that word."

"Let me guess, I have to figure it out for myself." Naomi nodded. "Fabulous." Shelby looked back down at the paper and the image sketched on the bottom. "I've seen this once before."

Naomi's eyes narrowed. "Just once?"

Shelby cocked her head to one side in thought. She remembered clearly seeing it on the wrist of the old man in the library in Rome, but that's the only time. Wasn't it? Was it in one of her weird dreams? Shelby shook her head. "I can't remember seeing it another time."

"Think, Shelby."

Shelby closed her eyes and pressed the paper between her palms. As she did, images from the past few days flashed through her mind. Finally, the roulette wheel of images slowed down and settled on one. Naomi sitting across a small table behind a glass of wine toying with her shirt, the scoop pulled slightly to one side. "You," Shelby answered meeting Naomi's face in a dead stare.

"Me." Naomi pulled the edge of her shirt to one side to reveal the same tattoo of the compass and clock.

"Why? Why didn't you tell me?"

"We don't usually come out and announce ourselves right away."

"So, you were just going to let me think I was crazy for telling you all of that? And that you must have thought I was insane? Or an idiot? Or both?" Shelby's voice was rising with each sentence in a decidedly uncool way. For two days she had been drinking with a Watcher who had let her ramble on like a half-crazed moron trying to justify her sanity to someone who damn sure knew it was the truth.

Naomi half-smiled, but her eyes remained still and serious. "No, Shelby. I was going to tell you. Just not in the middle of a crowded bar with your head spinning already."

"A whole day in Madrid, Naomi. A whole day!"

"Shelby, I know this isn't what you want to hear, but these things aren't easy to do."

"Neither is being electrocuted and jerked back in time!" Shelby's voice echoed off of the brick and stone in the plaza.

"I know. I mean, I don't, but I do."

Shelby stood staring at Naomi in silence. Her hands stung from holding the note, but she couldn't bring herself to put it down. Looking down at the image and words, she began to form another question. "The nun. What did you tell her to make her give me this?"

"I told her you were with me and would be needing answers. So, she gave you one. Or two, I suppose."

"I get the image now, but why the word?"

Naomi shrugged. "I wish I knew. Truly I do. You will know when you are supposed to."

Shelby stared back at her. "You sound like a smartass goddess I know."

Naomi's smile widened. "I'll take that as a compliment."

"And the cookie nuns?"

"Let's just say they have a connection to the universe unlike many others. It comes in handy."

Silence hung in the air between them. Naomi smiling and Shelby staring. "What now?" Shelby asked at last.

"Toledo."

CHAPTER 10

Sitting in the passenger seat of Naomi's Peugeot, Shelby watched the gilded old city fade into the modern low-rise brick abominations of the suburbs. Once again, she was brought back in her thoughts to Rome and the cab ride to Toscolano. She was pretty sure this drive wasn't going to end with a funky psychic grandma in a leisure suit, but she wasn't ruling anything out anymore. She leaned her head back on the upholstery and watched the suburbs fizzle out into the Spanish countryside.

Naomi said little, letting recent revelations settle into the recesses of Shelby's hungover mind. Nothing had happened in Milan, but Shelby was sure there was nothing accidental about the choice to go to Toledo. Seshat never said the Watchers were in on any great secrets. All she said was they are around to keep Travelers on track. Questions began to bubble to the surface as she stared out the window half seeing what was going by. How did the old man know she was a Traveler? How did Rafeeq know she needed to talk to Seshat? How does one become a Watcher? For once, it was Shelby who had questions for Naomi.

A heavy sigh drew Naomi's attention away from the road. "Benny again?" Naomi ventured carefully.

"Yes and no," Shelby replied vaguely.

"Why don't you call him?" Naomi asked with the simple innocence of someone who never questioned her own emotions or inner motivations. Someone who never faced or feared rejection.

"It's complicated. Besides, if he was interested in more than the sporadic trysts, he'd let me know."

Naomi shrugged. "Maybe. But it was you who did the leaving. Maybe he doesn't want to push too much into your life. Could be he just needs -"

"-permission to speak freely," Shelby finished. Shit. Just like Rafeeq, she'd managed to screw things up based solely on her own insecurities. How was she going to do great things if she couldn't even get the little things right?

Naomi stole a glance at Shelby and smiled. "How bad would it be to tell him you're ok? He must be worried. Rafeeq has likely told Carmelita some of what has happened, but only you can tell him everything."

She was right. God damn it. "And what do you suggest I tell him? 'Hey, you know the old library guy? Guess what? He comes in a sexy chick version, too!'"

Naomi laughed and the ice that had formed so solidly between them since the cookie nuns began to thaw in the Spanish sun. "It would definitely get a response."

"Maybe. Maybe later."

With a nod, Naomi let the subject of Benny drop and instead began to narrate some of the history of Castile as they made their way to Toledo, which was only an hour from Madrid. By the time they arrived in town, Shelby had learned two distinct things: she had little interest in the history of Castile, and Naomi was more genuine than Shelby was, even if she was a secret-keeping Watcher.

The Castilla-La Mancha horizon rose and fell in seductive undulations before rising to an intimidating height of fortified walls and towers standing sentinel above the natural moat of the Tagus River winding around the city of Toledo. The moss green water languidly drifted through sloping banks dotted with layers of scrubby trees and peachy Spanish rock. Stone walls draped down the city precipice entwining buildings and streets into a tangled ethnic lace of Moorish and Gothic influence. Approaching the city was like stepping back in time, but without the jolt of electrocution.

Naomi navigated the tight labyrinth of roads that threaded between buildings with the skill of a Roman cab driver. Their first stop was the cathedral standing spectacular and sanctimonious in the middle of the old town. It rose above the rabble of smaller buildings around it with towers reaching for the heaven from which it called down the saints. Opulence reached ethereal heights in the High Gothic structure. Naomi had to circle it before they were able to find a parking space which gave Shelby time to take in its intricate exterior.

Naomi found a space that barely accommodated her Peugeot and slid into it. They squeezed out of the doors trying not to scrape the paint on the cars on either side. Shelby wasn't holding out much hope for the spotless paint job on Naomi's car doors upon their return. On foot, the cathedral was staggeringly beautiful. Carvings covered the building like Holy Roman tattoos. Each corner and crevice seemed to tell a story. Shelby craned her neck trying to look at the towering height of the place. "I don't even know where look. It's overwhelming."

"Which was probably the idea. The faithful are intimidated and entranced at the same time," Naomi explained leading Shelby into the front doors of the church. There was a line of day-trippers from Madrid wrapping the outside of the church, but with a nod to the gatekeeper, Naomi led Shelby past the crowd and through the obtrusive carved doors. Once inside, the artwork became even more intricate. "The Catholic church claims the art teaches the illiterate people stories of faith. The Protestants called the art graven images and condemned the practice. Depends on who you talk to, I guess."

Shelby stood under the sweeping buttresses looking up at the vaults in the gilded ceiling then back down to the checkered stone floor trying to ignore the growing pain in her hands. Tucked high in the arches of the flanking sides were stained glass pictures that threw washes of color on the creamy ceiling panels. Every inch screamed with faith and power echoing through the cavernous space. The paleness of the milky stone was broken in places by shimmering gold. Somewhere inside, tiny fissures were forming in Shelby's cynical heart. "How many people could have been fed with the money it took to build this gorgeous monstrosity?"

Naomi smiled. "Spoken like someone with a heart for the people."

Shelby rolled her eyes and shoved her hands in her pockets to hide the blue sparks. "One thought about the pompousness of the papacy doesn't make me a leader. It makes me a cynic. Lives could have been changed with the gold in here, but I wouldn't be the one to take it from the Church like some sort of religious Robin Hood."

"If that's what you want to believe about yourself, then fine. Come, there's more to see."

Naomi led Shelby around the church showing her some of the more notable artwork and finally came to the High Altar of the sacristy. A large portrait of Christ with his eyes serenely heavenward surrounded by a press of violent humanity caught her eye. "This," Naomi explained, "is 'The Disrobing of Christ' by El Greco."

Shelby couldn't suppress the grin and snicker no matter how inappropriate it was for the location. "El Greco. Am I the only one who pictures him as one of those masked Mexican wrestlers?"

Naomi wrinkled her brow and half-grinned. "Probably. Of course, now I will, too. Thanks."

Gazing into the portrait, Shelby could see how the people could be inspired by such artwork, but couldn't get over the excessiveness of it all. It was time to move on. She pulled a stinging hand out of her pocket to brush back a stray piece of hair. As she did, a man with a camera in his face backed into her as he tried to frame his shot. Tangled in her own feet, she lost her balance for a moment and caught herself against the wall.

Instantly, she regretted not just going down to the ground. The familiar jolt of electricity shot up her arm and the white light surrounded her. In the distance, but growing louder, were hundreds of voices again. This time, instead of shouting, they were singing. As the light gave way and her sight cleared, she was disoriented. No longer was she facing the altar. Instead, she was turned to face the congregation. Gone was El Greco. The place seemed older and slightly less impressive. The congregation was on its feet singing in unison the prayers of high mass. Trying to get her bearings, she looked down at her clothes. A long white robe brushed the floor and peeked out from underneath a full-length black cape tied at her throat. In her free hand was a long wooden rosary. *A priest*, she thought. In the same moment, the high priest instructed the congregation to kneel. Instinctively, Shelby did as she was told, and dropped to her knees letting go of the wall. As she did, the singing faded again, and the white light jerked her back to her own reality.

Coming out of oblivion, she was sitting on the floor leaning against the wall she had grabbed and was surrounded by people. Naomi was babbling something to the worried man with the camera about Shelby being overcome with religious fervor and that he was not to blame for her collapse. Some woman with a lace scarf over her head crossed herself several times. Finally, as the color came back to Shelby's cheeks, they began to disperse convinced they had witnessed a spiritual event.

"Nice work," Shelby muttered to Naomi as she eased herself off the cold stone floor. "I'm a spectacle now."

Naomi shook her head. "Sometimes the best place to hide is in plain sight."

Shelby shrugged. Who was she to second guess a Watcher? "I guess."

"What was it this time?" Naomi asked quietly. Their voices seemed to echo in the voluminous space even with the ebbing and flowing of tourist groups milling about.

"It was mass. I wasn't facing the altar. Somehow, I was turned around and facing the congregation. Usually, when it happens, I'm facing the same way."

"Do you know who you were?"

"A priest."

Naomi thought for a moment. "Interesting. A man, then."

Shelby hadn't really considered the fact that in the memory she had changed gender. "I guess I would have had to be. Pretty sure I wasn't a nun."

Naomi shook her head. "No, they would have been cloistered most likely. So?" A grin was starting to peek out at the corner of her mouth.

Shelby stared at Naomi whose large dark eyes searched her expectantly. "Are you serious? You really want to know how it felt to be a man when I just got jerked back in time?" Shelby's head was throbbing and she wasn't in the mood for games.

"I didn't say that."

"You thought it," Shelby snapped.

Naomi's eyes widened. "Yes, I did. But I didn't say it." She tilted her head to one side and waited on it to dawn on Shelby who was never at her sharpest after an episode.

Shelby rubbed her hands trying to stifle some of the tingling in her fingers. "Then how could I know?"

"With every step closer, things change in you. And since I'm with you now, things may be stronger."

Shelby was getting frustrated at losing control of her life more and more every day. She learned more about what was happening to her, but it only created more questions. "So now I'm a half-cocked psychic like Carmelita?"

Naomi's smile was more like a mother trying to appease a petulant child. "I wouldn't go that far. But you are learning to listen to things around you, which can come in handy as you journey." It was as if Naomi could sense the heaviness of the conversation was only frustrating Shelby and she attempted to lighten the mood. "So, come on," she started playfully. "You have to tell me. What was being a man like? Does it feel different?"

Shelby stared at her for a second. "No. I mean, as a priest it wasn't like I was all that into communing with my machismo."

Naomi laughed. "Maybe, but you weren't a eunuch!"

Making their way out of the cathedral and into the sunlight did nothing for Shelby's headache. Naomi peppered her with anatomical questions about her gender-bending time warp as they headed toward their next destination, the Alcazar. As Shelby had been a man for mere seconds, she didn't have very titillating answers.

Riding the top of the hill above the city of Toledo, was the rigid brick square with spires on each of its corners. The dark points forming the corner spires were a sharp contrast to the peach-colored stone which was so dominant in the Castile-La Mancha and gave the already staunch building a feeling of intimidating size. There was little softness about the geometric wonder that had an air of foreboding without any of the grace of a castle. The stone levels of the Alcazar seemed to drip down the hillside in waves of brick walls. It was large enough to rarely only slip out of sight as they wound their way through the dizzying maze of streets and panted up the hillside. Shelby's hands began to sizzle, and she felt a strange sinking feeling in the pit of her stomach as they approached the Alcazar that she didn't understand.

Standing outside of the massive building, Shelby scanned the facade. It rose above in several stories of stone and brick intimidating the landscape below like the fortress it was. "It's been in use for centuries for many different things," Naomi explained. "Recently, it became a military museum."

"Sounds fascinating," Shelby said dryly. Other than the sheer size and staunch nature of the place, Shelby wasn't enthusiastic about the big square, and even less enthused about military history.

"But it's not really why we're here." Naomi walked into the little structure on the outside of the fortress where the line for tickets had formed. It was an atrocious modern afterthought to a place that was never intended for tourists. Once again, with a nod, Naomi managed to slip them both past the queue and into the Alcazar. Passing the levels of excavated Roman ruins made Shelby's hands surge, but they didn't linger long. Knowing there was no real reason to go into the updated typical museum rooms, Naomi led Shelby through the corridors and out into the covered walkways of the interior plaza. "Now, *this* is why we're here."

The fortress may have been imposing from the outside, but the interior was stunning. Around the four sides, two levels of arched stone openings were almost graceful as they concealed the checkered balcony walkways that rimmed a gleaming courtyard. A small centerpiece of layered steps in the center of the floor rose up to a statue holding a raised sword. Along the interior of the covered walkways at intervals were carved wooden doors.

"None of this is right," Shelby began. "It's too new. What I saw was older than this time."

"I know," Naomi answered quickly. "But this surface covers something older beneath. The ruins we passed coming in."

"Then why didn't we stop there?"

"Too public. We need corners that will conceal you when you touch it."

"But the building is too new," Shelby protested. "It won't work."

Naomi stopped and looked at her, then pulled the neck of her shirt aside revealing the tattoo again. "Trust me. Remember who you're with."

They found a corner of the portico that was less inhabited to try to send Shelby hurtling back in time. It was beginning to seem like Naomi was more hell-bent than Shelby to figure out what this life held for her. "Look, maybe I just need to leave things at me being a lowly priest in mass."

"And maybe it's all you were. There's only one way to find out."

Without another word, Naomi took Shelby's burning hand and placed it on the wall. White hot heat and light flooded her body. As the blinding light swirled around her, she felt a strange sensation of falling then a slow stop. Her surroundings eased into focus and she had to blink hard in the dim light to see. Old stone walls surrounded her with a single iron door that seemed like it was added later and roughly fit into the existing stones. Near the door, a torch was burning in a holder giving an eerie dancing pool of light to that area, but only a glimmer to the rest of the space. She looked down to see the same robes as before, but the rosary was not in her hand this time. Instead, she was holding a handle attached to a wooden gear mechanism. In the center of the room were two other priests on either side of a man who had been stripped to the waist. His hands were behind his back and his head hung low in silent resignation to his fate, whatever it was. Above his head, a rope rose up from behind him to the ceiling where a pulley was hung. The end of the rope wrapped around the wheel attached to the gear in front of her.

The priests in the center of the room spoke to the bound man. "You know the charges set against you, and you know the penalty you are facing. Now, who are the others?" one priest hissed in the man's ear. The other priest's mouth was moving in silent prayers as the older priest interrogated the prisoner. As it began to sink in what was going on around her, the first priest spoke to her. "Now. Two turns of the pulley."

Shelby hesitated as the horror of what she was involved in hit her.

"Or maybe you sympathize with this heretic?" snapped the priest.

"N-no," she stuttered, surprised at her own lower voice forgetting for a moment that she was a man.

"Two turns!"

With wide eyes in a silent apology to the prisoner, she began to slowly turn the crank in her hand. As she did, the man's hands raised up behind him. His face changed from resignation to fear and pain. Instinctively, he rose up on his toes trying to bring his body up to his arms which were unnaturally high behind him. At the end of the two turns, his arms were parallel with the cell floor.

"Now?" barked the priest. "Now, will you tell us who they are?"

The man cringed, but refused to make a sound.

Prayers continued to dribble from the lips of the priest on the other side of the prisoner.

The first priest grew impatient with the man's silent protest and ordered Shelby, "Two more turns of the wheel!"

Tears began to well up in Shelby's eyes and she gripped the handle in her hand. She instinctively knew if the priest saw her crying, she would find herself charged with heresy, so she looked away from the poor man. Watching only the turning of the gear and the winding of the rope, she turned the crank in her hand two times. From the center of the room came an agonized scream and a sickening popping sound as the man's arms pulled free of his shoulder sockets. Shelby's stomach rolled and she vomited at her feet. Weak from fear and revulsion, she sank back against the ancient stone wall that formed the holding cells for the Inquisition. As she slid down to the floor, she released her grip on the wooden handle and the white light surrounded her again.

Reality began to settle on her shaken body and mind as she opened her eyes. At least, she thought it was reality until she looked up into a pair of deep Roman eyes gazing down at her full of fear and something more. "Bella? Easy, now. You okay?" Benny asked taking her burning hands in his.

CHAPTER 11

The gut-wrenching sounds of the memory rang in her ears and the hangover feeling washed over Shelby's body. Her hands were a searing heat and the blue sparks raced along her fingertips. Emotionally, she was rocked. Nothing about that time trip was ok. Nothing at all. And now, she was disoriented as she looked up at Benny.

He was crouched next to her, holding her hand. Shelby could feel his touch through the pain. He was really there. Somewhere in the clouded recesses of her mind, she knew Benny was really there, but she was reeling too badly to put it all together. "Where am I?" she whispered.

"Toledo," he replied quietly. "The Alcazar."

"I-I don't understand," she said. Her head was swimming, and she was struggling to keep her eyes open suddenly afraid if she closed them, he would vanish.

Naomi looked over Benny's shoulders down at her. "I arranged it. Well, I called Dina and told her you were having a hard time leaving Rome behind. She asked what I thought you needed, so I told her."

"Then, she called me, and here I am," Benny finished.

"Dina did this? For me?"

Naomi smiled and nodded. "Apparently, she's got some romantic mixed in with her bohemian. I told you with your first glass of wine in Madrid. I told you I thought Rome should come to you."

Benny looked at Shelby with more seriousness than she remembered him possessing. "If this isn't okay, you say so, bella. No harm done."

Shelby reached up with her free hand and touched his face, as much to convince herself he was really there as to reassure him. "It's perfect." But too much for her just yet. A wave of nausea washed over her. Leaning back on the wall, she was careful not to touch it with her hand again. She didn't want to go back there. Ever.

Benny put the hand he had been holding in her lap to keep her from accidentally touching anything, then dug a water bottle out of her backpack. "Drink this."

Shelby took slow small sips and the nausea began to ebb. Naomi and Benny sat on either side of Shelby and let her collect herself before pressing her for details about the memory. Both knew enough to understand anything that knocked her on her ass that badly wasn't good. Most of the tourists were wandering the middle of the plaza and taking pictures of the architecture. The few who happened to stroll through the portico took little notice of the trio seated in the corner. It was shaded and cooler there, so there was no reason to question anything about them sitting out of the heat of the day. Mercifully, no one had seen Shelby's collapse to cause a scene.

Shelby knew she was going to have to tell Benny and Naomi what happened, but couldn't figure out how to explain the horrible thing she did. And she had done it. She turned that pulley. She broke that man. It wasn't someone else. It was her hand. Her memory. Her life.

Finally, she decided to get it over with. "It was the priest again."

"I'm sorry?" Benny asked.

"Shelby had a memory at the cathedral. She was a priest at a mass," Naomi explained.

"A man?" Benny asked.

Shelby nodded. "Apparently the universe doesn't care about gender when assigning lives. Or morals, either."

"How bad was it?" Naomi asked.

Shelby took a long slow breath to keep the nausea at bay. Getting through the memory without puking was going to take everything she had. Slowly, she told them the terrible details as tears streamed down her face. When she finished, they all sat in silence for several long moments. There were no words that could take the horror from Shelby.

Since Benny and Naomi had no idea what to say to her, it was Shelby who finally broke the silence. "Carmelita and Seshat said until I found my destiny, I would only be able to watch great things happen instead of making great things happen. How in the hell was that a great thing I was watching?"

Naomi shook her head. "Great doesn't always mean good. It could just mean something was significant historically. And the Spanish Inquisition was definitely that."

"I hurt that man," Shelby whispered. Benny wrapped his arms around her and pulled her close. Shelby melted into his embrace and broke down. There was a tenderness as he held her that had never been there before. Naomi the Watcher had known exactly what Shelby would need. And she needed Benny more than ever.

The Traveler, the Watcher, and the Roman sat outside of a small cafe in the Plaza de Zocodover just outside the walls of the Alcazar. Like in Rome, the cafes in the plaza had taken advantage of the Spanish weather and put tables and umbrellas outside. The sun was beginning to sit low on the hills casting long shadows. In the distance, clouds gathered and thunder rumbled. The storm was far enough away to only cool the air and make sitting outside more pleasant. Shelby was grateful for the movement in the air cooling her face and stinging hands.

The waiter set down three glasses of wine and a plate of fruit and cheeses, gave a slight bow, then went to tend to other tables. As at the cathedral, Naomi used to crowd of the outdoor cafe to hide in plain sight. The constant conversation around them would make anything they had to say difficult to follow if anyone happened to catch any of it.

"Benny," Naomi began, "I assume Rafeeq told Carmelita what happened in Egypt?"

"Some, yes, but likely not all." Benny related what Carmelita had told him of her conversation with Rafeeq. The Egyptian had been more thorough than Benny realized given the fact Shelby hadn't told Rafeeq everything. Shelby filled Benny in on what Seshat had said at the temple to finish out the details of that leg of her trip.

"I didn't tell Rafeeq what the goddess said, but maybe I should have. I just didn't trust him. He knew too much, but said too little. Seemed weird to me. And when Seshat said he wasn't officially one of the Watchers, I didn't know what to do."

"Understandable," Benny said.

"But you *could* trust him," Naomi added.

Shelby stared at her. "How do you know?" Shelby asked, forgetting for a moment what she was talking to.

"Seshat told you the truth. Rafeeq is not a Watcher. However, his father was."

"So that's how he knew who the library man was?"

Naomi nodded. "Right. You see, the Watchers have been around for eons and the gift is passed down through families. However, not all children of Watchers inherit it. Rafeeq wanted so much to follow his father as a Watcher. He studied hm and tried to learn all he could, but he didn't have the gift. Rafeeq's twin brother, Tavis, inherited it instead. Tavis had no interest in being a Watcher and squandered what he had been given. He only learned what his father forced him to and never developed the love for the Travelers his father had."

"Then why didn't Tavis find me in Egypt? Why was it Rafeeq?" Shelby asked.

"The gift wasn't the only thing Tavis squandered. By the time he was twenty, Tavis was in deep with some very bad people. He was in and out of prison for one thing after another, then, one day, he was found dead in a back alley in one of the slums in the suburbs. Stabbed several times. Since Tavis was in with such rough people, Rafeeq and his family feared investigating Tavis' death would bring those people to their doorstep, so they let it go. Without the gift, Rafeeq could only be a Watcher by proxy."

"Couldn't he be promoted or something?" Shelby asked.

Naomi shook her head. "No, it doesn't work that way. It's not enough to want to be a Watcher, or to even have the heart for it. There's a connection to the universe you must be born with."

"So," Shelby said as she processed what Naomi was saying, "he was really trying to help me. And I was such an ass to him."

Naomi smiled. "It's ok. He understands."

"You talked to him?" Benny asked.

Naomi nodded. "Yes. Don't worry about Rafeeq, Shelby. Really. He understands."

"Was there anything in the journal about Egypt?" Benny asked Shelby trying to change the subject.

"I don't know. I haven't read it all."

Benny's eyes got wide and Naomi wrinkled her brow. "All this time? Why not?" Benny asked.

"It hurts. And it freaks me out," Shelby answered rubbing her hands, more out of habit since it damn sure didn't make the burning go away. Thunder rolled gently over the Castilian hills and lightning danced along the clouds in the distance. A cool pocket of air rustled the napkins on the table and felt good on her fingers.

Naomi put her hand on Shelby's arm. "It's ok. But it might help if we knew more about what was in the diary."

Shelby realized she hadn't shown the journal to Naomi. "I have it, but I'm not sure this is the place to get it out." Shelby looked around at the crowd of people. Even hiding in plain sight, someone might notice blue sparks in the dimming light of twilight.

Benny nodded and waved his hand at the waiter. He paid for their drinks and food, then the three of them walked around the plaza. Across from the cafe from where he had been sitting, Benny saw a group of three trees growing closely together out of the stone plaza which would provide just enough privacy even though it was in the center of the open space. "How's this?" Benny asked Shelby.

"Should be fine. And the tourists are oblivious most of the time anyway. The people were just too close at the cafe. They would've seen the sparks." Benny and Naomi settled against the tree trunks while Shelby knelt down with her backpack. She set the bag on the ground and put one hand on the zipper to open it. The other hand she put flat on the ground to balance herself.

Instantly, she realized her mistake. Lightning streaked across the sky as the jolt flew up her arm and sent Shelby back in time again. Momentarily blinded, she could hear shouting and screaming all around her. As the white light cleared, she realized she was still on her knees in the middle of the plaza, with a torch in the hand the zipper had been in a second before. Black robes. She was still the priest.

As she got her bearings, she heard the crowd hush as a booming voice rang out over the crowd. It was the old priest from the cell. "...shall be condemned to die for your crimes of heresy. May God have mercy on your souls!" The crowd surged with shouting again. The voice had been behind her, but she knew it was the same priest who had ordered her to turn the wheel. She would never forget that voice.

Slowly she raised her eyes, afraid of what she would see after her experience in the cell. In front of her was a pile of wood stacked on end and leaning together around a large post. The wood smelled strange, like animal fat. It had been soaked with something in places. Tucked in between the large pieces were smaller pieces of kindling. There was a row with five pyres across the plaza between the bleachers with spectators. Standing on the pyre in front of Shelby, with hands and feet bound, and a chain and shackle going from the post to around her throat, was a child. She couldn't have been more than twelve. Maybe younger. She was silent, but scared.

"Ines Esteban," the priest yelled. The little girl's head jerked up at her name. "For spreading false prophecy of the coming of the Messiah and inciting conversos to practicing the heretical Jewish rituals- by order of the Holy Father and our Lord in Heaven, you are sentenced to death."

Little Ines turned wild frightened eyes on Shelby. The child was too terrified of the Inquisition to even beg for her life. Standing on the stack of lumber, chained to the post, the girl began to shake violently with fear. The booming voice of the priest spoke again. "You see the evil inside her fighting against the punishment handed down by the Church and the Lord God!" Shelby turned to look over her shoulder to see the priest in ceremonial robes flanked by lesser priests and monks. The lesser ones were mumbling prayers for the souls of the condemned. Shelby tried to pull her hand off of the stone beneath it to break free of the memory, but it was held fast. The old priest looked into her eyes and nodded at the torch in her hand. His thin lips parted slightly in what could almost pass for a sadistic smile as he gave her the silent order.

Shelby's heart fell and she sank onto her elbows as the weight of what she had to do hit her full force. She couldn't do it. They couldn't make her do it. She would die first. Her hand gripped the torch and she fought against the involuntary pull to move her arm toward the wood pile. It was no use. This memory and history would have its way whether Shelby wanted it to or not. She watched in horror as her own arm stretched out to the middle of the wood and thrust the torch into the kindling. As soon as the flame touched the animal fat, the fire leaped across the pile, popping and smoking.

Flames began to lick at the child's feet. Ines found her little voice, shrieking in fear and pain. Bloodcurdling wails echoed off the plaza buildings as Ines' dress caught fire. Cinders floated on the curling tendrils of smoke and settled in the little girl's hair, glowing orange, then smoldering as her hair began to singe. Ines struggled against the bindings trying to pull them loose as they burned, but the chain held fast. Smoke rose and swirled around the little girl, choking her as she screamed.

Another scream echoed along with that of the child. It was coming involuntarily from Shelby. She knew sympathizing with the little girl could get her killed, but she couldn't stop. She threw the torch as far away from her as she could get it and began tearing at the robes with her free hand. She pulled and pulled at the hand inexplicably connected to the ground desperate to break the connection to the memory, shrieking in terror as she fought against it. Tears flowed down her face and into her mouth. As the flames in front of her grew, the tears seemed to turn to steam, burning her cheeks as they fell.

Ines writhed against the growing flames for a moment more. Where her skin had blistered almost as soon as the flames touched her, it began to bubble in ghastly welts. Her hair had been completely burned away from her scalp. Coughing and screaming, the child's fight began to get weaker and weaker. Then, Ines went limp against the post, but her little body couldn't fall because of the chains holding her up. Her suffering was over, leaving only her corpse to burn as a warning to others.

Shelby's anguished screams reverberated through the plaza over the roar of the flames and the crowd. She lit that fire. She killed that child. It wasn't someone else. It was her hand. Her memory. Her life.

In a moment of blind panic and horror at what she'd done, Shelby lunged for the flames trying to throw herself on the pyre with little Ines Esteban. As she did, her hand pulled free and she was jerked out of the memory.

Lightning crashed as Shelby collapsed onto the plaza. The noise of the burnings was gone, but thunder rumbled overhead as the bottom fell out of the storm. Another streak of lightning shot across the sky as the world around her came into focus. Marble-sized hail ripped through the tops of the trees and bounced to the ground as the wind began to whip the branches.

"It's not safe here!" Naomi yelled over the storm. "Pick her up," she ordered Benny.

Shelby felt herself being scooped up in Benny's arms. "The book. It can't get wet," she said weakly.

Naomi dropped the backpack with the journal in it on top of Shelby and covered her with the jacket that had been tied around her waist as they bolted for the nearest covered walkway. It was only a few dozen feet, but it seemed like miles.

Once they were covered, Benny set Shelby down, pulling her hands into her lap so they didn't touch the ground again. Hail clattered. Thunder and lightning raged above them. The wind blew the rain in on them in a fine mist, but none of them cared. Shelby was pale and shaking, frightening Benny and Naomi.

"They're so much worse here," Benny said. He ran his hands through his thick dark hair, shaking out some of the rain.

"It depends on the life she's witnessing," Naomi replied kneeling next to Shelby. "This place holds both beauty and terror, depending on who you are."

"Terror," Shelby whispered.

By the time Shelby was able to say any more, the worst of the storm passed, leaving behind gently rumbling thunder and a drizzling rain. Like the Alcazar, Naomi and Benny sat on either side of her until she gained some of her strength back. The storm had cleared the plaza of tourists who had scattered like rats in a storm drain at the first drops of rain. Locals lingered in the porticoes a little longer, but once the lightning and hail passed and the rain stuck around, they eventually bailed out, too. Shopkeepers occasionally peeked out at the weather deciding to close up for the day or stay open in case the sun brought business back. Wait staff at the cafes loitered under awnings smoking and watching the raindrops bounce in puddles. With few ears to eavesdrop, Shelby could cry and stumble through her retelling of the memory without causing alarm or attracting stares.

Memories were seared into her mind leaving her with vivid images of Ines burning to death at her own hand. She told every detail as if she were in a trance with tears streaming down her face unchecked. As much as she didn't want to talk about it, the words kept coming, even though she wanted to keep the horror of it from Naomi and Benny. When she approached the lighting of the pyre, both went white. Shelby began to tremble as she told of watching Ines' little body burning and dying before her eyes. By the time she was finished and the trance broken, Shelby was barely conscious and the rain had stopped.

Naomi put her hand on Shelby's and looked up at Benny. "Stay with her. I'll go get the car. She needs to leave Toledo before it kills her."

By the time Naomi pulled up, Shelby had settled into a fitful sleep on Benny's shoulder. He gently picked her up and carried her to the car, laying her in the backseat. She whimpered softly, then calmed down and began breathing more evenly. Benny sat in the front seat then reached back to hold onto one of Shelby's hands while Naomi deftly navigated out of Toledo and plunged into the black night of the Castile-La Mancha headed for Madrid.

CHAPTER 12

A soft blue-white light filled the tiny room in the hostel as the sun eased itself over the horizon. The buildings set close together kept the glare of the morning at bay as long as their medieval height could hold back the rays. Even dedicated sentinels such as the structures of old town Madrid eventually had to succumb to the insistence of the Spanish sun. By mid-morning, yellow-gold sunbeams danced across the tiny bed and nudged Shelby awake. Shaking the deep sleep from her mind, she stirred gently. When she did, the arm around her tightened slightly. Benny.

Shelby stretched and realized they had spent the night in yesterday's clothes and on top of the duvet. Naomi slept in the chair in the corner, but was half-draped across the dressing table next to her. As she stretched, Benny's eyes opened and looked up at Shelby. "Morning, bella," he said smiling.

"Morning," Shelby answered returning his smile. Even having been through hell the day before, she couldn't resist that grin of his.

Naomi blinked a couple of times then arched her back trying to work out the kink from sleeping on the desk. "You look better today," she said to Shelby.

"I feel a little better."

Naomi nodded. "Good. Gave us a bit of a scare last night."

Shelby's smile faded. "Sorry."

"Don't apologize," Benny said. "There was nothing you could do."

Even though the morning sun had warmed the room, Shelby shuddered. "It was horrifying. To know I could do something like that-" She couldn't finish the sentence. Images of Ines Esteban surrounded by flames flashed into her mind as she tried valiantly to stop them.

Naomi got up and sat on the edge of the bed next to her. "We know, but the past is done. Things were different then. Terrible. You weren't the only one in history who did something horrible for fear of the Inquisition."

"Of course," Shelby began as she stood and paced a small circle in the tiny hostel room. "It's just that I can't get the image out of my head. Watching that little girl die. I could have saved her."

Benny sat up in the middle of the bed. "How, bella? How could you take on the Inquisition? Alone. With all the people there watching? She'd still die and you with her."

"I could have done *something!*" Shelby thrust her hands into her pockets in defiance of the helplessness she was feeling. How could she be destined for great things if she couldn't even keep herself from burning a child alive? Everything she saw in her memories made her feel less and less like the destiny she was supposed to have. Inquisition or not. It was murder.

She pulled her hands back out of her pockets and a small square of paper fluttered to the ground. Benny picked it up and handed it back to her. "What's that?" he asked.

"Oh," Shelby answered ceasing her caged-animal circling and flopping down on the bed. "Just the paper the cookie nuns gave me."

"Wait!" cried Naomi as Shelby was about to toss it onto the desk. "Open it up."

Shelby unfolded the paper and spread it out on her thigh. Benny noticed the drawing. "What's that supposed to be?"

Naomi pulled the neck of her shirt over revealing her tattoo. "Watchers all have one. It's what marks us for the Travelers and other Watchers."

"The word?" asked Benny.

"Perdón," Shelby answered. "It means 'forgiveness.'" She started to fold it back up, then stopped cold. Her fingers were sparking like crazy. Blue specks of light jumped from fingertip to fingertip then to the paper and back. More sparks than she'd ever seen before. As she stared down at her hands, they became almost completely covered in the dancing blue sparks.

Naomi whispered, "Open it, Shelby."

Slowly, Shelby opened it back up and the sparks targeted the word on the page like sniper fire. Forgiveness. Realization dawned on Shelby. "Forgiveness. That's why they gave me this." A weak smile mingled with tears falling down her face. One fell onto the paper in her hand. "They knew, didn't they?" she asked Naomi. "The nuns knew?"

Naomi nodded. "I suppose they did."

Benny's brow furrowed. "I don't understand."

Letting Shelby have her cry, Naomi explained. "The nuns must have known what Toledo held for Shelby. They couldn't tell her or stop her from experiencing her past life since it's what all Travelers must do, but knew she would need to be able to come back from that and keep going. They knew Shelby would need to know she was forgiven. She can never forget what she saw, but this can help her cope with it and keep going."

"But, keep going where?" Benny asked.

"For today," Naomi said, "Avila. And, Shelby, keep your hands in your pockets."

Through her tears, Shelby laughed. "That I can do."

✳

Shelby behaved herself and kept in her hands in her pockets throughout most of the day-trip to Avila which prevented any rogue outings to the past. Benny and Naomi did their level best to keep Shelby's mind off of Toledo and the horrors it held. By the time they made the trip back to Madrid, the mood was lighter. There was even time for tapas.

Once they settled into a table and ordered, Naomi asked, "So, when are you going to show me this journal of yours?"

"Crap. I forgot about it in all the other craziness. Not here, that's for sure."

"What good does this guy's story do for Shelby?" asked Benny. "He took a different path."

Naomi thought for a moment. "Well, that's true," she began. "However, there may be information to steer her where she needs to go."

"Dina does that for me," Shelby said. "All I do is go where she tells me to and wait for crazy shit to go down."

"Strange," Benny said more to himself than anything.

"What's strange?" asked Shelby. The waiter dropped off their drinks and a plate of hot bread.

Benny dipped a finger in the head of his beer and stuck it in his mouth, seeming to need the extra seconds to form his own thoughts. "Everywhere Dina sends you, something happens."

"There weren't any memories in Egypt," Shelby objected.

"No," Benny countered gently. "But there was a little thing with a goddess. Seems strange is all."

Shelby swirled the wine in her glass. Warm yellow lights from the bar bounced around the glass and illuminated the deep red liquid inside. "Dina has sent me all over the world, more than once to parts of it. Nothing happened before."

Naomi raised her glass to her lips and said over the rim, "The universe is full of coincidences."

Shelby shrugged. "Probably. Of course, the universe hasn't been all that forthcoming with me. Who's to say what tricks it has up its sleeve?"

"It's nothing," Benny said. "Forget I said it, bella."

Naomi grinned at Shelby. "So, let's see who all you have in your life these days." She began to count on her fingers. "A dead Victorian, a lecherous emperor, a smartass goddess, and a sadistic priest. Quite a collection you have there."

Shelby grinned. "You left out the 60s-glam psychic, enigmatic Egyptian, know-it-all cookie nuns, tattooed Watchers, and one hot Roman."

Naomi raised her wine glass. "A toast. To Shelby's magical menagerie."

Benny raised his glass, too. "I'll drink to that."

"I'll drink to anything," said Shelby and swigged the last of her wine.

⁎

Morning dawned gray and misty over Madrid. A chill danced among the buildings kicking up paper and twirling a few turns before changing partners. Locals silently made their way to work with heads bent against the wet wind, only their faces giving away their discontent with the weather. Little rivulets formed between the old stones and cracks in the pavement as the mist settled on the ground. Gone was the warm Spanish sun which had been so welcoming the morning before. If there was ever a day that made it easier to leave the old town, this was it.

Shelby, Benny, and Naomi had arranged to meet downstairs in the hostel lobby once they were dressed and packed to leave. Naomi chatted with the desk clerk while Shelby and Benny checked out of their rooms. Naomi chatted. The desk clerk flirted. Once again, Naomi was either oblivious or deftly polite.

Bags in hand, the three ducked into the mist. Benny and Shelby followed Naomi's shoes two or three blocks to a cafe that was beginning to clear out from the morning rush of locals stopping for coffee and pastries on their way to work. They found a corner table near enough to the door to make a hasty getaway should anything strange happen, but out of the way of any eyes that may notice the sparks on Shelby's hands. With her back to the restaurant, Shelby put her bag on the small table in front of them and opened it.

Her hands buzzed painfully and she was wishing she could have a drink first. Touching the damn thing sober was almost more than she could take. She certainly couldn't hold it to read it. Naomi would have to do it herself. Shelby reached into her backpack, pulled the journal out in a small cascade of blue sparks, and dropped it on the table.

Benny's eyes widened. "Didn't do that before."

"Nope," Shelby replied dryly. "It started in Egypt. Rafeeq said it was because I was getting closer. Whatever that means. He didn't say closer to what."

"He's right," said Naomi, "but could've explained it better. The closer you get to the end of your journey, the more intense your gifts become. Like knowing what I was thinking the other day."

Shelby wrinkled her nose. "This is a gift I could do without."

Naomi shrugged. "Travelers don't choose their gifts. And this one does have a purpose, like it or not." She picked up the book and turned it over in her hands before carefully opening it. Naomi handled it with less apprehension than Rafeeq. Apparently being a true Watcher meant you didn't have to worry about electric journal shocks. "It's gone through a lot," she said as she examined the worn cover and crinkled page edges.

"So did its owner," Shelby added.

Naomi opened the book and began to read.

Benny got up and went to order coffee for the three of them while Naomi caught up to what he had already read in Rome. By the time he returned, she was examining the map scrawled at the bottom of the page.

Shelby peeked over the top of the book. "Do you recognize the drawing? Is it a map?"

Naomi nodded. "I might. It is a map, but I'm not completely sure what the place is. I have an idea, but some of it isn't right. Maybe I'm wrong."

Benny set the coffees down on the table. "What do you think it is?" He slid back into his seat and studied the picture in the journal.

"It looks like a temple I've seen, but, like I said, there are some pretty significant details missing. I might be reading too much into it. Besides, it wouldn't have been something he would've seen that soon in his travels. Maybe it was just an ordinary dream."

Benny looked at Shelby. "You see things in dreams, too?"

Shelby shook her head. "Not like that. Most of my dreams are crazy remixes of memories and reality. Nothing at all helpful, which figures." Shelby sat back in her chair and ran her hands through her hair. "Why can't I get clues to all of this shit? Doesn't the universe know I'm not going to figure this out on my own?"

Naomi laughed. "The universe knows you can do it, but no one said it was going to be easy. Seshat told you that you have to grow through this to be ready for the life you were supposed to have."

Benny had said little since they started out from the hostel. Shelby knew there was something on his mind and she was pretty sure she knew what it was. She had been thinking it, too. The more time she spent with Benny, the more she didn't want to think about it. Finding the life she was supposed to have meant leaving this one. And everything in it.

Naomi kept reading and filling Benny in on parts Shelby already knew while Shelby sat watching tiny drops race each other down the window pane. Before long, Naomi got to the end of Eli's trip to Constantinople. "Is this the last part you read?"

Shelby declared the droplet on the left the winner and answered, "Yes. What's next?"

Naomi turned the page. "He's on a boat, sea sick."

"Great. That's helpful."

"More than you know," Naomi said scanning the next page. "He's headed for Egypt."

Without thinking, Shelby grabbed the journal and pain shot through her hands. Sparks flew from the journal to the turquoise bracelet on her wrist. "Seshat! Did he see her, too?" Cringing in agony as she held the book, she looked for the goddess' name on the page, but found nothing. Unable to take the electrocution anymore, she dropped the book. "Come on, Eli! Damn it! No one cares what you think you'll see at the monuments! They're huge. And old. We get it! Get to the fucking useful stuff!" Her outburst was louder than she intended and drew disdainful looks from the cafe owner who looked like he would have been happier anywhere else than standing behind the counter drying coffee cups. "Sorry," she apologized half-heartedly. She was too frustrated to give two shits what anyone in the stupid cafe thought of her.

"There may be more useful information in his ramblings than you give him credit for," Naomi said trying to pull Shelby back into the task at hand. "There's something significant he hasn't mentioned until just now."

Shelby rolled her eyes, completely fed up with Elijah Faircloth for the moment. "What is it?"

"A Watcher."

Benny sat forward. "How did he get that far without a Watcher helping?"

"I told you," Naomi said, "the universe is full of coincidences."

Shelby picked up her coffee cup. "It would be more helpful if the universe was full of clear directions."

Naomi smiled. "Likely. But a lot less interesting."

Benny moved the book a little closer to him. "Where does he mention the Watcher?"

"Here." Naomi pointed to a line in the middle of the page. "He doesn't know what the old man is, but the tattoo has caught his eye."

"How does him noticing the tattoo help?" Shelby asked.

"Well, at least we know for sure he's truly a Traveler. He wouldn't have noticed it if he wasn't."

"And the time warping wasn't enough to tell you for sure he was a Traveler?" Shelby asked indignantly.

"His story could have been-"

"Coincidence," Shelby spat. "I know."

Benny slid a hand onto her thigh and squeezed it gently. A shiver went up her spine. He had been so protective of her since he arrived in Spain that the heat from Rome had faded some. Benny had been more like a big brother lately. He even got his own room at the hostel rather than assume Shelby wanted him to stay with her. While it was thoughtful, it was far from the Latin lover whose bed she kept finding herself in. Shelby didn't realize until that moment how much she missed the heat. And maybe, just how much she needed it. "Bella, maybe it's enough of this for now?" Benny asked in an attempt to get Shelby out of her funk.

Shelby took the hint and tried to be a little less of a jerk about the whole mess. "It's ok. We can keep going. It's either sit here, or sit in the airport. I vote here. Besides, we won't have Naomi to explain things after this." Shelby let her hand rest on top of Benny's. Maybe he would take that the way she intended.

"Ok, then," said Naomi. "I'll skip the sea sick part and pick up when he gets to Egypt." Since there were three of them and Shelby couldn't hold the diary for long, Naomi read aloud.

The journey down the Nile was far preferable to the rolling of the Mediterranean Sea even if the small boat lacked the amenities of the larger ship. The wildlife at the water's edge was as exotic as the letters from Thomas said they were. Crocodiles sunned themselves on the banks or slid silently into the water and reeds. Birds nested in the vegetation watching for food to float by on the current. Sunsets from the deck of the boat brought the majesty of nature closer than I have ever felt it. Golds, reds, and oranges washed the evening skies and created beautiful silhouettes on the horizon.

I must remember to write to young Thomas about the beauty here. My paltry sketches will be of little interest to someone with such an eye as he, but nonetheless, I shall send them. Egypt has enthralled Thomas since he took over the care of the sarcophagus of Seti I in the museum of Sir John Sloane. It has always seemed strange to me that a renowned architect of modern Neoclassical design would have an interest in housing Egyptian relics, but Sloane's eccentricity has provided young Thomas with opportunity to advance his career in antiquities. As more of Egypt makes its way to the British museums and private collections, Thomas' knowledge will be in demand from those with money to pay for his expertise. My family's patronage of old Sloane's estate always seemed like a pointless waste of money which could be better used for more worthwhile endeavors, but it did manage to get Thomas the position. What good is having a ward if one cannot open doors for them? There are none of the parlor politics here on the Nile. No one clamoring for favors that money and position command. No false pretenses, secrets, and lies.

"Brace yourself, Eli," Shelby snorted.

There is something most diverting about the company of strangers. One could be anything one wants. There is a mischievous side of me that wants to tell a different name to everyone I meet, just because I can. Childish, yes, but tempting.

Last night, I dined on board the ship with the most interesting man. The meal was a simple one as the boat possessed only a meager galley, but the fare was delicious nonetheless. My companion was a local gentleman who in his younger years had helped with the excavation of Abu Simbel. His age had done nothing to quell his vitality, especially as he spoke about the great temple of Ramses II which had long been buried under the deep shifting sands of the Arabian desert. His stories about the giant of a man leading the excavation were especially amusing. From what I gathered, the giant had once been a circus performer. An odd choice for an archaeological dig, indeed!

As my companion told stories with considerable gusto, I happened to notice a small tattoo on the upper part of his forearm. I had seen tattoos on sailors and tribesmen in my travels, but they always seemed heavy and dark. This one was different. The lines were almost delicate, if I can be permitted the use of the word in a masculine description. It first appeared as a compass, such as sailor might fancy, but on a second look, it became clear it was also a clock. I remarked on the uniqueness of the design and my companion graciously accepted my compliment, but did not venture a story about its meaning. In my experience, body alterations have some deeper meaning and I must assume as much from this one as well. Since he did not offer an explanation, I thought it impolite to press him for one. It did spark my curiosity, however, and gave my imagination plenty of fodder.

As we drew near to Luxor, my companion approached me about my plans in the temple city. I mentioned I was exploring alone and he offered to be my guide to the ruins. His knowledge of Egyptian archaeology tempted me to accept his generous suggestion. I offered to pay him for his guidance, but he refused assuring me it was his pleasure to be of service. The refusal of my money is not something I am accustomed to. It seems most people I have encountered in my travels approach with an open palm.

"So, the Watcher has something he needs Eli to see," Shelby said thoughtfully.

"Exactly," said Naomi. "He goes on a little while about the temples at Luxor. You've been there, so I'll skip that part, too." Shelby nodded and let Naomi continue.

Standing among the columns of the hypostyle hall makes one feel remarkably small, which I'm sure was the intent of the pharaohs who constructed them. The grandness of the hall allows the vastness of the spirits to surround you in an ocean of ethereal power. It was almost as if I could feel it surging through me. The tingling in my fingers that has become so much of my daily experience began to intensify. I had attributed the tingling to poor circulation or fatigue from traveling abroad, but it seemed to be connected to this place. Madness again comes to mind, but truly it felt that way. The sensation intensified as I followed my new companion through the hall to a temple wall with beautiful relief carvings. My guide drew my attention to the carving of a man with the head of a bird. At the prompting of my companion, I raised my hand to touch the details of the piece. As my hand drew near, tiny blue specks of light appeared alarmingly at my fingertips, but I could not pull my hand away. It seemed drawn to the wall with a strength I could not resist.

The moment my hand came into contact with the wall, the now familiar white light and surge of pain enveloped me. Once the light faded and the world began to come into view, I was surprised to discover this was a different experience than the previous ones. It is difficult to explain, but I will attempt it. I was standing near the wall in the temple which had burst into vibrant color. Carvings were covered in colored paint bringing them to life. However, there was a distinct lack of life in this place. No sound, no movement, no sense of time and space. It was surreal. Like a dream, rather than a memory.

As I stood trying to determine what this new sensation was, I noticed movement in the shadows of the temple. It seemed to be the shape of a man, but as he emerged into the light, it was the living embodiment of the carving on the wall. A man with the head of a bird. A cloth of white and gold was wrapped around his waist and his torso bare. Around his neck, laying flat across his collarbone and shoulders, was an intricately beaded collar. Turquoise bands on his wrists, ankles and upper arms. He drew nearer and spoke. Not by using his voice and mouth, or beak as it were, but more like speaking through my mind. He said he was called Thoth and welcomed me by name. Holding out a hand, he guided me to a large stone against the wall and motioned for me to sit. As I did, I noticed more movement in the shadow. The shape of a woman appeared and leaned casually against the wall. She was stunning. Her dress was made of the skin of a spotted cat, leopard or cheetah- I'm not sure which. Black hair in tiny braids shone in the light. She had the same turquoise bands around her wrists and ankles, and, like the man, her feet were bare. As she settled into her place against the wall, her red lips parted slightly in a smile.

"Seshat!" breathed Shelby. Naomi smiled and Benny leaned forward in his chair.

Thoth introduced his consort as Seshat, the goddess of knowledge, and explained he was the god of wisdom and mediator between good and evil. Accepting that you are talking to a god does not happen quickly. I knew I must have completely succumbed to my madness, but Thoth assured me I had not. Indeed, he explained this was to be my moment of clarity. Unsure of how something this bizarre could bring clarity, I began asking questions like a curious child. Patiently, he answered all of them while including some questions of his own to guide my thinking as I mentally unraveled what he was telling me. Rather than include all of my questions, which were admittedly unintelligent much of the time, I will get straight to the point of the conversation. Thoth explained that what has happened to me is unique to people known as Travelers. People who were born in the wrong time through some twist of universal energy and are searching for their destinies. They will continue to live life after life until they are able to gain the knowledge and experience that will lead them to the life they were *meant for. Their journey is guided by Watchers who keep them on their way once the universe has connected the Travelers to the path home. What I was unable to learn was how the Travelers get back to their destiny. The god spoke largely in metaphor which made gaining information difficult. His words in answer to the question were, 'The sages caution the Traveler. The serpent rests in the sweet breath of the god of truth and light. The Traveler follows the serpent.'*

"What the hell does that even mean?" asked Shelby. "It sounds terrible!"

Benny shrugged. "But it's more than we knew before."

Shelby sat back in her chair. "Why didn't Seshat tell me this? I asked her, too."

"Why would she tell you when you already had the answer?" Naomi asked.

"Why would I ask a question I had the answer to? Now *you're* talking in riddles," Shelby snapped.

Naomi held up the book and cocked her head to one side.

"But I can't hold the damn thing to read it. If you weren't reading it now, who knows when I ever would have gotten this far?"

"And," Benny added, "we don't have any idea what Thoth meant. So, not much of an answer."

Naomi sighed. "Not a literal one, no. But it's the answer. When you figure that out, you will know what to do." She sat back and wrinkled her nose as she thought. "Have you ever heard of a Japanese puzzle box?"

Shelby was getting tired of feeling stupid. "I think so. Vaguely."

Benny's badly veiled confusion prompted Naomi to explain. "The ornate boxes are deceptively simple, until you look closely. Then, you see they are full of secrets locked away inside by a puzzle. Steps have to be followed precisely to open it. It takes time and patience to figure out, and you will only open it when the puzzle is complete. Then, the secrets inside are revealed."

"What does this have to do with me?"

"Your journey is the puzzle box and Thoth's words are the puzzle key. You will know what to do when the clues are deciphered and the time is right. Until then, you have steps to take and growing to do. Seshat knew you had the answer in your hand. She also knows you have it in you to figure it out. That's part of your journey."

"Great. We all know how brilliant I am at figuring things out. I haven't known what was going on for weeks now."

Benny had been pouring over the words in the diary much like he had poured over the Latin in the book at Carmelita's. "Sages. Serpent. Sweet breath. God of truth and light. Sounds biblical."

"Except for the sages. Not sure those are in the Bible," Shelby replied.

Naomi winked. "Now you're thinking about it. You're on your way."

"And so are we," Benny said checking the time. "Airport."

"Shit," said Shelby. "Just as we were getting somewhere."

Naomi smiled as she slid the diary into Shelby's backpack. "More than you know. Come on. We'll get a cab."

CHAPTER 13

There was something liberating about sitting in the airport. Other than the multitude of international germs, there was nothing stopping Shelby from touching anything she damn well pleased. Any danger of being jerked back in time was eliminated within the stainless steel and fiberglass walls of an airport. No issues with picking something up off of the dingy indoor-outdoor carpet square floors. No ancient thrones materializing in place of the vinyl covered molded chairs bolted together on a metal bar. For most travelers, airports are stressful places. For one Traveler, airports are relaxing places. By the time Shelby and Benny settled into their seats on the plane, thoughts of Thoth, Seshat, and Eli were comfortably in the back of their minds.

A couple of hours later, they were back in the risky world of history on every corner. "I need a drink," Shelby groaned as she gazed up at all of the buildings and potential time trips that surrounded her in the heart of old Paris. Her hands tingled uncomfortably as the cab wound through the streets. Part of her wanted to remember where they were when the pain intensified, and the other part wanted to close her eyes and pretend there was nothing happening. "Antoine said there was a pub around the corner from the hotel." Her French guide knew what was really important.

"Or room service," Benny suggested with a wink that made Shelby Starling do stupid things.

"Or room service."

The desk clerk at the hotel in the Latin Quarter looked at Shelby's license. "Oui, mademoiselle. One room for Mademoiselle Shelby Starling and Monsieur Benito Moretti paid in advance by Delphine Temple at Pioneer Tours."

"One room?" Shelby asked.

"Oui, mademoiselle. Is this not correct?"

Shelby glanced over at Benny who was clearly not wanting to put Shelby in an uncomfortable position, but was over his big-brother-ness enough to not suggest a second room. "No, one room is perfect," Shelby answered with a wink at the hot Roman next to her.

"Delphine?" Benny asked.

Shelby nodded. "Dina's a nickname. Here," she said tearing her attention away from what she hoped was coming later, and back to the desk clerk, "let me give you my card for room service and incidentals."

The clerk shook his head. "No need. Mademoiselle Temple insisted all charges were to go to her." He smiled. "Enjoy your stay. Should you need anything, please call."

Shelby tossed her bag and backpack into the corner of the simple but well-appointed hotel room. A light breeze drifted through the window hanging slightly ajar bringing with it the smells of the restaurants below and a soft hum of distant conversation. Benny closed the door behind them and set his own bag down as Shelby walked over to the window and pushed the curtain aside. "Not bad," she said. "Nice view from here."

"Yes, it is," Benny said from behind her. He slid his arm around her waist, pulled her dark hair aside, and kissed the curve of her neck.

Her hands hummed and her heart raced as she leaned back onto his chest. "I think Dina knew what she was doing."

"I know she did." Benny turned her around and held her face in his hands.

His rich Roman eyes looked at her as if they were seeing her for the first time. Scanning her face, his eyes settled on her own. A shadow of a smile flickered on his lips as they met hers. The high intensity of something that felt good but was definitely wrong was gone, replaced by warmth and a comfortableness Shelby had never experienced. For a second, she almost pulled back as her New York self-preservation threatened to surface, but she railed against it and let herself sink into the moment. Six months ago, she would have come up with some lame excuse to duck out and avoid anything that resembled a meaningful encounter. Instead, she wrapped her arms around the man who held her and gave in to feelings she never acknowledged before.

❋

The sun was setting over the buildings of the Latin Quarter as Shelby lay curled up next to Benny. Music drifted through the window signaling the opening of the bars in the neighborhood below. If they had just been in Paris on vacation, Shelby would have stayed right where she was running her tingling hand across Benny's chest while he curled a strand of her hair around his finger. Time may bend for her, but it definitely doesn't stand still, so the moment of contentment was fleeting. The spell was broken with a chime on her phone and Antoine's message that he would see them downstairs in an hour. Shelby sighed and tore herself away from heaven and got into the shower.

Jeans, white t-shirt, Chucks, and a ponytail were as dressed up as she was willing to do. The most American in Paris headed downstairs with a Roman on her arm. Antoine waved her and Benny over to the small table where he was sipping wine with a man Shelby didn't recognize. "Shelby, good to see you!" Her French guide was of an age which was difficult to put a number to on first glance. His face was slightly worn and his hair was a silvery salt and pepper, but he carried himself with the lightness of a young man.

With the traditional two cheek kiss and a smile exchanged, introductions were in order. "Antoine, Benito Moretti."

"And this is Gael Dardenne. Unfortunately, I've had something come up that I cannot avoid. Gael is another local guide who has been kind enough to step in for me."

"If it's okay with you, Shelby, of course," Gael jumped in with smooth English in his French accent. Gael was a stark contrast to Antoine. Where Antoine was shorter and thicker built, Gael was tall and slender. His movements graceful and refined without being off-putting and stuffy. His dark hair curled slightly on his forehead drawing attention to clear blue eyes seeming to take in everything around them.

"Of course! I hope it's nothing serious, Antoine."

Antoine shook his head. "No, but if you ask my mother, she will tell you the world is ending."

Shelby smiled. "When Mama calls, you go. I understand. I'm sure we'll be in good hands with Gael."

Benny asked, "Do you at least have time to join us for dinner?"

Antoine smiled and nodded. "I know just the place. There's a small cafe around the corner. Great food and even better wine."

The four made their way out into the Paris night with Gael holding the hotel door open for them to pass. As he did, the cuff of his sleeve pulled slightly up his arm revealing the edge of a tattoo. Like Naomi's, just enough to make one curious about what it could be, but with a look Shelby and Benny saw enough to know exactly what it was. A quick glance at one another and a silent agreement was reached not to say a word about what they knew just yet. There was no way to know if Antoine knew what Gael was and changed the plans intentionally, or if the change of plans had been orchestrated by the Watcher. The answer to the riddle would have to wait.

Paris is known for high fashion, money, and historical elegance, but the Latin Quarter was definitely more Shelby's speed. Old narrow streets seemed to be stuck in a cozy part of the past that was welcoming and casual. Music and delicious smells poured from the bars and cafes lining the bottom floors of the historic French architecture. Like in Madrid, the different buildings were designated by subtle variances in the shade of the stone and the shape of the wrought iron balconies instead of any spaces between them. There was nothing posh or trendy about the neighborhood on the bank of the Seine. Just a quirky twist on old Paris.

Shelby and Benny did their best to keep things light and normal as Antoine and Gael entertained the two of them, but neither one could forget about the tattoo. They walked through the night in the warm glow of lights streaming from the windows of shops and eateries, and under the neon of the unobtrusive signs lining the lower floors. Glowing modern versions of medieval shingles. Awnings would have shaded passersby from the midday sun, but the narrow streets made them really more for looks than sun-blocking functionality. Finally, passing galleries, bakeries, and several ethnic restaurants, they came upon a bar with rich dark wood framing the door and windows, but a bright welcoming interior. It reminded Shelby of where she had first spilled her guts to Naomi in Madrid. Maybe she should guard her tongue a bit closer this time.

Antoine nodded at the bartender who waved a waitress over to the small table in the corner where the four of them sat down. "So, how was Madrid? I can gather how Rome was," Antoine said with a wink at Benny.

Shelby found herself absurdly blushing as she answered, "Madrid was good. Nothing really spectacular." Gael raised an eyebrow as if he wasn't really buying her story. "Toledo and Avila were nice. Hadn't been there before." Shelby chose to pretend to ignore the look from Gael and keep things normal. As normal as her normal could be.

"Well," said Antoine, "I'm sure Gael will be able to find you some excitement in Paris."

Shelby's eyes locked with Gael's. "I'm sure he will." Gael winked and raised his wine glass in a silent toast. He knew she knew.

Dinner passed with conversation about places Antoine had planned for Shelby to visit that Gael would now be touring her and Benny through as well as some places they might go for meals and some night life. Gael seemed to realize before long that Benny knew exactly what was going on, and the three exchanged enough looks to also realize Antoine was oblivious to it all. Gael had been the puppet master for whatever had pulled Antoine back home to the French countryside and his mother. There was a reason the Watcher needed to be with her in Paris, which meant more memories. Maybe these wouldn't be as soul-sucking as Toledo.

⁕

Shelby sat in the window sill looking out at the night lights of Paris, at least as many as she could see through the narrow gaps in the buildings. The curtain behind her blew lazily in the breeze as if it was tired and ready for bed. With her knees pulled up to her chin and her arms resting on them, Shelby sat deep in thought.

Benny rolled over and reached for her only to find empty sheets. "Bella, come back to bed."

Shelby smiled from the window. "Sorry, Benny. I didn't mean to wake you. Couldn't sleep."

He propped himself on his elbow and smiled back at the silhouette in the dark. "I know, but tomorrow is busy. Rest, bella."

Shelby turned back to the window. "I'm not sure I want to go out there."

"Then don't."

"It's my job, Benny," she sighed. "Even if I wanted to stay here in bed for the next two days, I have a job to do. I have to go. I just don't want to."

"What are you afraid of?"

"Toledo."

Benny slid out of bed and put his arms around Shelby. "Bella, you have no idea what memories are here. Good, bad, whatever. They're yours, and you have to find them. You've come too far to stop now."

Shelby buried her face in his chest. She knew he was right, damn him, but she didn't want to go through that again. The memories only got more stressful. More terrible. Seshat said she had to learn from her memories. You don't learn from sunshine and roses. You learn from heartache.

"But what if I just stopped here? There would be other lives to live and get there. I could just stay here. With you."

Benny pushed back a little to look at her as a tear slid down Shelby's face. Wiping it away, he said, "I'm here for you every step of the way, but I will *not* be the reason you stop this journey. Do you understand me?"

Shelby nodded. "It's strange. I worry about losing something I didn't even know I wanted a few months ago."

"Shelby. Every life we live, we have people we love and who love us. No matter if you finish this now or another life, there will be reasons not to."

"Is the world really so bad that I need to go do great things and change history? Would the world be so bad if I just walked away?"

Benny shrugged. "No, probably not. Maybe it's not so much about what is, and more about what could be."

Shelby laid her head back down on Benny's chest. This whole mess was draining her more than she cared to admit. When she slept, an eleven-year-old girl on fire haunted her dreams. Waking hours were spent in fear of touching anything and thoughts of losing the one thing that felt like it belonged in her life. There were so many reasons to pretend this wasn't happening, and so far, no good reasons for embracing it.

"Come, bella. Maybe the sun will bring you clarity. Until then, come back to bed." Benny took her hands and turned them palms up. They surged with pain and she wanted to pull her hands away, but he held onto them. Gently, he opened her fingers and softly kissed her palms. Blue sparks jumped from her hands to his in a wash of color and light. Benny didn't flinch. Still holding her hands, he led her back to the bed and laid her down.

✳

"Bon jour, Shelby. Ça va?" Gael asked. "Benny?"

"We're good, thanks," Shelby answered understanding more French than she spoke. "Where do we start this morning?"

"Breakfast." Gael led them out into the cobbled street to a bakery cafe with a perky red and white striped awning. Small wooden tables and chairs were set close together under it as if every square inch was sacred and must be used. "This is one of my favorite places. Great bread, good coffee."

"Sounds perfect," Benny said politely. Shelby knew whatever passed as coffee in Paris was going to be a far cry from the cappuccinos Benny was used to. Part of her ached for the morning she opened her eyes from the edge of the Trevi fountain to see him standing over her with a cup of coffee. This morning seemed so far removed from that one.

The glass case filled with pastries, breads, and other baked goods was definitely everything she hoped it would be from the outside of the boulangerie. Baskets hanging on the wall behind the case were piled high with loaves of different shapes and sizes, all freshly baked. The smell inside was intoxicating. A line had formed inside as busy employees handed wrapped loaves of bread across the case to the customers, greeting almost every one of them by name. "With so many pastries, why is everyone leaving with a loaf of bread?" Shelby asked.

"A loaf of bread is a more common thing for the French. We love our decadent pastries, but the bread itself is tradition," Gael explained, "especially for breakfast." When it was their turn, Shelby and Benny gladly left the ordering to Gael.

Moments later, the three of them sat squished in one of the tables on the street side patio with sliced bread, fresh butter, jam, and coffee which was more like an Italian espresso than the milky café au lait Shelby had been expecting. "So," Shelby began as she melted butter on a hot slice of bread, "what's the plan today? I mean, Antoine had a plan, but something tells me you may have a different agenda, Gael."

Her new French guide stopped mid-sip and lowered his coffee cup. "You're right, of course. You knew last night. How?"

Benny replied bluntly, "The tattoo. You don't hide it very well."

Gael chuckled. "No, I suppose I didn't, did I?" He leaned back in the chair as much as the tight quarters would allow. "Then, I should explain. Part of it, it seems, you already gathered."

"We know what you are, at least. From that, the logical guess is there's some reason I'm here beyond my job."

"Perhaps," Gael said. "Perhaps not. None of us can predict where your journey will take you. Watchers know some things, but not all. What we *do* know is you have had enough happen lately it's a safe bet here would be the same."

"And Antoine wouldn't know what was going on if it did."

"Right."

Benny wrinkled his forehead in thought. "But how did you get his mother to call him home to her?"

Gael laughed. "That part was easy enough. Antoine's nephew got himself in with some questionable people doing some equally questionable things. All it took was making sure the boy's grandmother got wind of it, as you say. Since Antoine's sister couldn't keep her kid out of trouble, we knew grandma would make sure Antoine dealt with him."

Shelby's eyes widened. "You ratted the kid out just to swap places with Antoine?"

"Oui, but it's not so bad. The kid will get out of trouble, and you don't have as much explaining to do."

Shelby stuffed a piece of bread into her mouth to keep from telling Gael what a piece of shit thing it was to do to the kid. Of course, she was thrilled she wouldn't have to explain weirdness to Antoine, but she felt bad for the boy.

Benny asked, "How much do you know?"

"Enough. Naomi told me what she knew." Gael leaned forward and said softly, "Shelby, I know it's hard for you to trust someone else, but there was nothing Antoine could have done to help you here. You know yourself how hard hiding what happens to you can be. Tarek was easy enough to avoid and there was only Seshat for you in Egypt. There were no other episodes. Here- well, who knows what's here? Antoine wouldn't be easily fooled."

Shelby knew he was right about everything. He was right about her struggling with trusting a new Watcher. Naomi was different. She was familiar, not a new person thrust on her by throwing some poor kid under the bus. Gael was a stranger who knew more about her than she seemed to. Nothing about that was easy to swallow.

"Come," Gael said tossing his napkin in his plate. "Notre Dame awaits."

Religion and history are intricately woven together all over the world in a rich and blood-stained tapestry. The two have birthed stories both beautiful and terrifying. An eternity of leaders have wreaked horror in the name of their god, and even more have created masterpieces trying to make themselves gods. Notre Dame is France's pièce de résistance.

In the middle of the Seine in the heart of Paris, the cathedral rose up toward the heavens. Centuries of history and stories were immortalized in its architecture, and even more in its art. As they approached the west facade, the depth of Notre Dame was hidden behind the imposing twin towers and sweeping ornate arches. Shelby did her best to avoid references to Quasimodo that may have been off-color, and was smugly congratulating herself on her success while Gael explained the nuances of the carvings around the arches. She couldn't deny there was something both imposing and inspiring about the cathedral, but apprehension was preventing her from enjoying the moment. As she approached the entrance passing through the portal of the last judgement, her hands burned painfully signaling something was waiting for her inside. Layers of carved figures looked on as though they knew but were sentenced to stony silence.

"You okay, bella?" Benny whispered in her ear as they followed Gael inside.

Shelby nodded. "I think so. It hurts, though."

Benny took her hand and gently squeezed it. Sparks danced along their fingertips as he laced his fingers through hers.

Inside, the ceiling swept upward, arches meeting in points overhead. The checkered center aisle reached out in front of them toward the main altar and tremendous organ. Rows of columns added strength to the sides of the hugely open space. Thick pointed arches formed every opening from windows to alcoves. High stained-glass windows let cool colors dance around the ceiling while tremendous chandeliers bathed the lower spaces in warm golden light. The north and south ends of the massive structure were anchored by the spectacular rose windows which were synonymous with the cathedral itself. Gael, putting on his tour guide hat for the time being, explained the history and story in the glass panes, including them being removed and hidden from the Nazis, as Shelby took photos for Dina.

Even though they had arrived shortly after opening, the cathedral was quickly filling with tourists and spiritual pilgrims. Not being religious in the least, Shelby always felt weirdly out of place in churches, especially ones that seemed to thrust religion on visitors with every brick and statue. As in every other cathedral and temple she visited, tourists were too oblivious to anything but the majesty surrounding them to notice anyone or anything else. With her burning hands heralding an episode any minute, Shelby knew their cluelessness was her saving grace.

"It feels different here," she said quietly, not so much out of reverence, but confusion.

"How so?" asked Gael leading them to the main altar.

"It's a pull sort of. Like something I can't see is tugging at me."

"Where do you feel it? Your hands?" Benny asked.

Shelby shook her head as she walked. "No, not like I can feel someone touching me. I feel disconnected. Like I'm not really here. Hollow." The aisle opened up as they reached the front of the intricate altar. Shelby's hands pulsed wildly and sparks shot from her fingertips to the tile under her feet. "No-"

The altar vanished in a flood of white light while pain surged through her body unchecked for what seemed like minutes rather than the seconds of the past. Finally, the pain released its grip on the unwitting victim. *This isn't right. I didn't touch anything. I didn't-* The church came into focus as a choir began singing in complex harmony. The pews, sparsely populated seconds earlier, were full of people dressed in rich jewel tone gowns and tunics. Sprays of flowers filled the center aisle. Candles and torches replaced the chandeliers in the alcoves. Incense hung heavy in the air. Near the altar stood a priest in medieval ceremonial robes with his hands raised in invocation of the Spirit. Guards, or were they knights, stood with one hand on the hilt of their swords flanking the young man to one side of the priest. Other men stood in front of the guards on either side of the altar in richly made tunics. The young man stared down the center aisle as the choir reached a crescendo, and Shelby noticed a ring of jeweled gold set on top of his dark curls. A king, but who? Glancing down, she realized she was wearing a tunic with an embroidered fleur-de-lis emblem matching that of the guards. A page. She was a page, but whose page? One of the knights'? The king's?

As one body, the congregation stood and turned at the sound of heavy wooden doors opening at the far end of the aisle. Slowly came a procession of guards with a different emblem on their chest followed by women in tall hats with scarves flowing behind them with every step. Behind them walked a woman alone with her head held high, the long hem of her gown being carried by two handmaids. Beyond her were more guards and ladies in waiting. As she passed, the congregation knelt. Reaching the opening in front of the altar, the guards split and flanked each side, turning in unison to face the congregation. The court of the young woman took their places on either side of the couple. A few ladies gave shy smiles to some of the men standing with the king. As she looked on, Shelby swore the bride winked at a dark-haired young man standing next to the king before she took her place in front of the priest. The cleric brought his arms down as the bride and groom took each other's hands and knelt.

When their knees touched the ground, white light poured into the cathedral wiping out the happy scene before her. Shelby's vision slowly returned. The flowers were gone and dark shrouds with fleur-de-lis crests hung in their place. A woman was still kneeling at the altar, but she was older and heavy. She was praying, but surprisingly not upset given the fact that where the priest had been moments before was a coffin. It was the queen she had seen coming down the aisle at the wedding, and the king was dead. In the shadow of one of the alcoves, an older version of the man who stood beside the dark-haired man she winked at leaned against a column. Another man approached him from behind and whispered something in his ear. The first man never looked back while a smile slowly curled his lips then vanished into a false somberness more appropriate for the setting as the other man faded into the shadows. He remained watching the widow intently as she murmured her prayers. Shelby tore her gaze from the man in the alcove and back to the funerary scene at the altar. Candles surrounded the casket draped in the same fleur de lis she was wearing. Still a page? Or now a knight? Or something else? What the hell was going on? This was not greatness or terror. This was just life. Royal medieval life.

The queen slowly raised her head and looked at Shelby with a smile that was tired and worn. "It's over," she said quietly, but the words rang in the emptiness of the stone room. "He's free. I'm free. Let the people come." With a nod to the man in the alcove, the queen walked back out alone down the main aisle she had walked up moments before in procession. As Shelby watched her go, Notre Dame shimmered like heat before fading into white nothingness.

When the light finally dissipated, Shelby was being held standing up on either side by Benny and Gael facing the altar. Her head had dropped forward and they were doing their level best to make it look like she was rapt in prayer. The hand Benny was holding was sparking wildly between their fingers and Seshat's bracelet. Her hand in Gael's was stinging, but the sparks were dwindling. "Don't understand," she whispered.

Benny and Gael sat her down in a front pew. Shelby gripped Benny's hand tight. "Neither do we, bella. Neither do we."

Gael gave Shelby's other hand to Benny and sparks cascaded over it from the other hand. "Naomi said you touched things to bring the memories. Did you touch anything?"

"No," she said watching the sparks. They were trying to get her attention, but why? "Felt weird, then-" Shelby was weak and talking was draining what little energy she had left. Benny assumed his role as protector and wrapped an arm around her and let her rest on his shoulder.

Gael leaned back on the pew. "She's getting more powerful."

"How can you say that?" Benny snapped. "Look at her!" Glares from tourists shushed Benny's indignance. "They've always taken a lot out of her, but she's struggling more to come out of them. How's that powerful?"

"Not physically powerful. Her connection to the universe. She doesn't have to touch the history to feel it anymore."

Benny stroked Shelby's dark hair. "So, she's not safe anywhere. She doesn't have control of when she gets pulled back in time."

"No," Gael said quietly. Soft footfalls on the tile floor and hushed voices of travelers filled the silence settling over the three of them.

⁕

The slow walk around the exterior of Notre Dame in the fresh air cleared the haze in Shelby's head but the memories still rang in her ears. The last few weeks were blurring together. The choir in Notre Dame, the surge of the crowd in the Colosseum, and the screams of a child burning to death in Toledo. The sound was thick, like a wall of sound she was trapped behind. Shelby wanted to push through to hear what Benny and Gael were talking about, but they seemed so far away. "...could come from anywhere now..." Singing. "...ruins get paved over..." Shouts. "...won't see it coming..." Screams.

Benny stopped walking and took both of her hands. Sparks. "Shelby?"

She closed her eyes and concentrated on his voice to pull it out of the din. "Yes?"

"Bella, we need your help."

"Shelby," Gael said, "can you tell us what you saw?"

The tidal wave of sound gently ebbed back into the ocean of memories as she focused on the two men standing in front of her. "A wedding. Royals." Words. Where were her words? What the hell was happening to her mind?

Gael took her hand. No sparks. "There were many royal weddings here. Do you know who they were? When it was?"

Shelby shook her head. "Medieval wedding." Why the hell was she talking like a toddler?

Gael smiled. "Well, that's something! Anything else?"

"Funeral." Way to go, Rain Man.

Benny stared at her for a second. "Wedding you mean."

"Yes. And funeral. Same people." Getting better.

"What royals are buried here?" Benny asked Gael.

"None," Gael said. "Some religious figures, but no royals. The kings and queens of France rest at Saint Denis north of the city."

"The crest," Shelby said. "On my tunic."

"Would you know it if you saw it again?" Gael asked.

Benny answered for her as Shelby visibly struggled for words. "She can't forget anything from the memories. She'd know it." Shelby nodded.

"Come. I know just the place. Bibliothèque Nationale. Medieval collection." Gael was starting to sound like Shelby.

CHAPTER 14

The Bibliothèque Nationale de France made the stunning little library in Rome look homely. Intricate, gilded, and modern spaces intertwined with older tired rooms awaiting the attention of the architect overseeing the ongoing and staggering renovations. The main room of the le site Richelieu was immense but airy with the cream and silver arches and domes giving light to the ceiling creating a feeling of cool openness. The space was anchored by rows of desks and reading lamps whose straight lines were in beautiful contrast to the carved white and gold details above the top rows of books seemingly several stories above the heads of the patrons. As stunning as this place was, they were only passing through.

Gael wove through the library, up flights of stairs, and over a glass bridge to a pair of heavy doors. Like much of France, they were anything but simple elegance. Warm wood panels were covered in a lace of carved ebony overlay. In the center of each door was another carving covered in gold. They were made for passing through, but the doors would stop most people on the threshold to spend a moment in their beauty. While Shelby gawked, Gael pushed them open as if they had been nothing more than a sliding glass door at a supermarket.

The room behind the spectacular doors was more spacious than the antique book room of the quaint Roman library, but just as cozy. A wall of tall windows poured in natural light onto the rows of desks with felted tops for protecting the contents of the shelves that wrapped the room. In one corner, nestled in among the rich woodwork, was a small curving staircase tucked into to a tiny wooden turret leading up to a balcony with more shelves, many empty.

Across the room, sitting at one of the wooden desks pouring over a thick book with wavy pages full of brilliant illuminations, was a small woman with silver hair and a kind smile. A female French version of the little man from Rome. A few words from Gael produced a volume bound in leather with gold and green accents on the spine. Letters had been painted on the front in gold at one time, but only shadows and flecks remained anymore.

Gently, as though it were made of the thinnest glass, Gael opened it. "Now, Shelby," he began, "I need you to think about what you saw. This book contains the coats of arms of French kings over the ages. I'll turn the pages. You tell us if you see anything familiar or feel anything."

Shelby's hands had calmed down since the cathedral, and she wasn't excited about aggravating them on purpose. "Fine."

Pages turned full of colorful crests and family trees. Lists of offspring and the occasional branches of illegitimacy, some of which contained the names of more kings who managed to usurp the throne. The pages worked their way back through the eons. Most of the crests had common repeated elements and many contained the fleur de lis from the livery of those in Notre Dame, but each was represented in a different way. Gael continued to slowly turn the pages, studying Shelby's reaction more than the images on the paper.

Shelby winced in pain as he turned the page one more time. Sparks swam across her fingertips. "That one!" On a royal blue field, was a gold fleur de lis on the top left, and half of one lower down and in the center. The other half of the field was covered in a checkerboard of gold diamonds.

Gael read the name at the top of the page. "Are you sure it's this one?"

"Positive. It was everywhere. On my tunic, the nights, the robe of the king."

Benny looked at the name on the page. "Charles VI. What does it say after that?"

"Charles the Beloved," Gael translated.

"That sounds good. Why do you look like Shelby should be worried?"

"Because of what it says after it. 'Charles the Mad King.'"

Shelby's attention had been on the crest, but at those words, her head snapped up to look at Gael. "Mad? What kind of mad?"

"Any definition of the word you please would fit him at some point or another. There's legend, but who knows how much is true. Like any king, there were many who sought to take the throne from him or secure it for a successor they would choose. Politics often cloud the truth, so it's difficult to say how mad he really was."

Shelby refused to let it go that simply. "What do you believe?"

"I believe the legends. You say you were a page in his court?"

"As best I could tell."

Gael closed the book. "Then you may be able to tell us how much of the legends are true by the time you're finished here. But you must be careful. Madness is unpredictable."

Benny chimed in. "And so are her memories. How are we going to protect her when they can come from anywhere, not just what she touches?"

"By staying close enough to catch her when they happen."

Shelby rolled her eyes. "That won't look weird or anything. One more of us and we'd look like The Monkees walking around town. There must be some other way."

Gael shook his head. "No, I wish there was. Most of the ruins of Charles' day have been demolished and built over. Some places remain, but most have become something else. His palace, Saint-Pol, spanned a large area on the bank of the Seine, but it was demolished not long after his death, so its foundations lie under the more modern city buildings and streets now."

"So," Shelby said, "I can't deliberately bring these memories on by touching something, but I can't really avoid them if I plan on doing the job I came to do, either."

Gael shrugged. "I'd say that pretty much sums it up."

"Well, this just gets better and better. So, now where?"

"Let's go be tourists and give you a break for now. Eiffel Tower and Arc de Triomphe. Both of those are new enough to not pose much of a risk. Tomorrow, we'll track down the Mad King." Gael said it as if they were looking for lost car keys. Time bending mental torture was hardly something Shelby took lightly.

⁕

True to his word, there was nothing to worry about at the Eiffel Tower. By the time the three of them finished the climb to the top, Shelby had relaxed enough to almost enjoy it, at least as relaxed as someone whose physical activity level revolved around Benny and copious amounts of wine. Benny and Gael had spent the walk through the city talking shop and telling stories of some of the strangest tours they'd given, which took the edge off of the insanity of Notre Dame. Shelby slowly began to thaw with Gael as Benny warmed up to him. It wasn't so much that she didn't like Gael, but baring her soul wasn't something she was comfortable with in the first place and it was happening all too often lately.

Coming down from the top, Gael made the best suggestion so far. "How about we put the Arc off for today, have dinner here at the Tower, and watch the city lights come on over a glass of wine?"

"Make it a bottle of wine, and I'm there," Shelby laughed.

"Done."

Perched fifty-seven meters above the ground amid the lace of the Eiffel Tower supports, Shelby and Benny sat sipping wine with Gael while the sun eased down below the city rooftops. The glass walls of the restaurant allowed visitors to experience the beauty of the city while suspended above the noise, traffic, and smells of the old town. Lights began to wink on in the distance as ones in the restaurant were dimmed to make the most of the sparkling horizon.

"It's hard to believe somewhere out there is madness and terror," Shelby said stuffing hot buttered bread into her mouth.

"Not tonight," Gael insisted. "Tonight, there is only Paris. Let yourself get to know her for what she is."

"Good luck with that," Benny snorted. "I tried to tell her the same thing about Rome."

Gael looked at Shelby over the flickering candle. His blue eyes sparkled and a curl fell onto his forehead. If she hadn't already lost everything she was to Benito Moretti, Gael would have been difficult to resist. She felt a pang of guilt sitting there with Benny and mentally falling into bed with Gael. Which was new. The guilt, not the falling into bed with tour guides. "Tell me something, Shelby. Why do you run from yourself?" the Frenchman asked her.

Shelby resisted the urge to tell the Watcher it was none of his goddamn business, and replied instead, "Because if I walked, I would catch me."

Benny shrugged and rolled his eyes. He knew Shelby well enough to know she was masking her irritation at the personal question behind sarcasm like she had done with Naomi. "You won't get it out of her," he said. "I don't think she knows."

"Of course, I know."

"Well, then?" Gael asked leaning forward across the table.

Did she really know why she did the things she did? Why she ran? Yes. Was she proud of it? No. It was weak. What business was it of his? Why should Gael know what drove her to run in terror from what she could be? "It's complicated."

A shrug and a raised glass was Benny's silent 'I told you so.'

Gael never took his eyes off her as he sat back in his chair, unwilling to admit defeat, but not wanting to push her away just as he was making some progress. "In your own time, then."

Shelby held his stare also unwilling to admit defeat. "Is any time really my own anymore?"

A grin broke the intensity of Gael's stare-down. "No, I don't suppose it is." He toasted her moxy and poured her another glass. "If you won't bear your soul to me, fine. Maybe a different subject." He winked. "Read any good books lately?"

Shelby shot a look at Benny. The diary. "I'd say yes, but I can't actually read it, myself."

"Naomi said it hurts you to hold it?"

"Yeah. With a good buzz I can get through it, but not sober."

"Many things are better with a good buzz, no?" Gael said smirking as Benny shifted uncomfortably in his seat.

Shelby slid a hand onto Benny's thigh to ease his budding jealousy. As much fun as it would have normally been to have two gorgeous guys flirting with her, she was surprised to discover that Gael's innuendo put her on the defensive for Benny. But that feeling wasn't her. She was a self-absorbed smart-ass. Wasn't she? She'd spent so much time being other people, she felt like she was slowly losing her grip on who she was anymore. Blue sparks flickered along Seshat's bracelet trying to get her attention. Maybe Seshat was trying to tell her feeling this way was part of the journey.

His hand on hers, Benny kissed Shelby just under her ear. A shiver ran through her as his lips brushed her neck. "Bella, maybe it's a good time to show him the journal," Benny whispered.

Shelby looked around. Tourists and locals were deep in conversation or pointing at landmarks illuminated outside the massive panes of glass. This was as close to hiding in plain sight as they could get. She nodded and opened the backpack at her feet. The pain of hundreds of tiny hot needles stung her fingers as they wrapped around the leather binding. Only able to hold it for a second, she dropped it on the table in front of her. "Gael, meet Elijah Faircloth. Here," she said, "you'll have to take it yourself." She waved her hand above the book in a gesture for him to take it, but as she did, the book slid several inches across the table.

The three of them instinctively pulled away from the table in shock, Shelby's chair narrowly missing a collision with a waiter. "What the hell?" Benny whispered. He looked at Shelby for explanation, but she was staring wild-eyed at the book as if it were a three-headed dog. Her mouth gaped open twitching slightly as if hunting words that continued to elude her. Gael was doing his best to make everything look normal, speaking just loudly enough that any guests startled by the sudden lurch of chairs would think there had been a close call with a bumped wine glass.

"I'm sorry," Shelby managed to say at last. Where the words came from, she couldn't tell, but she was grateful for anything that interrupted the stupid voiceless babbling her mouth had been doing.

"No, it's quite alright," Gael continued speaking slightly louder than necessary. "Come, let me refill your glass. This is a marvelous vintage. It should not go to waste." He picked up the bottle and poured. Under his breath, he hissed, "Drink it, Shelby. Now."

Shelby obediently picked up the glass which reflected and distorted the sparks on her fingertips. Part of her wanted to grip the glass tightly in her shaking hand, but another part of her feared shattering it. So, she concentrated on holding it gently and steadily as she brought it to her lips. Benny and Gael did their best to soothe Shelby's shattered nerves with small talk while carefully averting their eyes from the book as if it was laying in the middle of the table stark naked. Shelby couldn't tear her eyes away from it as she drank down the rich liquid. She was going to need a lot more wine. By the bottom of the glass, her hands were shaking less and stinging more. Gael refilled it before she had a chance to ask. Her head was swimming, but there was no way to tell if it was the wine or the weirdness.

"I moved it? How did I move it?" she asked softly, more to herself than anything.

"Bella?"

"Benny, did I move that book?"

Benny looked at her with pity, and Shelby hated it. She didn't want his pity. She didn't want any of this. She wanted to be drunk laying on the edge of a fountain in Rome. "Yes, bella. You moved it. I don't know how, but it had to be you."

"Gael?"

The Watcher looked at her with the same pity, damn him. "Shelby, I wish there was another explanation, but there isn't. Did you notice anything before it happened? Feel different? See anything?"

The bracelet. "Yes. Sparks on the bracelet."

"But that isn't different," Benny said. "It happens a lot."

"It's all I've got right now. The sparks get my attention. That's all I know about them. Seshat was less than helpful on some points."

Gael's eyebrows came together as he thought about what he just witnessed. "If they are to get your attention, try to think back to that moment. What were you thinking?"

Shelby closed her eyes. Even in the darkness behind her lids, she could still see the sparkling of the City of Lights. Pushing the image from her mind, she tried to recall what she was thinking before she moved the book. Nonsense. It had to be utter nonsense. So much of her thoughts were anymore, but what was it this time? Benny? Maybe? Wait... "I was thinking I was losing my grip on who I am, or who I was. Things that would have amused me before make me feel...different now. I don't like it. I mean, I do, but-"

"Shelby," Benny began, "I don't understand."

Shelby's face reddened a little as she opened her eyes. Gael looked steadily at her for a moment and smiled as his eyes flickered to Benny and back to her. "It's fine, Shelby." He knew exactly what she meant. Damn his smile. It was dangerous and he knew it. With a shadow of a wink, the Watcher changed the subject. "Then, perhaps we should be paying attention to the diary."

"Maybe so. Clearly, I have no idea what I'm talking about. I guess Notre Dame took more out of me than I thought."

Benny, who had been awkwardly trying to figure out what the hell was going on, chimed in. "How much do you know about the diary, Gael?"

The Frenchman swirled his wine and stared at it for a moment before he spoke. "Naomi told me very little. She was more concerned about protecting Shelby than what some dead Englishman babbled about. Although, she did say there were things in his ramblings that could prove useful."

"Quite," Benny said trying to match the smooth aloofness of the Watcher. "But we've been left with more questions the more we read."

Gael engaged the duel of manners. "Then, since it takes so much out of Shelby, perhaps you would fill me in on the tale of the wandering Victorian?"

"Of course," Benny replied, only mildly veiling the Latin heat that was bubbling to the surface in a tide of jealousy.

Shelby normally would have been secretly entertained by the international macho warfare shrouded in decorum happening at the table, but it was making her uncomfortable. Benny had her heart, but he was no match for the silkiness of Gael. She had to put a stop to it. "Maybe this isn't the best place for this after all."

Gael signaled the waiter to bring the check. "Of course, you're right. Perhaps some night air would do you good. The air here is a bit close."

Shelby nodded. "Great idea." Benny took her hand and laced his fingers through hers. Sparks between their fingertips caused a raised eyebrow from Gael across the table, but he kept his thoughts to himself.

Moments later, they were looking up at the full height of the Eiffel Tower illuminated spectacularly in the night. It had been cold metal when she first looked up at it in the daylight, but now it seemed to pulse with life as the light threw shadows. "It really is beautiful," she whispered, becoming more enamored than she expected with something she had heretofore considered one man's compensation for an area in which he must surely have been ill-equipped.

"Yes," Gael said standing next to her. "Paris is full of beauty tonight." The corner of his mouth twitched with a smile. Her chest tightened and her stomach fluttered. His hand almost imperceptibly brushed the small of her back as he strode away from her toward the cab line. Shelby's breath caught in her chest. She could still feel Gael's touch as he opened the door for her and Benny helped her into the backseat. The Watcher gave an address to the driver while Shelby sat silently beating herself senseless over the thoughts going through her mind as she settled into the crook of Benny's arm.

* * *

Rooftop bars had recently become all the rage in Paris, but Shelby would have been happier if picking up dog crap had been the latest fashion instead. Piles were easy enough to avoid in the daytime, but at night the sidewalks were full of landmines. Steering around them made a tea-totaling pedestrian look like a drunk and, since Shelby was less than sober, she was grateful the cab was able to drop them a few paces from the bar.

The queue in front of the unmarked door stretched to the end of the block, but there was no anxious shuffling of feet or craning of necks indicating the inability of those in line to await admittance into the rooftop bar. Instead, people talked quietly, always quietly in Paris, and waited patiently. Nothing in France seemed to move quickly, especially when it revolved around food and wine. It was meant to be savored, and so it was.

Just as Shelby was realizing she was far too American to wait in the infernal line, the host glanced over at Gael and jerked his head towards another door out of the glow of the neon sign. Without a word, the Watcher led them inside and up a dark back staircase. Several flights later, the three of them emerged onto a patio full of wood slat folding tables and chairs, strings of lights, and a jungle of potted palms. Curls of cigarette smoke rose over the heads of people who chatted while nursing cocktails and wine. There was nothing stuffy or swanky about the place, but the view of the city rooftops was staggering. Since tablespace was at a premium, Gael motioned to a low wall surrounding a small patio garden near the bar.

"I'll be right back," Gael said and went to order drinks from the bar since they had no waitress on their wall.

Shelby's mind raced looking for something to say to Benny to reassure herself about how she felt. He was clueless to the sensations that had rocked her at the Eiffel Tower, but she still felt guilty. Not that she had done anything wrong. There had never been anything before but playful attraction with Benny. Nothing serious or long-term. Now, there was a lot more, even though nothing had ever been said. Small talk seemed silly, but she couldn't think of anything with any substance to say, so she said nothing.

Benny picked at an invisible stain on his pant leg in the silence between them. "Nice night," was all he managed to say.

"It is," Shelby answered dully. This was ridiculous. "Benny-" she began, but cut off by Gael holding out one hand with two wine glasses balanced between his fingers and handing a beer to Benny. She took one of the glasses of wine, only slightly grateful for the interruption, and drank a deep swallow.

"A little wine and fresh air should do you some good, Shelby," Gael said sitting on the other side of her. He was too close. Goosebumps stood up on her skin. "Now," he began, pausing to take a sip of his wine, "tell me about our helpful Brit."

At least it was conversation, not mind-numbing small talk, and it involved Benny, which broke some of the awkwardness settling over them. Between the two of them, Shelby and Benny brought Gael up to speed on the misadventures of Elijah Faircloth. Gael listened intently, interrupting once in a while to ask for details when they glossed over parts they knew too well. A few drinks later, Gael was caught up with as much as they knew.

"Benny, have you read the whole diary?" Gael asked.

Benny seemed a little offended by the question. "No, why?"

"I just thought, since Shelby can't hold it, maybe you read it yourself to see what secrets it holds."

"That wouldn't be right. It's her journey, not mine."

Gael raised an eyebrow. "Really? You seem to be in this almost as much as she is. I mean no offense, of course, but wouldn't you think it would be more helpful if one of you finished the diary?"

Goddamn him, the Watcher had a point, but Benny refused to back down. "No, the other Watcher led Shelby to the book. It's hers."

"But she can't even hold it."

"No, but when she's ready, she can have one of us read it to her."

Shelby said quietly, "Maybe I don't have to hold it to read it."

"Well, no," Benny said, suddenly aware he had let his machismo get the better of him rather than letting Shelby speak for herself. "I could hold it for you to read, if you want."

She shook her head. "No, that's not what I mean. If I can move it across the table, maybe I can read it without touching it."

Benny and Gael looked at each other for a beat. They had been too busy trying to one-up each other that they hadn't actually thought it through. Gael spoke first. "Makes sense."

"Maybe that's the real reason I could move it. So I don't have to touch it to read it. I don't care what Naomi says, there aren't as many coincidences as she likes to say there are."

Benny shrugged. "You could be right. Do you want to try it?"

Shelby nodded, "But not here."

"No," Gael said. "Not here. There's likely to be sparks, and they wouldn't go unnoticed."

"Then, where?" Benny asked.

Shelby looked expectantly at Gael to know what to do. He thought for a moment. "The back stairs."

The trio put on a weak performance in an attempt to look as casual as possible with their departure, and headed toward the back staircase. It was dark with only some small sconce lights here and there. Pools of golden light illuminated a few stairs, then left more in the dark with just shades of shadow to show where they were. One light happened to fall on a landing about halfway down the flights. "Here," Gael said sitting on the top step.

Shelby and Benny followed suit. She set the backpack down, and unzipped it. Sparks glowed bright blue in the small pool of dingy light. Her hands buzzed with electricity and she couldn't bring herself to lift the leather-bound book out of its resting place. "Benny-"

Benny put his hand inside and pulled the book out. He laid it gently on the wooden landing as if it were made of antique glass. "What do we do now?" he asked.

Gael looked at Shelby. "Do what feels good."

Had he been talking to the old Shelby, there was a perfect opportunity for smart-ass flirting, but she only faintly considered it. Instead, she focused her mind on the book and her hands. The tingling changed. It wasn't just electrical buzzing. There was a pull, like a magnet in her palms, that seemed to be drawn to the book. Slowly, she moved her hand, palm down, toward the book. It didn't move with her hand. It just laid there as inanimate as always, but then, she hadn't really wanted to move it. She glanced up at Gael. "I don't know what to do. It feels different, but I don't know what I'm supposed to do."

"Try to move it," the Watcher instructed. "Concentrate on where you want it to go."

Slowly, she pushed her palm away from her. Equally slowly, the book slid haltingly against the wooden floorboards as though connected to her hand. Sparks jumped from her fingertips to the book and back making the connection visible.

"Pull it back to you."

She pulled her hand back toward her and the book followed.

"Open it."

Instinctively, Shelby put both hands over the book and moved one away from the other. The cover of the book lifted and settled flat on the floor.

"Turn the page."

A flick of her finger and the page turned. Again, and another page.

Benny, whose eyes were flitting from Shelby to the book, whispered, "She was right." Gael nodded in reply. "Does it hurt, bella?"

Shelby shook her head. "No more than the usual stinging in my hands. Not like actually touching it."

Gael smiled. "Now, we can get somewhere." Shelby leaned back against the wall, exhausted from wine and concentrating. "But not tonight."

CHAPTER 15

Dawn slipped through the curtains in the Latin Quarter and mercilessly accosted Shelby and her hangover. Burying her face in Benny's chest, she made a sleepy effort to rail against the coming of the day. Morning, however, was stronger than she was.

Benny chuckled at her as she squeaked and stretched like a kitten with bedhead. "Good thing Dina didn't ask you to do a Sunrises of the World Tour."

Shelby yawned. "Would've been a short tour."

Benny threw on some pants and a t-shirt then went down to the lobby to find some coffee. Shelby promised she would be up and in the shower by the time he got back with it, but he had his doubts. A cold shower, hot coffee, and an hour later, they were downstairs waiting for a cab with Gael.

Shelby wasn't exactly enthused about the day, but she had a job to do and not much time to do it. When the cab stopped and she stepped out, she looked up at Notre Dame up ahead and shuddered. She had almost forgotten about the memory and its aftermath in all the chaos with the journal. Almost.

Walking through the city had a strange effect on Shelby. The wall of sound from the day before was more like a veil of whispers. Unable to make out what they were saying, she let them drift into the back of her mind and tried to focus her attention and her camera on what Gael was narrating. In the 4th arrondissement, the modern Pompidou Centre and the Renaissance square Place des Vosges both sat comfortably in the neighborhood of eclectic ethnicities and sexualities, ruled by the morality and excess of Notre Dame. Somehow, amid all of that, the whispers didn't seem so out of place.

"You okay, bella?" Benny asked quietly.

"Fine," she lied.

The further they walked, the louder the voices became. Before long, it was like a family reunion with twelve meaningless conversations going on at once and a couple of arguments thrown in for good measure. As they crossed Rue Saint-Antoine, the din was almost unbearable. Gael's voice had long since faded into the background lost in the swell of sound. Benny watched her carefully for any sign of time-warping.

Rounding a corner, Shelby froze. Light washed over her and a surge of electricity shot from her fingertips, through her body, and down to her feet rooting her to the ground. Shimmering into existence, stone walls surrounded her where she stood once again dressed in the fleur de lis livery. Above her hung banners with the familiar crest from Notre Dame. Music was playing and people in medieval dress were talking and laughing. Drinks and food were being brought in and set on large banquet tables along the walls with huge candelabra lighting up each side of the room. There were iron holders on the stone walls for torches, but none were in place making the room feel close and dark even with the high ceilings. The woman from the church stood with several other nobles and ladies in waiting, laughing. A party. But where was the king?

A door on one end of the grand hall burst open. Several people in costumes created to make the wearers look like wild shaggy creatures entered with fanfare from the musicians that transitioned into a raucous song. The masked creatures began a strange dance, both frightening and flirty depending on who they were engaging at the moment. As they drew nearer, Shelby could see the costumes were covered in a waxy substance holding some sort of straw onto the fabric. The masks were covered the same way. As the dance continued, more and more of the spectators got into the spirit of the masquerade. The men challenged the dancers with bravado and the women feigned swoons into the arms of nearby knights. The queen watched with dignified amusement, but remained detached from the debauchery. On one side of her was a young girl, maybe fifteen years old. On the other was the man from the church who had been watching her from the shadows.

Another group strode into the hall with boisterous laughter. All eyes snapped to the new group, whose leader was holding a torch in one hand. He and his friends were clearly sloshed, even more so than the rest of the party. The shaggy wild men tried to keep up their act, but the young leader of the new group strode brazenly over to the queen and kissed her hand, lingering a moment too long.

One of the dancers said something to him Shelby couldn't hear and the young man with the torch wheeled around to face him. As he did, flaming resin dripped from the torch onto the straw of the dancer's costume igniting it. The queen shrieked and drew back as the dancer frantically spun around trying to put the flame out but only managed to spread the blaze to dancers around him. Soon all of them were alight and flailing wildly. The mask of the first flaming dancer fell off to reveal the king's terrified face. Shelby wanted to do something, but her feet wouldn't move. The face of a little girl burning to death took the place of the king for a moment and fear seized her. The young noble girl who had stood by the queen sprang into action and used her voluminous skirts to smother the blaze that enveloped the king, singeing her hands in the process. Another dancer leaped into a vat of wine, which then ignited, but soon burned itself out and doused the flames.

The young man who held the torch had joined the rest of the court in trying to put out the fires. Someone threw open windows and doors to let the building smoke cloud escape as the nobles and servants began choking. Eventually, the flames were extinguished, but one man lay dead and several others were critically injured. On all fours weeping over the king, who was struggling to breathe, was the young man with the torch. From across the room, the queen stared daggers at Shelby who had stood frozen in her fear through the whole ordeal, but said nothing. The haze of smoke faded into the blinding white light that brought her back to reality.

Benny and Gael led her to a stoop and sat her down to get her bearings. Her ears rang from the screams and her lungs stung from smoke even as she sat there. She could see they were talking to her, but she couldn't hear them. Eyes closed against the noise in her head, she tried desperately to focus on what they were saying, but she couldn't get the images of the burning little girl and king out of her mind.

"...okay, bella?" Benny was talking. She tried to nod, but wasn't sure if she moved.

Gael looked down at her, but stopped talking. His face was patient, but expectant. After a moment, he spoke. "Shelby, what did you see?"

"Fire."

Benny's eyes widened and he shot a look at Gael. He knew how much Toledo took out of her. "Not again."

Shelby shook her head. "Party." She tried to find more words. "Went wrong. Dancers. Torch." Shit, where were her words? They were in her head. Why couldn't they find her damn mouth?

"The same king?" Gael asked. Shelby nodded. He smiled. "I know what it was. The Bal des Ardents."

Benny tried to hide his confusion, but finally had to ask. "What's that?"

Gael explained as much to Shelby as Benny. "During the reign of the Mad King, Charles VI, the queen, Isabeau, threw a party for one of her ladies in waiting to celebrate her remarriage. When a widow married, there were usually wild parties, as much as a joke as celebration. The king and some other nobles decided to have some fun and dress up as wild men. The Duke of Orleans managed to catch them on fire with a torch. The king and one other lived, but the others died of their injuries."

Shelby found some words. "One was dead. Others hurt."

Gael shook his head. "They died later. One, it is written, screamed curses at the court for three days before he finally succumbed to his injuries."

"One hell of a party," Benny said shaking his head.

"That put an end to parties for a long time. The court even had to do public penance for it at Notre Dame. The people were outraged by the whole thing."

"What were you doing there, Shelby?" Benny asked.

"Watching."

"You weren't involved this time?"

She shook her head. "No. Couldn't help. The queen looked at me. Angry." Words were coming easier now. "I saw the little girl. Burning. It was the king, but I saw her face instead. Too scared to move." Tears rolled down her face as the thought of the burning child swept over her mind. She wanted to push it away, but couldn't. "How can I do great things if I'm too scared?" Dropping her face into her hands, all of the emotion poured out of her in a tidal wave. Benny wrapped his arms around her, while Gael deflected looks from passers-by. Eventually, she cried herself out and slowly regained her strength.

"Shelby," Gael said, "I hate to do this, but I think there's somewhere we need to go. There's more to the story of the Mad King. I doubt the memory is finished with you, and we could get it all out at once."

She raised her eyes to meet his. "Where?"

"The necropolis at Saint-Denis."

"Fabulous."

A short cab ride later and the three of them stood in front of yet another cathedral just north of Paris. For someone with no real sense of religion, Shelby spent a lot of time walking into churches. Saint-Denis, like Notre Dame, was intricately carved and gothic. Flying buttresses added a sense of openness and height to the rooms. Huge ribs of stone swept upward allowing for massive walls full of stained glass, including a large rose window similar to the famous one in Notre Dame. Light passed through and bathed the cold stone interior in warm color making the dozens of marble figures reposing all over the place look weirdly out of place and delicately beautiful at the same time. Crypts were everywhere Shelby looked, laying amid columns as if it was the most normal thing in the world for the inside of a church.

"This way." Gael led them to the right into an alcove. There, on a slab of black marble, lay polished white carvings of the king and queen splashed with reds and blues from the stained glass. "The recumbent statues of Charles VI and his queen, Isabeau."

Shelby's hands burned and sparks began their familiar leaping around on her fingers and wrist. "Strange. Most people would think the statues look life-like, except for the whole lack of actual color bit, but they seem so cold and dead. I saw them living and breathing not an hour ago." Shelby couldn't take her eyes off the statues lying there. Isabeau seemed more peaceful and pious in her polished marble wimple than the queen she knew. Charles' eyes looked sad and vacant where vitality had been before.

Benny put his arm around her waist. "Do you feel anything here?"

"No," Shelby said shrugging. "It's odd. It's them, but I don't feel them. It's more like a shadow of them." Benny narrowed his eyes. "I know, it doesn't make sense."

"Actually," Gael chimed in, "you're right. They were here, but now they aren't. Well, not right here in this tomb anyway."

"Why do all Watchers talk in riddles?"

Gael apologized. "Revolutionaries sacked Saint-Denis. Tombs were desecrated and bodies dumped. Bones and hair taken as souvenirs. Then, whatever remains were left were tossed into a pit with quicklime to get rid of them. Eventually, the monks were able to dig the remains up, but there was so much decay and no way to tell who was who to put them back where they belonged."

"Where did they put whatever was left?" Shelby asked.

"In an ossuary. Come on." Gael led them through the main part of the cathedral and down into the crypt.

As they entered the space, Shelby began to feel the same weird feeling of detachment she felt walking through Notre Dame. She took Benny's hand and squeezed it trying to hang on to some sense of reality for as long as she could. Tucked in a corner, was a small dark doorway and large black plaques mounted in the stone on either side. A genealogy that would rival the Old Testament was written for each of the royal French dynasties interred there. From the middle of her chest, Shelby felt a pull toward the door which was harder to resist by the minute.

"Inside. They're in that room." Shelby could feel them as if they were standing in front of her.

Gael nodded. "Whatever was left of them is inside. This is as close as you're going to get to the Mad King in this lifetime."

Shelby took a step toward the ossuary. As her foot touched the ground, electricity shot through her and the church vanished in white light. She stood against the wall in the king's bedchamber. In the middle of the bed, crouched like an animal, was Charles VI. Cautious servants and noblemen inched slowly toward the bed, but recoiled when the king turned on them.

"Villains!" the king shouted. "Traitors! You'd see me dead! All of you! You'd see me shattered to bits!" A man Shelby could only assume was the physician spoke calmly. "Sire, you are flesh and blood. Not glass. You will not shatter at their touch."

Charles wheeled around to lash out at the doctor but got tangled in the sheets. He lost his balance and fell shrieking onto the bed. As he struggled to free himself, the nobles and servants leaped into action and restrained the monarch grabbing whatever flailing limbs they could get hold of.

"You!" an older man barked at Shelby. "The vial. Now!" He pointed to a small bottle on a table next to her. She grabbed it and brought it to the doctor as the king continued his thrashing. For someone made of glass, he was strong. It was taking four men to hold him down, and their grip on him was precarious at best. The doctor held out a cloth while Shelby poured the contents of the vial onto it. Then, the physician held it over the king's mouth and nose. As Charles began to calm down, he looked up at Shelby with fear and sadness in his eyes before they rolled back in his head and his body went still.

Another flash of light and the king was standing at the foot of his bed glaring at the queen standing silently in front of him. He was looking her up and down, snarling insults at her about her figure and her face. Horrible things. Yet, she stood there and bore it silently.

"Your Grace," the man who had stood next to the queen at the party said, "the queen came to see how you were feeling today." The man didn't acknowledge the insults any more than Isabeau did.

"The queen?" Charles spat. "This is no queen! This is a gutter whore! Where is my queen?" he demanded.

"Charles, I am Isabeau. Your queen," she said softly. She raised a hand to touch the king's face, but he slapped it away.

"No! Take this tired old wench away and bring me my Isabeau. Hang this one for treason to the crown!"

The noble sighed. "What is her crime, Majesty?"

"Impersonating the queen. And lying to the king!"

The other man sighed again and spoke softly to the queen. "If we hung people for lying to him, we'd all be dead." Then louder for the benefit of the deranged monarch, "Come, woman. Be gone with you." He took her by the arm and walked toward the door.

As soon as the door closed behind them, Charles turned his attention to Shelby. "Wine," he ordered. Shelby filled a goblet and brought it to the king as he sat on the foot of the massive bed. He drained the glass in one gulp and seemed to calm as the liquid coursed through him. *Well, there's something we have in common,* Shelby thought. The king looked up at her. "You're a pretty thing, boy. Won't make much of a man."

"I should hope not," Shelby answered forgetting herself for a second. "I mean, if you say so, Sire."

The Mad King laughed. "Your first answer was better." He rubbed his head with one hand and held his goblet out with the other. Shelby refilled it. "Thank you."

Shelby wasn't sure what to do with herself as the king drank his wine. She was alone in a room with a man who didn't recognize his own wife and thought she was a pretty boy. Her palms began to sweat and her stomach knotted up. *Think of something, you idiot*, she thought. "Shall I fetch someone else to keep you company, your Majesty?"

A low laugh rumbled in the king's chest. "No, I have all the company I need."

White light flashed again and Shelby found herself alone in an empty corridor running toward or away from something. She had no idea which. Torches flickered overhead throwing eerie light on the curves as she raced forward for no apparent reason. Then, ahead of her, she heard laughter and the padding of bare feet. The laugh was familiar. The king. After what she had just seen, she wanted to run as far away from him as she could, but her body wouldn't change direction. She was being forced forward toward the laughter. Rounding a corner, she could finally see what she was chasing. It was definitely the king, and he was definitely naked. He looked over his shoulder at her, then burst through a side door. Shelby had no choice but to follow.

She found herself in a courtyard garden with lush grass and flowers lining narrow winding paths. Laughter was filtering through the leaves and blossoms, but it echoed off the stone walls surrounding her making it difficult to know where the king had gone. Shelby wandered the paths pushing branches, leaves, and flowers out of the way like a medieval Indiana Jones hunting treasure in a jungle. Movement, laughter, whispers. Over and over.

This was ridiculous. She wasn't going to find the king this way and wasn't even sure why she was trying to. Charles was as stark raving mad as he was stark naked. Yet, she felt sorry for him. There had been fear in his eyes when she helped to knock him out. Shelby stopped and sat down on one of the crossroads of the paths. "I won't look for you anymore, Sire. Run if you want to, but I'm tired of this game."

Shelby listened. No movement, no laughter, no whispers. Then, a rustle in the plants next to her. "I win?" Charles asked poking his head out of the purple flowers that settled on the top of his head like a crown.

"Yes, Sire. You win."

"And you lose?"

"I lose. You're very good at this game, but I wonder if it wouldn't be easier to hide in the shrubbery with clothes on. Surely you must have thorns in your ass." She immediately regretted that.

The king's face disappeared and his royal rump took its place. "Do I?" he asked. The lecherousness from the bedroom was gone. This man was more like a child needing help from his nurse.

Shelby pretended to attend to his problem. "No, I don't believe you do this time."

His face reappeared. "Then, there is no reason for me to wear those stupid clothes. They itch and they smell funny." Charles climbed out of the shrubbery and sat next to her. He laid his head on her shoulder. "I like you."

Shelby smiled. "I like you, too." The garden began to shimmer, and for once, Shelby was sad to let the memory go.

✦

Coming back to reality didn't take as much out of her this time. "I don't understand why," Shelby said to Gael hoping the Watcher had an answer.

He shook his head and knelt down by her on the floor of the crypt. "Maybe it has something to do with the memories themselves rather than just having one?"

Benny sat cross-legged in front of her rubbing her hands that sparked wildly when he took them. "I wonder if you would have suffered more coming out if the beginning was all you saw. By the time you came out of it, you weren't under any strain."

Gael agreed and Shelby nodded. "Maybe so. It's strange. All this time, I've wondered if I was going mad. Each time I get yanked back in time, I think, 'Is this it? Is this the mental breakdown?'" She let her head drop and looked at her hands. "Madness looks very different. It's frightening to watch. Exhausting to care for." Arching her back, she stood up and went to the names on the ossuary plaque. Her hand reached for Charles' name, but she was too afraid of getting sucked back in time to actually touch it. "The memories. They're lessons, aren't they?" she asked tearing her eyes away from the names and looking Gael in the eye.

"As far as I know, yes."

"Then, we focus on unraveling those. If I don't know what I'm supposed to be learning, this will never end." Something had changed in Shelby, and she wasn't entirely certain how it had happened. There was a resignation about what was happening to her. Madness wasn't the answer. She had seen madness, and this wasn't it. What was happening to her had purpose, even if she didn't know what it was yet.

CHAPTER 16

If they were going to sort out what was happening to Shelby, they needed to get some answers from Eli. Since the only way for Shelby to read the journal was by not holding it, they convened in the hotel room. Shelby, Benny, and Gael sat on the bed with the book in the middle of their circle as if it were a literary Ouija board at the center of a seance. The curtain had been pulled to block the daylight so the blue sparks would be easier to see. If there was something they needed to pay attention to, they would need the sparks to guide them. A lamp on the nightstand was the only light in the room except for a halo of sunshine trying to sneak around the edges of the drapes.

"So," Shelby began, "we left off with him in Egypt. Thoth had just given him the cryptic answer to his question about how we are supposed to figure out our destiny."

Gael asked, "What was the answer exactly?"

"*The sages caution the Traveler. The serpent rests in the sweet breath of the god of truth and light. The Traveler follows the serpent.*" Shelby shrugged. "I still have no idea what it means."

"You have to love the old gods and their mysterious ways," Gael said shaking his head.

"Which is weird since Seshat was so blunt about everything else," Shelby added. "She seemed so down to earth. Snarky even. But damn if she didn't talk in riddles about this part, too."

Benny rubbed his hands on his thighs absently. "I get that you have to figure it out on your own, but it's like they're making it confusing on purpose."

Running a finger across the leather diary cover, Gael said quietly, "The answers are in here somewhere. They have to be."

Shelby put her stinging hands out over the book. "Then let's find them." She was sick of being confused and scared. She may not know what the lessons were that she was supposed to be learning, but she was over being clueless. If walking around Paris had taught her anything, it was she couldn't run from this and go through life with her hands in her pockets. Shelby's destiny was coming for her whether she liked it or not. It was time to meet it head on.

With a wave of her hand, the cover eased open and pages fluttered to the place where Thoth spoke the riddle. "Woah," Shelby whispered.

If I had known storms were going to settle over the Mediterranean Sea two days into our trip from Alexandria to Rome, I would never have boarded the blasted boat. Not that I was looking forward to a week of seasickness anyway. Why I decided to cross the sea again after the last time is beyond me. It was as though I had a deep desire to be in Rome and nothing else would do, but it was far from a hasty decision. Days spent in Alexandria wandering the city with my hands thrust firmly in my pockets afforded me time to think and freedom from fear of being yanked into some bizarre fold in time. Although, I couldn't help but wonder what I might experience if I did decide to touch something. Would I find myself face-to-face with Alexander himself? Of course, given my previous experiences, I would more likely find myself on the pointy end of a spear. So, I kept my hands in my pockets and wandered.

The first day, I thought a great deal about going to Greece. It seemed like where I should be going, but then, I was indeed in Alexandria. Perhaps it was just the legend of the great Greek himself which inspired the thought. Now that I think about it, with all which has transpired since that thought, I should have listened to myself and gone to Greece. No, instead, I wandered into a bar. Understand that no good decisions are made after wandering into a bar.

For a while, I sat in the back corner of the dimly lit hovel of a place. I thought it would give me time alone with my thoughts and for a while it did. By the bottom of my second scotch, I had enough of my own thoughts and welcomed the company of a young lad who was vainly looking for an empty table. Feeling sorry for the young man, I offered him the chair opposite mine, and we struck up a conversation. Before long, he was telling me about his beloved Rome. The city that might well have been the love of his life. I had never before heard someone speak with such passion about a place! Women, yes. A city, no.

"And you thought it was just me," Benny said with a wink at Shelby.

Who knows how many drinks we had sitting there? Needless to say, inebriation must have played a part in the fact that I made up my mind to see Rome for myself and let her woo me as she had seduced the young Roman across from me. Staggering out of the bar and into a cab, I made plans to depart for Rome as soon as I could book passage. As the hotel had a very capable concierge, it was easier than I expected. As the hotel concierge was available around the clock, it was quicker than I expected. Before making it to my room to sleep off the alcohol, I had a reservation for the following afternoon.

Once my head cleared the next morning, I was berating myself for my decidedly un-British impulsivity. Clearly, I had to cancel my reservation and think this through. There had been no planning and no consideration of seasickness. There had also been no recollection of a plan to meet the young Roman for luncheon. Fearing looking like an old fool, I decided not to change plans. Stupid, stupid old fool that I am. He seemed so excited for me to experience Rome and his homesickness fueled his enthusiasm. It would be another six months before his business concluded in Egypt and he could return home. Next time, I must remember not to give a damn about sentimentality.

On a good day, I don't do well on the open sea, but there were no good days on this journey. Storm swells were building overnight, and by dawn the ship was pitching wildly. Passengers were instructed to stay off of the open decks, but many feared being below decks if the ship were to take on water. I was too sick to care one way or the other. At that point, death seemed like a welcome respite from my misery.

No one could say exactly how it happened, but the steam engines began to struggle until one gave out completely. My guess was the captain trying to push them too hard against the swells. By the time night fell, we were down one engine and limping in the open ocean on an engine sputtering pitifully. We survived through the night, and the next day. Soon, we had to find land and any land would do. Well after midnight, the ship found harbor.

More than anything else, I was thrilled to be off of the ship and on solid ground wherever that ground was. Imagine my relief to find myself in a British colony. Dawn came and the island of Malta welcomed the ship's passengers and crew. We were brought to a small hotel, offered baths and food, and given beds until the ship engine could be repaired. Spending two days sick at sea, I was most grateful for the bed. After a restful few hours, the island beckoned me to explore.

Oddly enough, as much as the sea does not love me, I do love the sea - from the shore. The city of Valletta sits on a peninsula with narrow straits on either side creating staggering seaside views that pulled me to the port. The stone city shone golden in the setting sun shimmering on the water of the Mediterranean Sea as I made my way to the sea wall. Scrub brush dotted the cracks in the stone paths. Boats bobbed in the water, sunlight glinting off of wet bows. Buildings themselves seemed to be carved out of the very rock that rose straight out of the water. The only softness was the domed roof of the Carmelite church rising above rooftops. It was an island hardened by history and weather, but it was my haven from the open sea.

And yet, there was an intrinsic beauty in the place which required investigating along my trek to the water. While the exteriors of the buildings are formidable and stark, once inside there are richly Baroque interiors that stagger the imagination. Nestled in the fortress city is art rivaling that in the great European museums. Indeed, some of the greatest artists of the modern era have worked their magic in Malta. Interwoven throughout the city architecture is the famous eight-point Maltese Cross of the Knights of St. John. More than the famous symbol, the knights were responsible largely for what this great city became. It was also this symbol which resulted in my coming face-to-face with the knights themselves.

I blame the lingering exhaustion from my miserable days at sea for my forgetfulness regarding keeping my hands in my pockets. Or perhaps it was the trance of the waves in the harbor that befuddled me. Whatever the reason, I became fascinated with a carving of a Maltese Cross in the stone wall running alongside the path I walked overlooking the strait whilst the sun set and lights winked on across the cityscape. Being so dimly lit, I decided to run my hands along the carving to fully appreciate it, paying no mind to the surge of burning in my hands that had become a constant companion. Instantly I regretted my carelessness.

Once again, the familiar white light and shock washed over me. It took longer than usual for the light to clear. When it did, my surroundings shimmered into focus. Once again, I found myself in the middle of a battle. In the water, ships fired relentlessly towards the land. Shells landed in the rocks above where I stood. Having no idea whether or not these memories could cause me any real harm, I dove flat on my stomach and covered my head in time to shield myself from gravel that rained down. Looking through my fingers at the assailants, they appeared to be Turks from their dress and general violence. This wasn't my first run-in with the Turks and I was less than enthusiastic about being so close to the fighting this time. From the looks of things, the fighting had been going on for days. Both sides were haggard. The ships and shore had taken heavy damage.

Realizing the Turks were across the harbour for the time being, I rose up some to get my bearings. In the distance, smoke hung in a haze over fires that had been burning for some time. In the midst of the fighting, I could see the Turks vastly outnumbered the local forces. Flashes of red tunics were more scarce, but seemed to be the most skilled. They barked orders and organized the others. The Knights of St. John. Under the red tunics bearing the iconic white cross was chainmail more common for professional soldiers. Proper helmets, shields, and swords in addition to superior training put the knights at the head of the charge.

"You!" barked an older man to my left.

I looked around and could see no one else, so apparently, I was the 'you' in question.

"Get down, you imbecile!" As he said it, a cannon fired and I jumped. Something looking more like wadding flew from the cannon and out over the water toward the ships. Three more cannons shot off with similar results. Nothing exploded but shouts and curses from the ships below. More cannon fire. More curses.

One of the knights came down to check the targeting and I stopped him to ask what was going on. He replied, "The Turks are getting back what they sent us. The demons thought they could float headless knights over to us, so Valletta is sending them some more heads for their collection- Ottoman heads. Bastards." The young knight looked out over the water to where the Ottomans were stationed in St. Elmo and waved back at the infantry. More canon fire. More heads being shot at the Turks.

I turned to look toward the direction the firing was coming from. On the hill was a line of Turks being held by Maltese soldiers. Valletta, I assumed by the confidence with which he gave orders and his carriage, strode back and forth in front of the Turkish prisoners considering his next round of ammunition. The sword in his hand dripped thickly. This was not a man who commanded by rank alone. A nod signaled the Maltese soldier to duck as Valletta's sword took the Turk's head off in one fluid motion.

My stomach rolled as the man's head hit the ground and was gathered up to be stuffed into the waiting canon. Blood spurted as the Turk went limp. The Maltese soldier let the body fall rather than struggle against the dead weight. Valletta never flinched. Never hesitated. It was staggering to watch. The violent valor of the Knight leading by vicious example. The Christian seemed to have forgotten his gentle values and instead met his enemy on their terms for the greater good. Valletta was relentless and ruthless, and yet, he was an incredible leader. Having learned some history along my journey to the harbour, I knew that Valletta somehow managed to emerge victorious, even when outnumbered. Looking up at him in action, I had no question as to how he did it. But was Valletta the savage in civilized clothing he seemed to be? As my surroundings began to shimmer and the shock began to surge again, Valletta turned, used the corner of his tunic to wipe his face of the blood spatter, and looked *down at me. There was anguish in his face. For a moment, his shoulders heaved with a stifled sob. Another once-over of his face with the tunic edge. Then he set his shoulders straight and strong, turned, and swung his sword once more. Light flashed and I was alone overlooking the harbor, trembling and jerking with the echoes of canons.*

Next time, I will follow my instincts and go to Greece.

Shelby stopped reading, exhausted from focusing energy on the book and turning pages. Benny pulled her to him and let her collapse on his shoulder.

"Well," Gael said quietly, "looks like we know what Elijah Faircloth was meant to learn."

Shelby cut her eyes at the Watcher. "What's that?"

"Leadership in battle," Gael answered simply.

❦

The sun had begun to set on Shelby's last day in Paris and no more answers than she had leaving Spain. A crazy new talent, sure, but no answers. Eli's purpose was becoming clearer, but hers was just as foggy as ever.

"Come," Gael said, "let's go get some dinner. And maybe a drink."

"Definitely a drink," Shelby answered.

Benny laughed and picked up a jacket for Shelby. Her hands may have been burning, but she was shivering from exertion. "Sounds good."

A few minutes later found the three of them at a corner cafe sipping wine and buttering hot bread. Gael ordered several courses that he claimed were specialties of the chef. Shelby didn't care so long as it wasn't something weird like snails. Moments later, the server arrived with bowls of broth which seemed a tad anticlimactic from what Shelby had come to expect from French cuisine. One sip, though, and she understood what Gael was going on about.

"There is nothing quite like a good meal," Gael was saying, "to put the world back in its place."

Shelby looked over her spoon at him. "What puts the universe back in its place?"

"Wine."

Shelby slurped her soup and raised her glass to that.

Knowing she would never be able to let the chaos go, Gael and Benny decided to use the more relaxed meal to help sort through details. Once again, hiding in plain sight in the middle of a cafe. The hotel room seemed too close and intense for the conversation. Shelby needed the momentary distractions of the coming and going of waiters and the comfort of good food. Damn good food.

Gael was the first to broach the subject of her lessons. "I suppose we should start with the first memory and go from there, yes?"

"Might as well," Shelby answered swigging the end of her wine.

"A gladiator, right?" Gael asked. Shelby nodded. "That you knew?"

Benny answered this time, looking at Shelby. "She knew him. She loved him." There was something almost sad when he said it.

"Well," Gael said trying to lighten the mood, "there's no accounting for taste. Especially in ancient Rome."

"Ancient anywhere," Benny answered trying his best to veil the bitterness that seeped into exchanges with Gael.

Shelby jumped in to keep the conversation civil. "I don't think the lesson is about how I felt about the gladiator. The other visions centered on Hadrian. It has to do with him."

"Alright, let's focus on the emperor, then." Gael disengaged the budding confrontation with Benny and focused on Shelby. "He gave the order for the other gladiator to die."

"In a pompous show of power."

"That's something, then. What next?

"The ceremony where he walked out to greet the crowd as almost a god."

"Pompousness again. Then?" Gael pushed.

"The Circus. The race had ended. It wasn't about the ceremony that time. He-he wanted me."

"Did he try to seduce you?" Gael asked.

Benny shook his head. "No, nothing as classy as that. It was an order."

Gael raised an eyebrow, and took a slow sip of his wine. "I see a theme emerging. Don't you?"

"What lesson can I learn for my destiny about pompous assery?" Shelby asked dryly.

Gael shook his head. "Surface details, Shelby. What does it mean? Really mean?"

Shelby flagged a waiter who refilled her glass as she turned over the events in her head. Benny was thinking, too, but knew she would have to come to it on her own, so he said nothing. Hadrian had been in control. Murderously at first, then regally, then personally. Hadrian may have been a royal ass, but he had incredible control over the people of Rome, both on a public level and a private level. He knew how to motivate them and inspire them. Confident in his position and his command to the point where it took only a word from him to have what he wanted. Yet, even as she witnessed his power over others, she was repulsed by it. The emperor played at civility, but embodied savagery.

"Power. The power in appearances and control," Shelby answered slowly. "Civil savagery."

A smile began to curl the corner of the Watcher's mouth. "Good. Let's hold onto that thought and see what we find in the others."

Benny broke his silence. "Egypt was next. We know what Seshat said."

"No reason to go through that one. It wasn't one of Shelby's memories, so there wouldn't be a lesson. After that was Spain. Toledo?"

Shelby shuddered. "I don't like to think about Toledo."

Benny gave her hand a squeeze. "I know, bella. There was a lesson, though. A purpose to it all. If we don't figure that out, then you suffer with that memory for nothing."

Damn him, he was right. She sighed and nodded.

"Good," Gael said. "What was first?"

The cathedral. "Mass. I was a priest. Not a high priest or anything. There wasn't much to it. It was Mass. The high priest said to kneel and we knelt. That was it."

"Ok, so not much to go on. What happened next?"

Shelby's breathing was becoming shallow. She hated the Toledo memories more than any others. More than the gushing wounds of the gladiator. "The chamber. I pulled the lever that broke a man."

Gael looked steadily at her. His eyes never wavered from hers. "On your own, or by order?"

Defiantly, Shelby spat, "On order."

Gael's head twitched minutely to the side. "Are you sure?"

Shelby's eyes blazed, but she kept control of the anger surging from her core. "Positive."

"Good," the Watcher said quietly leaning back in his chair. "And the girl? Another order?"

Shelby blinked hard to keep the tears stinging her eyes from escaping. "Yes." It was barely a whisper. "I fought it. Tried so hard to pull my hand back." Benny took her hand again. Sparks jumped wildly but she didn't care. She needed his strength. "I couldn't fight it."

Gael's face softened and he pushed his hair out of his face. "Shelby," he said gently, "you can't change the memories. Mentally, you can rail against them all you want, but you can never change your past. You couldn't save her then and you couldn't save her now. Learn from it. That's all you can do to honor the memory of that girl."

She looked up at him from under glistening eyelashes. She was tired and emotional. Ordinarily she would have made fun of herself for being such a girl. Now, though, she didn't feel as silly getting weepy over the memory of the innocent child. "You're right. But what's the lesson?"

"What did you feel in those memories?"

"Fear. Helplessness. Anger." Insanity. Benny's grip tightened as she weakened. "So, a similar lesson, then?"

Trying to think beyond the surface meaning of the events was not something she was used to. Shelby Starling was nothing if not shallow. At least, she had always been before. Knowing what she was doing was wrong- even in the memory she knew it- she still went through with the orders she was given. She had no choice. The prisoner would have died at the hands of the head priest anyway, and she would have been killed, too. Somehow, she felt like her soul was tied up in this one in a way it wasn't in Rome or Paris. "Control using fear and faith. Violent, pious control."

Gael grinned and her chest tightened. "Good, Shelby. Now, Paris. What has the Mad King taught you?"

Shelby didn't need to think about that one. It was a feeling that had been with her since Saint-Denis. This one was easy. "Compassion."

"But that doesn't fit," Benny said.

Gael shook his head. "Not as such. But combined, there may be a bigger lesson."

This was a level of thinking Shelby was certain she had never done before. Compassion wasn't hard to wrap her head around, even if it wasn't a quality she would say she possessed before now. Connecting it to the violent power and intimate total control of Hadrian and the Inquisition was tougher. She was going to have to talk it out and hope to hell that the Watcher could help connect the dots. "Hadrian ruled with ceremony and savagery. Total power and control of the masses and the individuals. The Inquisition held power even Hadrian couldn't claim - power over the souls of those under their control. Control deeper than the death they doled out. Charles was tortured by his own thoughts. No control at all. A person trapped in a broken mind. Sad and pitiful even when he was fearsome in his rage. Chaos in his mind but clamoring for order and civility." Shelby fell silent. Slowly, the image was coming into focus like a Polaroid. At first in shades of thought before the clarity settled in her mind. "I have to change something. Something controlled by violence. Change it to order and compassion. Focus on the civilized individual rather than the chaos of the hoard."

Somewhere inside her, something released. Her hands surged with pain. Instinctively, she pulled them close and rubbed them. Sparks covered the bracelet and spun around in a mass like a school of fish moving in unison. Destiny. Her insides quivered and it radiated outward until she was sitting in her chair shivering again. Benny wrapped her jacket around her shoulders trying to stop the trembling, but it was no use. A jacket was only effective against the chilly night air. This chill came from deep within.

Gael smiled calmly as Benny, clearly shaken himself by what was happening to her, tended to Shelby. "Excuse me," Gael said quietly. He pushed his chair back, gave her another grin, then weaved his way to the back of the cafe.

"Shitty time to walk away," Shelby muttered.

Benny smiled. "It's okay. I'm here."

Laying her head on his shoulder, she let Benny take care of her. She could think of nothing she wanted more than to fade into him, letting Paris and the rest of the world vanish. Her hand in her lap was mostly hidden by the tablecloth, but as she leaned on Benny, she could see the swirling blue swarm of sparks. It was stunning. Seshat knew how to make a statement.

By the time Gael returned, Shelby had turned everything over in her mind and was slowly coming to grips with the lessons, even if she had no idea what to do with the information. Having had enough deep thought for one night, she pushed the past into the past where it belonged for the time being.

"I'm sorry," the Frenchman began when he returned to the table, "there was something I needed to take care of before it slipped my mind with all of this occupying my thoughts so often."

"It's fine," Shelby said perking up some as the waiter brought the main course. Plates were set down in front of them with a flourish. "I don't know whether to eat it or just look at it," Shelby said staring at the intricate dish in front of her.

"Eat it. Trust me." Gael answered with that damn sexy smile of his.

Shelby grinned back and proceeded to decipher what was garnish and what was part of the dish. Soon, conversation had turned away from her destiny to the meal and a gamut of food-related innuendo. Gael was intentionally flirting with her in front of Benny and thoroughly enjoying the reactions he was getting. Soon, Benny figured out it was all in fun and began to engage in the battle of wits. Shelby, well at the bottom of one bottle of wine and diving into her second, found herself wondering how far either of them would actually take it.

✳

The small alarm clock on the side table was saved from the certain destruction of slamming into the wall only by its short cord plugged snugly into the wall outlet by the bed. Shelby had protested more violently than usual to the cheerful beeping by sending the poor thing flying to make it shut up. It thudded on the carpet, rolled under the nightstand, and proceeded to make muffled beeps in defiance of Shelby. It was quieter, but the damage was done. Slowly, Shelby peeled open her eyelids as the hotel room came into focus.

Hanging on the chair in front of the dressing table across from the foot of the bed was her shirt from the night before. Her jeans lay crumpled on the floor on top of a pile of dirty clothes. On the dressing table were Benny's clothes loosely folded. She was a mess and he had it together, down to how they ditched their clothes. Tossed on the desk by Benny's stack was Gael's shirt and slacks, not folded, but not in a heap either. The wine had left her muddled and thick, but there is nothing like discovering there's a second man in the room to sober a person up.

She jerked the sheet up to her chin and closed her eyes tightly. Someone was in the bed with her and she had to make herself look to see who it was. Through a crack in her eyelids, she peered at the sleeping figure next to her and let out a slow breath. Benny. Opening her eyes more, she looked past Benny, who was beginning to stir, to the chair under the window. Gael slept curled in a ball wearing Benny's t-shirt and sweatpants. His hair had slipped down on his forehead, and even in his sleep he pushed it back. Reaching for a tank and shorts on the floor by the bed, Shelby slipped out of the covers and into the bathroom to get dressed, kicking the offending alarm clock further under the nightstand.

Splashing water on her face, Shelby began to try to piece together the end of the evening, but wasn't having much luck. She looked like hell and felt worse. She remembered flirting over the entree and dessert, but couldn't picture leaving the cafe. What the hell had she done? Popping several aspirin into her mouth and gulping down some water to wash them down, she decided whatever happened had happened and there was nothing for it now. She turned on the shower and looked at her face in the mirror. "You're a picture this morning," she said sarcastically to the face looking back at her. Circles under her eyes gave away the stress she wasn't willing to admit to herself. Slowly the mirror began to fog over, removing any trace of the girl in the glass.

The shower did a lot to clear the mind even if answers about the evening continued to elude her. Feeling a bit more like herself, she drew a face in the steamy glass, winked at it, and opened the door. Benny was up sorting dirty clothes and folding them into his suitcase. Gael had shed Benny's clothes and replaced them with his own. He sat with one leg dangling over the arm of the chair he slept in and watched Benny's progress. "You're looking better this morning," he said with a wicked wink.

"Thanks. Apparently, I feel better."

"Wouldn't take much for that," Benny laughed.

Shelby looked from one to the other. "Someone please tell me what happened after desert."

Gael laughed and swung his long leg back over the arm of the chair. "Shelby," he said, "by the time we made it back here, you were half asleep where you stood. Benny tucked you in, then we spent another hour talking shop. That's all."

Benny laughed. "It really is. What'd you think happened?" He grinned at her.

"I have more fun in my imagination than I do in real life."

Shelby plopped on the foot of the bed and gathered up her clothes. Pulling a shirt off the floor under the dressing table chair, she uncovered her computer. With the shirt tossed in the general direction of her suitcase, Shelby opened the screen. As it went through its login routine, she stuffed some clothes into her bag and fished one of her shoes out from under the bed. Halfway packed, she opened her email. "Good lord, Dina. Thanks for the notice," she grumbled to herself.

"What is it?" Benny asked.

"We've been re-routed."

"To where?" Gael asked.

"Greece," Shelby said unenthusiastically. Her hands began to burn and sparks flew to the bracelet. "Greece," she whispered. Shelby raised her eyes and look squarely at the Watcher. "Elijah Faircloth wanted to go to Greece."

Gael shrugged. "The universe is full of coincidences." With remarkable resolve, Shelby did not knock the perfect teeth out of the face of the Watcher.

CHAPTER 17

Outside the hotel, the three of them stood in front of the waiting cab. Benny and the driver loaded the suitcases into the trunk leaving Shelby and Gael to themselves for a moment. "You know," Gael began, "I can see why he won't leave your side." With a topiary that was supposed to give rustic charm to the front of the building between them and Benny, Gael slipped his arm around Shelby's waist. She resisted. A little. "If this had been any other time-"

Shelby put her hand on his arm. "But it isn't." Damn him for making her want things she couldn't and shouldn't have.

He smiled and her heart pounded in her chest. She wondered if he was close enough to feel it. For an instant, he pulled her to him and was inches away from her face when the sound of the cab trunk closing broke the moment. Gael released her waist, took her hand, and kissed each cheek. Shelby hoped Benny didn't notice the Watcher lingering a bit longer than he should have on the second cheek. Apparently, he didn't since Benny took Gael's hand and shook it. "Thanks for all you've done," Benny said.

"My pleasure," he answered cutting his eyes at Shelby. "My pleasure."

She felt like a silly school girl hiding her blush as she climbed into the cab. As much help as he had been, Gael was a dangerous distraction. Not to mention the temptation. She needed to put some distance between her and the Watcher and she hoped Greece was far enough.

"You okay, bella?" Benny asked. "You seem far away."

"Hmm? Oh, sorry." Shelby said coming back out of her own thoughts. "I was just wondering why Dina changed the itinerary at the last minute."

Benny's forehead wrinkled slightly as he thought about it. "Is that unusual for her?"

"Not really. I mean, she's always sending me all over the place without much of a system to it, but she always has a reason when she changes plans. She didn't this time. Just a short email with new tickets."

Benny patted her thigh. "I wouldn't worry about it. Maybe she was just busy. Probably a tour guide wasn't available or something."

Shelby leaned back on the cab seat. "Yeah, he probably had to go deal with a wayward nephew."

The ride through Paris was full of the familiar rise and fall of stinging in her hands as they passed locations that would have somehow been connected to Charles. As painful as most of her memories were, she willingly let her mind drift back to the Mad King. Of all the strange things she had experienced, the memory of him sitting next to her like a child was the hardest to shake. For that moment, he was real to her and it broke her heart. In this city, it wasn't terror that shook her to her core, but pity.

✦

The sun was sinking in blazing glory over the tiled rooftops of Athens as the plane banked for approach giving Shelby and Benny a breathtaking view through the small grimy window. Backlit clouds were silver-lined in the brilliant blue of the Mediterranean sky. Orange and gold rays shot through spaces between them. Below, inlets of the Adriatic Sea sparkled a deep turquoise. A maze of short modern buildings filled spaces once occupied by an ancient city just as magnificent. Towering on hillsides and tucked in among the concrete, ruins stood as silent sentinels of the city of the old gods.

Shelby instinctively rubbed her stinging hands together as the plane began its descent. By the time the wheels bounced on the tarmac, her chest was tight and her hands buzzed savagely. Whatever was here, it was powerful. As passengers started to deplane, she began to feel trapped like a caged animal. She knew it was all in her head and fought the urge to climb over the seats and get the hell off the plane. Benny noticed her agitation and gave her hand a squeeze. When he did, blue sparks swirled around their hands. Passengers focused on phones and overhead bins were oblivious to the mini light show in row P.

Just outside the gate area heading toward baggage claim, a small gray-haired older man stood wearing a white shirt and black slacks. The shirt was pulled snuggly over his slightly portly belly, and his pants were puddling at his ankles since it apparently took a larger size to get around his middle and he lacked the height to fill the legs. In his hands was a small sign that read 'Starling - Pioneer Tours.'

Shelby looked up at Benny and grinned. "Looks like our ride is here."

Benny laughed. "I sure feel safer with this guy at the wheel."

Shelby waved at the little man who bobbed in greeting as he held out his hand to her. "Welcome to Athens, Miss Starling. Mr. Moretti. I'm Apollo, your guide."

Shelby smiled at him and shook his hand. "Shelby and Benny, please. We don't stand on formalities."

Apollo bobbed again. "So sorry. Shelby and Benny it is, then. Come, we'll get your things and get you settled for the night. Tomorrow, we see the Acropolis early before the crazy tourist crowds."

Shelby and Benny nodded and followed the little man to baggage claim and then out to his waiting car. As they went through the automatic doors of the terminal, Shelby couldn't resist anymore. She cut her eyes over at Benny and said, "Somehow, I thought if I met Apollo, he'd be taller." Benny snorted and turned it into a cough out of politeness to his Greek counterpart.

The forty-five-minute ride to the city center was filled with an increasing sensation of duality for Shelby. She was in the car zipping through town amid drivers that would give the Roman scooter girl a run for her money, but she was also removed from it all. Benny noticed something wasn't quite right about her. "Bella?"

The turn to look at him seemed as if she were underwater. Slow, fluid, and distorted. "Notre Dame, only worse," she said. The words seemed to echo in her own head a beat behind her mouth. Benny took Shelby's hand and let the sparks leap unchecked and unhidden between them. It didn't matter if Apollo saw them or not. She was all that mattered now.

The closer they got to the city center, the more her hands burned. The disconnected feeling never intensified, but never abated either. It felt as though she were floating slightly above herself, watching rather than participating in what was going on. Once in a while, Apollo would glance at her in the rearview mirror, but he said nothing. Without even seeing a tattoo, Shelby knew he had to be a Watcher. No one else would be able to sense what was happening to her, and he definitely seemed to know.

Apollo pulled up to a small boutique hotel and hopped out to open the door for Shelby. "I will see you settled, then bid you goodnight. An early start tomorrow will let you have some time before the tour busses descend on the Acropolis. Once they arrive, it can be difficult to move around without being in a throng of people." There was more to that statement and Shelby knew it. So did Benny. He cut his eyes over at Shelby, nodded, but said nothing.

Since Shelby was still feeling strange, Benny took care of checking them in. She nodded vaguely at questions directed at her, but said little. By the time Benny had deposited their bags in the corner of their small, but cozy room, she was spent.

"Bella," Benny called from the window, "you have to see this."

With tremendous concentration, Shelby managed to get one foot in front of the other to the window. He held the sheer curtain back and revealed the Parthenon lit up magnificently on top of the Acropolis. She let out a slow hiss between her teeth as her world began to settle into focus. Somehow, looking up at the ancient temple grounded the duality some. "It's incredible. And it seems to help."

"It does?"

"I can't explain it, but yes." Shelby shrugged. "At this point, I'll take what I can get, even if I don't understand it. It's the weirdest feeling."

Benny looked down at her wrist. "It must have something to with that."

The swirling mass of sparks had returned around Seshat's bracelet. "I guess so. Who knows?"

Benny wrinkled his brow. "I'd bet Apollo knows."

Shelby nodded. "And you'd win. He has to be a Watcher. Did you see anything?

"No," Benny answered shaking his head. "Long sleeves and a shirt buttoned up. There's no telling where the tattoo is, but it wasn't somewhere we could see tonight."

Shelby sighed as exhaustion washed over her. Benny put his hand on the small of her back and led her to the bed. Any other time that would have stirred the heat she loved to feel with him. This time she felt more like a child being taken care of and was oddly okay with that. As she got ready for bed, he set the alarm. "Sleep, bella. Who knows what tomorrow will bring?" She closed her eyes and the image of the Parthenon was etched into the backs of her eyelids. It was weird, but it seemed to keep the duality at bay. She hoped it was enough to get her through the night.

With dawn came Apollo. Once more dressed in the long sleeves and slacks, just different colors, it was impossible to notice the clock and compass tattoo that labeled the Watchers. Without it, Shelby and Benny didn't want to breach the subject on their own. If they were wrong, there would be too many questions. All they could hope for was for him to reveal himself like Naomi did, or for there not to be any memories that made it necessary to explain her catharsis.

White buildings gleamed in the early morning sunshine that looked warmer than it was. Shelby pulled her jacket tightly around her as they get out of the car at the base of the Acropolis and looked down at the Athens city center below.

"We're going in at the southeast entrance. No lines there like the other side. The tour busses unload there and it can get crowded quickly." Shelby and Benny nodded and followed Apollo to the small ticket building outside the gate happy for anything that would avoid a crush of people.

The Parthenon continued to ground Shelby and keep the feeling of duality at bay. She didn't understand it, but was beyond trying to rationally explain things anymore. Logic had gone by the wayside in Rome and there was slim chance Athens was going to restore it. The best she could hope for was another layer of understanding.

Shelby, Benny, and Apollo began the trek up the hill towards the ruins along the cobblestone path lined with trees and the occasional guard rail fence to keep travelers on the path. The stone walkway was wide enough to accommodate a crowd, but it was almost deserted except for a couple of back-packed tourists in khaki sun hats ahead of them. Apollo explained that in ancient times, this same path would have been used in procession as the people came to pay homage to the city's patron goddess, Athena. Nearing the top, the path narrowed considerably. While the stone path was narrower, the view was panoramic. Hills and the valley between them were emerging in the dawn sunshine. Mist rose above the tree-covered hills and reminded Shelby of the morning in Jamaica when it seemed as if the whole earth was exhaling.

Coming over the top of the hill, she could see ruins that seemed to disappear off the side of the cliff. Getting closer, she saw that it was an amphitheater sunk into the side of the hill. "This," said Apollo, "is the Odeon of Herodes Atticus."

"What are those?" Benny asked pointing down at some large shapes among the semi-circle of stone bleachers.

"Thrones. Different rulers had their own thrones installed to watch the performances and orators. At one time, this was more wood than stone, including the roof that would have shaded them. Unfortunately, much of it was lost until the Romans rebuilt it," he explained with a nod to the Roman standing next to him.

Shelby's eyes narrowed. "Romans? Here?"

Benny laughed. "You really didn't pay much attention in history class, did you?"

"Nope. Perhaps if the teacher hadn't droned on like the window unit in the back of the room, I would have hung on to a nugget or two."

Benny sighed and grinned. "There was a time when Greece was controlled by Rome."

"Yes," Apollo added. Shelby saw a lecture coming, so she pulled out her water bottle and decided now was as good a time as any for a break. "The Battle of Corinth was the final blow. The Corinthians lost-"

"Wait. Corinthians like in the Bible?" Shelby interrupted.

Benny laughed again. "So, you were as alert in church as in history class?"

Shelby rolled her eyes at him and opened her water bottle.

"Yes," Apollo began again, "Corinthians like in the Bible. At first, it seemed as if the Romans intended to leave things as they were in Greece, but that soon changed. To make sure the Greeks were well aware of who was in control, the Emperor Hadrian marched into Athens."

Shelby almost choked on her water. "Hadrian?"

Apollo nodded. "Did I say something wrong?"

"No," she answered shaking her head and wiping water off of her chin. "Are you sure it was Hadrian?"

Apollo stifled a chuckle. "I'm positive. There's even an arch to prove it."

Benny and Shelby exchanged looks, but said nothing.

Before long, the path gave out completely and a dusty foot-worn space opened up at the base of more ruins rising above them. Approaching them, Shelby's hands began to burn and a fleeting instance of duality washed over her.

"Bella?" Benny asked noticing the hesitation in her steps.

"I'm ok. Not sure what that was, but it's gone now," she replied taking Benny's hand for stability on the slick uneven terrain. Apollo glanced at her and opened his mouth to say something, but then shut it again. Shelby wished he would say something that would let them know if they were right about what he was. Why was this Watcher being so much more cautious than the others when he definitely knew what was happening?

Assured that Shelby was alright, Apollo continued his narration about the history of the Erechtheion temple, from playing host to the wooden statue of Athena to the cult of the mythical king Erechtheus. As he talked, they climbed up and down the steps and stones that connected various levels and blocks of the temple, pausing now and then for Shelby to take photos of the parts not clad in scaffolding from the Acropolis' constant state of restoration. Shrines were dotted around the complex, including the spot where Poseidon struck the earth with his trident and created a spring. Next to that, the olive tree Athena brought forth to win the contest for patronage of the city of Athens. "There were several sacred spots that needed to be preserved while building this temple that was most often used for religious events, even though people think that was the role of the Parthenon."

"So that's why this looks like it's made out of a child's block set?" Benny asked.

"Looks like a suburban modular home, but with some ancient stone flair," Shelby added flippantly.

Apollo nodded with a grin. "You could say that. It was the only way to work with both the terrain and the shrines. The statues and the Ionic columns give it some 'flair.' It would have had a bit more flair in its prime, but most of the frieze work was taken to England. Same with the Parthenon. But we do have the Caryatids. Come, I'll show you." Apollo led them around the Erechtheion to a striking porch whose roof seemed to be resting gently on the heads of six statues of togaed women casually standing there looking out over the city of modern Athens.

"I've seen these before," Shelby said. Benny shot a look at her, but she shook her head, letting him know she didn't mean that in a time-warpy kind of way.

"I wouldn't be surprised," Apollo mused. "They are popular photos for Greek restaurants in America. Like the Parthenon."

"Yep, I bet that's it. The ladies look almost sultry standing here in stone."

"Indeed, which may have been the inspiration for the place being used to house a hareem at one point. Togas that cling as if they were wet, and the hips relaxed. At one time, the arms would have held pitchers, perhaps for pouring wine. We only know because of the copies of them in Rome," Apollo explained with a glance at Benny, who shrugged. "These are replicas as well."

"What happened to the originals?" Shelby asked less out of curiosity and more because she felt like it would be polite to.

Apollo gestured vaguely in a direction away from the porch. "Five are in the Acropolis museum. Another in England. Copies or not, they are lovelier to imagine here on the hill." With that, it was time to move on to the main event.

Coming around the Erechtheion, the Parthenon's mighty columns loomed into view. Looking up at the hollow shell of the place to the blue sky where a roof should have sheltered Athena, a wave of sadness washed over Shelby. Rubble amid scaffolding in the place of what should have been the elegant opulence of an incredible society. She turned in a slow circle away from the Parthenon towards the modern city below. "What makes us so special?" she whispered. "Rome. Egypt. Greece. Great powers that all fell. What makes us invincible?" One of the many cats that sunned themselves on the ancient stones lazily looked up at her as if to answer, 'Nothing,' then went back to sleep.

Benny walked up behind her but it wasn't until he slipped his arm around her waist that she realized he was there. "You seem far away, bella."

"I am, and I'm not," she answered turning away from the city. "Benny, we've seen a lot of old things. Ruins, I mean. None of them has ever made me sad."

"But this does?"

She nodded. "Yeah, and I'll be damned if I know why. It's like someone I loved died. You know, like realizing how fleeting time is and all that crap people talk about at funerals. It feels like that. Like, if it could happen to the great civilizations, what makes us think it won't happen to ours?"

Apollo had walked over in time to hear the last part of what she said. "The downfall of any great civilization is only unnoticed by the powers in charge who focus too much on staying in power to see what the cost to the people is. The people always see it coming. Few do anything about it." He shrugged, dusted off his sagging trousers, and walked back toward the monument.

With a slight pressure on the small of her back, Benny nudged Shelby back to the Parthenon. "Forget I said anything," she mumbled. "Silly stuff."

"No, but you can't solve the world's problems on your own. Best to enjoy the moment you're in," Benny answered. Typical Roman. Carpe diem and all that shit. He wasn't wrong, though.

Even if she couldn't shake the sadness of the place, she was grateful for the relief from the duality as she walked around. It was as though the Acropolis needed her focused for some reason. She had yet to try touching anything and the needle pricks in her hands certainly weren't going away. Of course, now it didn't matter if she touched anything or not. If history wanted her back, it reached out and grabbed her. The camera had been a good enough excuse to keep her hands to herself just to be on the safe side. Since they couldn't be completely sure what Apollo was, neither she or Benny was willing to risk an episode. Something, though, was connecting her to the place.

Apollo led them to the Parthenon and explained the function of the building over time. "There," he said pointing to one end, "would have been where the goddess stood."

Shelby looked around at the scaffolding and crumbling stone trying to imagine what the ancients saw. The sun glinted over the top of a column and blinded her for a second making her blink hard. When she did, for an instant, she was standing inside the temple in all its former glory. Opening her eyes, it was gone. No time warp. Just a flash of an image. She blinked again and for a split second, she was looking up at the statue of Athena, then ruins again. With every blink, she was seeing some twisted slide show of the temple shifting from splendor to rubble. Vibrant color to shades of tan. At first it was only the inside of the temple. Then, people in frozen states of running in fear. More blinking revealed soldiers, but not Greeks. Invaders. Trying to hold her eyes open, she turned to look at Apollo who was looking back at her with a strange half-smile. "What's happening?" Shelby asked.

"Perhaps we should rest," he answered deliberately dodging her question.

Benny nodded. "Good idea." Apollo motioned toward some stones shaded by the shadow of the temple and led the way. "What's going on, bella?" Benny whispered.

"Flashes. Only when I blink. Static images. Nothing moving. Like snapshots of another time."

"A memory?"

"I don't think so. I don't know what it is, but I think our dowdy little guide does."

Benny's expression darkened. "Why does he let you suffer in silence? Why doesn't he say what he is?"

Shelby shook her head. "Who knows?" The further she walked from the temple the fewer flashes there were, until they reached Apollo, and then they were completely gone. Shelby took a deep breath and sat down on the ancient stone half-expecting to be yanked into the temple battle. She knew damn well that if something were going to happen, it would have by now, but she couldn't help feeling like a dog on the Fourth of July.

Apollo looked up at the Parthenon. "As often as I come here, it never fails to amaze me. Did you know this wasn't the original temple here?"

Shelby shook her head. "No, I didn't."

"According to the archaeologists working the site, there was a smaller temple much like this one that sat in the same place. Layers and layers of history. Being an archaeologist must be like being able to go back in time." Benny glanced at Shelby, but said nothing. "Ah, well," the little man said slapping a hand on his thigh and standing up. "I suppose we should get going. More to see in the city." Obediently, Shelby and Benny rose to go.

Apollo led them back down the path, pausing for a moment to point out the ancient Agora market in the valley below. What once was a bustling hub of ancient Athenian commerce now looked like a giant Lego set that had been scattered across a playroom. At the base of the Acropolis, they climbed back into Apollo's tiny car and weaved through the city to their next stop.

CHAPTER 18

The further they got from the Parthenon, the more the duality began to set in. Now and again, they would turn a corner and the Acropolis would come into view and give her some relief. "Almost there, now," Apollo said over his shoulder to Shelby who had chosen to let Benny sit in front where there was more leg room.

Shelby nodded but said nothing. Her hands in her lap were stinging badly and the sparks began leaping from her fingertips to the bracelet. Seshat was trying to get her attention but she didn't know why. Something here was familiar.

Soon, their destination loomed into view. Standing almost sixty feet in the air, it was hard to miss. Getting out of the car, Shelby let her gaze drift the full height of the massive columns in front of her. "Holy shit."

Apollo nodded and helped her out of the backseat seemingly oblivious to the sparks dancing along her wrist. "Indeed. It was once considered one of the wonders of the ancient world. Welcome, Shelby, to the Temple of Olympian Zeus."

Shelby lost her balance slightly and rocked back a step before catching herself. Benny's arm went to her waist to steady her. "Okay, bella?" Apollo raised an eyebrow.

"I'm fine. Thanks. Just a little dizzying looking that high up." She wrapped her arm around Benny as much to steady herself as to hide the increasing flood of sparks around her hands.

"Come," Apollo said, "it's even better up close." Off went the tiny man to the colossal temple, tugging at the waistband of his sagging pants. If she hadn't been feeling so strangely, Shelby would have had a hard time keeping her giggling in check.

Benny was awe-struck. "Just look at the size of those columns."

"Impressive, isn't it?" Apollo asked leading them towards the monument. "Can you imagine what it must have looked like when all the columns stood here? There were once one hundred and four of them. Now, only fifteen remain. Well, sixteen counting that one." He pointed to one side of the property where a column whose marble discs it was made of lay on the ground like fallen dominoes.

"What happened to that one?" Shelby asked.

"Wind storm. I know, seems unlikely that wind could topple one of these, but there it is. Nature will have her way, I suppose," Apollo said with a sigh.

Shelby had been fighting a strange mix of feelings since she got out of the car and was struggling to think clearly. Once more, she felt as though she was floating just above her body watching herself go through the movements of walking and talking. The three of them approached the temple and Shelby felt the air around her, that had been still and cool, begin to shift. Warm air floated around her as the temple started to shimmer. There was a pulse of music and shouts in the distance. She tried to look around to see where the sounds were coming from. Turning her head back to the monument, the white light flooded over her and electricity shot up from the ground through her body. When the light subsided, Shelby could see throngs of people gathered around cheering. There were ribbons streaming from tall poles in the crowd, music playing, and delicious smells of street food. It was a celebration, but for what?

She stood at the base of the colossal temple looking up at the complete structure. It was staggeringly huge and equally beautiful.

"Come, my beauty, the people won't wait forever," said a familiar voice behind her. Shelby spun around and saw a face she knew well. Strong jaw, straight nose, dark curls, and the laurel crown. Hadrian.

"What?" she asked stupidly. "I don't understand." She couldn't wrap her head around what she was seeing. She was in Greece. What the hell was Hadrian doing here?

"The dedication ceremony, beauty. It's time." Hadrian linked her arm through his and walked her up to the front of the temple into the shadow of one of the massive columns. He lifted her hair and kissed her neck. A shiver ran through her but she was oddly not horrified. Somehow, in the midst of the time warping insanity, there was something almost nice about seeing a familiar face, even if it was a lecherous emperor. As Hadrian kissed her again, she saw a dark look on the face of a young man over the emperor's shoulder. With a nod, Hadrian left her in the shadows to preside over the ceremony.

The noise of the crowd swelled as he took his place with the priests. He was in his element. Adored. Worshipped. A stately woman was standing beside Hadrian, but was completely disinterested in anything he was saying as he commanded the attention of the throng of Greeks. Her eyes drifted toward a younger man standing to one side making a pathetic attempt to be inconspicuous. Her lover. It had to be.

The young man who had been glaring at Shelby since Hadrian kissed her could no longer control his tongue. "What do you think you're doing?" he hissed at her.

"Excuse me? Who the hell are you?" she shot back.

"Don't play coy, harlot! How dare you try to take the place of Antinous. Barely cold in his grave and you try to take his place as the emperor's lover?"

"*His* place?"

The young man was getting angrier and Shelby was getting fed up with his insolence. The storm in his eyes raged. "You may warm his bed, but never his heart. Remember that, wench."

Shelby was done with this guy. "Jealous? Would *you* rather warm his bed?"

His hand whipped upwards and he checked it just before it flew to her face. Apparently, he thought better of slapping Hadrian's consort and shoved his way through the crowd and vanished.

For a moment, Shelby felt some satisfaction in having dispatched her rival for the emperor's affection. Who was she to tell Hadrian who he should sleep with? Looked to her like the great leader would take it wherever he could get it. Her, the dead loverboy, maybe the angry guy. He was the emperor of the Roman Empire. He could do whatever the hell he wanted.

From the shadow of the column, Shelby watched Hadrian captivate the masses. He was passionate and commanding. They loved him, and she could have sworn he loved them, too. Conquered people or not, Hadrian had a soft spot for the Greeks. As the ceremony ended, the empress was led away on the arm of the young man from the crowd. Hadrian nodded at her, but made no move to follow her. Instead, he turned to Shelby and grinned. "Now, my girl, come keep me company." His arm slid around her waist by way of her ass before leading her to a waiting covered litter. He held the curtain back as one of the bearers helped her inside. She settled among the pillows as Hadrian climbed in beside her. Inside, it was shaded from the sun, but the air was still and close. With one fluid movement, the bearers hoisted the litter up. When they began to move, she could hear the creak of leather and clink of metal as the soldiers marched on all sides of them through the crowd outside the gargantuan temple.

Hadrian gently slid the gathered fabric from her shoulder and kissed her bare skin. "What was young Pelonius wanting with you earlier?" Hadrian said into the curve of her neck as he worked his way up. His hands found their way through the folds of her garment as if it was familiar territory. "He didn't seem too happy. He didn't upset you, did he?"

Shelby chuckled. "No, Highness. He just doesn't approve of me."

Hadrian looked up at her. His dark eyes met hers. His playfulness ebbed some as the meaning of her words became clear. "Antinous?" Shelby nodded. "No one will ever replace him, you know that, don't you?" She nodded again and the twinkle returned to his eyes. "I'm sure Pelonius would love to try." Hadrian pushed the cloth off of her other shoulder and a soft deep laugh creased the corners of his eyes, for a moment showing his age. "Shall we give him something to be jealous of?" The emperor lifted her chin and kissed her, sliding his arm around her back pulling her against him. As he did, the sound of the crowd and marching soldiers began to fade. The curtains that had been swaying with the steps of the litter bearers away from the Olympian Zeus shimmered and blurred. In a flash of white light and surge of electricity, Hadrian was gone and Shelby was laying in the grass at the base of the massive columns.

Benny and Apollo were crouched on either side of her. "Bella," Benny whispered, "what happened?"

Shelby cut her eyes over at Apollo. "I guess the morning took a lot out of me," she lied. Her hands burned and she instinctively rubbed them, which did no good at all. Benny took a bottle of water from her backpack and gave it to her.

"Perhaps that's enough for one day. How about some rest, then dinner?" Apollo suggested.

Using Benny as a crutch, Shelby slowly stood. "Sure. Sounds perfect."

Apollo nodded, gave her a shy smile, then walked ahead of the two of them to the car.

With their quirky guide out of earshot, Benny asked, "What really happened back there?"

"Hadrian."

"What?"

"He's a pretty big deal here."

"I mean, yeah. There's the library, arch, and all that, but what were *you* doing here with him?" Benny asked.

Shelby wasn't sure she really wanted to tell him, but if he was going to help her, Benny needed all the information she had. "Remember the Circus?"

Benny's expression darkened. "Yes."

"Well, apparently, that was the start of something." Shelby dropped her eyes as if she had done something wrong, even though she knew she hadn't. "I'm sorry, Benny."

Benny struggled to look at her and said nothing for a minute. "There's nothing you can do about your memories," he said, but Shelby could sense he was hurt.

"It wasn't what you're thinking, Benny. Not in that memory. Maybe he never really got what he wanted." Feeling like a total schmuck, she was trying desperately to reassure him, but now he seemed far away. "Benny, please. Emperor of the Roman Empire or not, I could never love Hadrian. I-" Shelby stopped before the words came out of her mouth, surprised at what she almost said.

He stopped walking and turned to look at her. "You what?"

As much as she wanted to say it, she couldn't. Benny was in this mess, too, deep as it was. She knew what the end was, and it was going to be painful enough. She didn't want to make it worse by telling him how she really felt. "I-I don't like the way he looks at me." Nice recovery. Sort of.

Benny took her hands in his and the sparks swirled between them glinting faintly in the sunlight. Benny brought her hands together and raised them to his lips, kissing them softly. Sparks reflected in his dark eyes. His mouth slowly curved into a smile. "I know." He winked at her, kissed the corner of her mouth, and dropped one of her hands. "Come on, before Apollo wonders what's going on."

⚜

Shelby lay in the hotel bed curled up in Benny's arms looking at the Parthenon out the window. The lowering sun made it a vibrant orange that began to fade into a warm glow from the spotlights that came on as the sky began to darken. There was power in that building, even in the crumbling state it was in. It held the duality at bay, but showed her glimpses into another time like no monument had before. Something was different here. Very different.

Benny had drifted off and the slow rise and fall of his breathing lulled her into a calmness that let her mind wander back to the diary and Elijah Faircloth. He had wanted to come to Greece. Something told him to, but he hadn't listened. Not listening to his intuition had gotten him shipwrecked on Malta, but also led him to a memory there. Maybe the universe was more in control than it seemed. But did he ever get to Greece? Part of her wanted to find out, but she didn't want to get up and wake Benny. Besides, she liked being wrapped up in him.

"Well, kid, let's see what you can do," she whispered. Shelby held her hand out over the side of the bed where her backpack rested on the floor. It was unzipped and slightly open. She closed her eyes, pictured the worn leather cover of the journal, and slowly raised her hand. The book nudged its way out of the opening and hovered slightly above the edge of the bed. "Shit," she breathed, opening her eyes. "It worked." Moving her hand over the bed in front of her, she brought the book down gently. Another wave of her hand opened it to where she left off before. It all sapped some of the strength the rest had restored, but not as badly as the first time in Paris.

It didn't take much effort to book passage to Athens on one of the multitude of ships crisscrossing the Mediterranean. After some consideration, I decided to give up on going to Rome. From the experience getting to Malta, it became apparent that Rome was not where I was supposed to be. I was certainly not looking forward to more time at sea, but I had to get off the island. Mercifully, the ship I secured a berth on was large enough to withstand some battering from the sea. As stunning as Malta was, and as refreshing as it had been to find that almost everyone spoke English, something spurred me on to Greece. Perhaps I needed to put some distance between me and the cannons. The vessel was a Greek ship returning back to Athens following trade in Rome and Malta. Her crew had made good money and was returning home in high spirits.

Once settled and heading out to sea, I went on deck to watch the island fade into the horizon. The sea spread out around us like a deep blue blanket, smooth and silky. As far as I could see, there were no swells to speak of. Just glassy water. Becoming more superstitious with all that had transpired recently, I took that as a good omen.

The first two days of the voyage passed in relative quiet. No mechanical crises or storms. After a while, the peace became dull as I became more restless and eager to get to Athens. I began pacing the deck regularly, scouring the horizon for land even though I knew we were still a day or two away. My pensive strolls caught the attention of one of the crew. He was older than the other sailors on board. Weathered bronze skin gave away years at sea in the salty wind and sun. The man was smaller in stature than the others and made my modest height look tall by comparison. His pants seemed to be too long for his legs, but barely made it around the slight paunch at his waist. The buttons on his stained once-white shirt strained slightly. On top of his gray curls, was a black hat with a small brim not big enough to shade his face that was typical of the Greek sailors. He introduced himself, and I had to hold back a chuckle as he certainly bore little resemblance to the Greek god he was named for. Apollo-

"Shit!" Shelby yelled and sent the book flying across the room.

Benny woke with a start. "Bella! What happened?"

Shelby stared at the book laying on the floor. She pointed a stinging trembling finger at it. "Apollo."

"Where?"

"In the journal. Talking to Eli."

Benny's eyes grew wide. "That's not possible. The journal was written in 1871. It couldn't be the same man."

Shelby shrugged. "I know it doesn't make sense, but it freaked me out. The description-"

He got up and brought the book back to her. Laying it on the bed in front of her, he opened it back up and read the pages she had already read. Shelby stared out at the Parthenon. "Where did you stop?" Benny asked.

"At the first mention of his name."

Benny read a few more lines and looked up at her. "The description fits, but you can't be sure it's him from just that. Come on, keep reading."

Apollo, like so many sailors, was a great storyteller of the myths and legends of his home and the sea. Having studied some ancient mythology at university, it was enchanting to hear more colorful versions from a local. Between his duties, we would meet and he would pass the time with the scandalous proclivities of the ancient gods and the humans they mingled with. His tales gave such personality to each of the deities that was sorely lacking in the textbooks. It was as though he had known each of them once upon a time. As anxious as I had been to arrive in Greece, it was with some sadness that I thought of going ashore without so lively a companion.

"See, it couldn't be the same Apollo. 'Lively' isn't exactly how I would describe him."

Shelby half-shrugged. "Maybe not."

Sailing through the Greek isles off the mainland coast, Apollo pointed out locations where some of his stories had taken place, which added to the depth of his tales. Soon enough, the mainland appeared on the horizon as a dark shadow that seemed to rise from the sea itself. Our vessel was nearing the Cape of Sounion and more of the crew began to join us on deck. It was a tradition on board that apparently went back to ancient times to get a glimpse of Poseidon's temple as the ship neared home. Sitting atop a craggy spur of the shoreline, a gleaming white marble temple ruled the coast and sea. Sailing nearer, I could see how the ancients must have been awe struck by the temple. It was impressive even in its incomplete state. There were only fifteen or sixteen remaining columns and no roof to speak of, but the position it commanded on the Cape gave it power nonetheless. I began to see why Lord Byron was so taken with the place.

It was difficult to tear myself away from the spectacular Greek coast to gather my belongings from my berth. Once I had everything ready to disembark, I resumed my position at the deck rail to watch the Greek coast slide past as we approached Athens and the port of Piraeus. As the crew assembled to unload the ship, Apollo stopped to say his farewells. He gave me several things I should see during my time in Athens, but was rather insistent that I venture outside the city to see some of the most enjoyable ruins, specifically Delphi, where he lived. Given his enthusiasm and friendship, I promised I would make the trip and visit him there after my time in Athens.

The bedside clock alarm began to beep insistently. "Crap. That's our alarm to get ready for dinner," Shelby grumbled.

Benny shut the diary. "It's not like Eli won't be here for us when we get back. We don't want to keep Apollo waiting," Benny said with a twinkle in his eye, "just in case."

"God forbid," Shelby said with a snort.

Apollo held the door to the tavern open for Shelby and Benny. Warm savory smells poured out of the place along with a ripple of laughter and voices. Inside, the restaurant was cozy. Soft golden light from covered lamps hanging from the low ceiling washed over the white plaster walls. Dark wooden chairs sat around small tables. Several had been pulled together for a larger group in the back corner. A number of wine bottles and half-empty plates were scattered across their tables. Plates were passed as their voices rose and fell in several conversations going at once. Eating in Greece was much like eating in France. It took a while, and involved copious amounts of alcohol. Also like France, you rarely saw an obnoxiously drunk Greek. The constant flow of mezes, or appetizers like tapas in Spain, kept the alcohol in check.

The waiter sat the three of them at a table in a far corner from the noisier group in the back. "Wine?" he asked.

Apollo ordered a Greek wine Shelby had never heard of, then looked at Shelby. "My apologies, I should have asked. Is wine alright with you?"

She smiled at her blushing guide. "Of course. Wine is always good." With a nod, the waiter scurried off.

The meal passed as a relative non-event aside from the brilliant food choices Apollo made. He insisted they try the most popular dishes that made up the canon of Greek comfort foods. Moussaka, tzatziki, dolmades, and Shelby's favorite dish of fried cheese called saganaki. As the food and wine came course after course, Apollo began to loosen up some. His stories turned from the typical textbook histories that they had been getting earlier in the day to more colorful myths and legends. By dessert, they were laughing at some of the more obscure foibles of the Greek pantheon.

"It must be fascinating growing up here with so much history around you and the stories that go with it," Benny said.

Apollo laughed and took a quick sip of his wine. "No more so than you, Benny. You grew up surrounded with the same thing. The Colosseum and the Roman gods. Same stories, different names, yes?"

Benny nodded and raised his glass in salute. "Good point. I managed to absorb the history, but not the personality of the stories like you did."

"Well, Athens and the legends always fascinated me as a child. They are what truly brought me to the city."

Shelby popped an olive into her mouth. "You didn't grow up here?"

"No," Apollo said, "but was still surrounded by history now that I am older and wise enough to see my home for the wonder that it is. You'll see. We're going there tomorrow. I'm from Delphi."

Shelby choked on her olive, coughing and sputtering for a moment. Benny handed her some water and rose to help her, but she waved him away. Apollo looked at her with only mild concern, and a strange look of suspicion as though she knew something she shouldn't. By the time she quit coughing, he has regained his passive expression. "Sorry," Shelby said catching her breath, "juicy olive."

"Indeed," Apollo said flatly. "Coffee?"

"I don't understand it," Shelby said as Benny unlocked the door to their room. "He has to be the same Apollo from the journal. But, how in the hell can that be? There are too many coincidences for him not to be. Do Watchers not die?"

"They die. Rafeeq's brother was killed."

"He was murdered. Maybe they don't die if nothing happens to them?"

Benny shrugged. "I guess anything is possible. Hell, all of this is strange. Who knows what all can happen that we haven't thought of yet?"

"Why doesn't the little man just tell me what he is? Seems like he'd be a damn sight more helpful if we could actually talk to him about all this shit." Shelby tossed her backpack on the chair, frustrated. Peeling off her shirt and jeans, she kicked them into a corner and flopped down on the bed.

Benny shook his head, tossed his clothes over the arm of the chair, and stretched out next to her. "You could always ask him," he said twirling a piece of her hair around his finger.

"Right. And if he isn't what we think he is, I look as insane as I feel. Not gonna happen."

"Well then, there's only one thing to do."

Shelby raised up on one elbow and looked at Benny. "What's that?"

"Take your mind off it," he said with a wink.

CHAPTER 19

Apollo arrived mid-morning outside the hotel with two cups of coffee. "Delphi is a few hours from here by car," he explained. "Most people will be there early then go into the other nearby towns on their way back. I've made arrangements for us to stay later at the ruins, so we can take our time and do some exploring of the countryside on the way. Krya is a beautiful little neighborhood and they have wonderful souvlaki for a late lunch before we go on to Delphi."

"Sounds like a plan," Shelby replied as she got in the car. Benny slid in beside her, and they were soon winding through the Greek countryside.

Riding through Athens, Shelby's hands burned and tingled, but as long as she was within sight of the Acropolis, she was mercifully free of the strange feeling of being there and not being there. Riding out of the city and into the country brought the feeling back. She leaned on Benny's shoulder and looked out at the changing landscape trying not to think about how weird she felt. Craggy tan peaks with scrubby trees like freckles on the mountainside rose up on either side of them as they wound through inland Greece. Most of the ride passed in relative silence, but once in a while, Apollo would mention something historic or unique about a town they were going past.

It should have been a relaxing drive through a picturesque setting, but Shelby spent the trip doing battle against a kaleidoscope of mental images. The duality prevented her from controlling much of what played through her mind. Flashes of memories. Hadrian's hand on her cheek, Seshat's red lips parted slightly in a smile, the Mad King in his crown of flowers, a terrified child and a torch in Shelby's hand. The last one sent a chill through her. Apollo noticed the shiver and adjusted the air conditioning as if it would do any good. Her burning hands were pulsing with each of the visions. Ebbing and surging with the intensity of the images.

After a couple of hours, they arrived in Livadeia. The small valley town was fairly modern compared to some of the older places that dotted the landscape on the way up from Athens. Apollo drove through the city center highlighting some notable features, such the Cathedral of St. George, whose head was said to reside there after having been returned to the church from Venice. Before long, the townscape began to change as they came into the neighborhood of Krya.

The modernness faded giving way to something more reminiscent of a fairytale land than a Greek village. Small grottoes, springs, and waterfalls added charm to the quaint little town made of small stone and stucco buildings. Trees swept overhead shading the village in cool emerald lushness. Greenery flowed down to the water's edge around the streams and waterwheels. It was the perfect place to kill a few hours while the tourists overran Delphi a few miles down the road. Shelby was really in no mood or condition for sightseeing, but the distraction served to push the images back into the recesses of her mind, even if the duality persisted. Some shopping, strolling, and a good souvlaki later and they were ready to get back on the road.

Nearing Delphi on Mount Parnassus, the bulk of the traffic was headed in the opposite direction on the winding mountain road. "The site closes early, but we have run of the place as long as we like," Apollo explained. "Nothing like the ruins as sunset."

By the time they had parked at the base of the site, most of the tourists were gone. One last bus was loading and a few cars lingered until the last possible minute. The bus group was the usual conglomeration of snappy-dressed Brits, Eastern Europeans in retro 80s wear with sunburns, and Americans in cargo shorts. "I don't know why tourists always amuse me," Shelby said to Benny while Apollo went to talk to his friend who was letting them in late.

"Me either, since you make a living as a tourist," Benny replied grinning.

"Smart ass."

Apollo waved them over to the entrance and launched straight into tour guide mode. "Welcome to Delphi. The god Zeus determined this to be the center of the earth. The Omphalos, or navel. Even before it was associated with the oracle you know, it was holy as the place of Gaia, the mother earth goddess. Much to see," the little man said waving them toward a trail. "Come, come. First we go to the spring."

Apollo led them through the entrance to the site and down a pathway. The hike wound through a valley lush with trees nestled between steep mountain cliffs. Ahead, they could see ruins carved into the cliffside, and bridges and steps built in an area in front of them. A small spring trickled through. Apollo knelt beside the spring and put his hand in the water. Slowly, he let the water run through his fingers. For a moment, he seemed far away. Once the water had left his hand, he turned back to Shelby and Benny. "This was an important first stop for anyone visiting Delphi. Different parts were built at different times with the oldest being the carved cliff arches. The openings were for offerings that people would leave here before going to the Oracle. The spring was sacred, and anyone wishing to see the Oracle would wash here first. Even the Pythia and her attending priests."

"Pythia?" Shelby asked.

Apollo answered, "Pythia, sybil, oracle. All names for the one the gods would speak through. The name Pythia comes from this spring actually. Apollo is known for being a god of truth, light, and art. Few really focus on how much he cared about the people of Greece and was fiercely protective of them. Like most of the gods, Apollo was strong, courageous, and captivated by beauty. Over his shoulder, he carried a silver bow and a quiver of golden arrows, as beautiful as they were powerful. They could dry up rivers and take down entire armies, which made them feared by many.

"The legend says that Apollo was saddened by the plight of the people in this valley who were being tormented in the night by a serpent that would slither into the village and poison them in their sleep. There was so much fear and sorrow that Apollo could not help but intervene."

"Not quite the image I had of him," Shelby interrupted. "Myths always make the gods out to be a bunch of self-absorbed asses."

Apollo nodded. "That's what I mean. So many people don't know who he really is- was."

Shelby and Benny glanced at each other unsure if that was the Watcher slipping up or a language issue. 'Is' and 'was' are very different things where the universe is concerned.

Apollo continued on. "He had gone more than a few rounds with the serpent Python and the beast had always managed to escape the death Apollo wanted so badly to deliver. This time, the god was determined that the snake would cause no more trouble. The problem was that Python knew the valley and its caves so well that he could be almost invisible when he wanted to, making him a formidable enemy. No one could find the beast during the day when it hid, and they were too afraid to go seeking it at night when the serpent would prowl. Apollo knew his one chance to kill the beast would be to destroy Python where he slept.

"So, the god took his arrows up on top of these cliffs and waited for Python to emerge from hiding to hunt the villagers. But Python didn't come out into the open as Apollo had hoped, so he went in search of the monster." Their guide pointed up at the cliffs around them. "There are caves and cracks in these mountains all around. Python could have been anywhere. The god was not afraid for himself, but feared that while he hunted the beast, it would slip out and hunt in the village. He pressed quickly on, searching every crevice. At long last, he came upon one that was larger than the others with a shimmering ceiling of precious stone that glinted in the sunlight. Apollo was too wary a warrior to take chances on being ambushed, so he shot an arrow into the cave. The arrow missed its target and only served to enrage the beast who was coiled inside the cave. Python struck out at Apollo, narrowly missing him, then slithered into the mountain up to the temple of the oracle of Gaia, the earth goddess mother of the Titans. Apollo was so focused on destroying the enemy he had hunted for so long, that he followed the serpent into the chamber where the oracle herself sat balanced on a low tripod chair over a crack in the limestone. Python had made a crucial mistake. He had nowhere to go. Apollo stood in front of him with a shining arrow poised in his bow, and the rock cliff behind him. The serpent's only choice was to fight.

"Apollo took no chances and fired his arrow into the beast as it rose to strike. The oracle shrieked about sacrilege and went into a raving fit as Python's body quivered, becoming almost liquid, and slid into the crack in the earth. The ground shook with the raging anger of Gaia over the violation of her temple. Zeus placated the goddess by making Apollo preside over the Pythian games held at Delphi as penance for defiling the oracle's sacred space with the murder of Python. When we go up, you can see the arena where the games were held. It was quite spectacular in its time, though sadly little is left of it today.

"Eventually, Delphi became so associated with Apollo that a temple was constructed and the oracle became his rather than Gaia's. I'll show you that, too. Apollo's oracle was so accurate that the great and powerful from the far reaches of the ancient world would travel here to see her, making Delphi one of the most influential temples in antiquity." Apollo paused and glanced at the trail back to the temple.

"Are we ready, then?" Benny asked.

Shelby had been sitting next to the spring silently listening to Apollo's story. Her hands burned and sparks had been swirling around her bracelet. Some began to jump into the water in front of her. "Almost," she answered softly.

The water. There was something she was supposed to do with the water. More sparks leaped into the stream. Shelby reached her hand out over it and felt a pull from the center of her palm. Letting her hand lead her, she placed it on the surface. The water was cool and clear. Sparks danced happily on the ripples around her hand. Her other hand began to sting, so she put it in the water. They pulled towards each other guiding her to cup her hands to hold the water. It was as though Seshat was walking her through a ritual using the tugging on her hands. Following the goddess' lead, she raised the water to her lips and drank it. As the cold water went down, the feeling of duality subsided. "Woah," she whispered.

"What is it?" Benny asked.

"The water," Shelby began looking at Apollo, "it-" Damn him. Why wouldn't he tell her what he was so she could say what she wanted? "It's cleaner than I expected," was all she could think to say. Benny knelt by Shelby, cupped his hand, and sipped the cool clear water.

"It's holy water, of sorts," Apollo said as if that was the explanation for the sanitary nature of the spring. "That's what makes it good for blessings." He paused and locked eyes with Shelby. "Among other things."

"Yes," she said slowly. "Yes, it does." Apollo nodded and a faint smile twitched at the edge of his mouth before he turned to walk back to the path towards the main site.

Like the Acropolis, Delphi was reached by way of a processional path that tested the endurance of the tourists who made the climb each day. The last of the visitors had gone and the dirt road was deserted except for the three of them. For the ancients, the arduous climb to the temples must have been a testament to the sincerity of their desire to see the oracle. Along the path, ruins were scattered of smaller buildings that had been constructed as tributes to the oracle for some success gained from her advice. Much of the site had been built into the mountain side, climbing the peak and nestling into nooks and crannies. Little was still standing, but the plethora of stone blocks scattered all over was proof of the number of buildings that once surrounded the larger structures. Small pads of stone and bits of walls gave some shape to the surroundings. High on the mountain was a large amphitheater built into the rock itself. On a large flat space, there was an arena where the Pythian games were held. "They would have had similar events to the ancient Olympics in Athens. All designed to demonstrate the perfection and strength of the human body. The Classical Greeks were fascinated with the balance and beauty of the body," Apollo explained. "Much like the Romans of the time," he added for Benny's benefit.

"They picked a hell of a spot for it," Shelby said looking out over the mountains and valleys surrounding the site. Delphi was perched high on Mount Parnassus looking out at mountaintops that were becoming shrouded in mist as the sun began to drop behind the taller peaks bringing a coolness to the valleys. Below was an expanse of olive trees carpeting the valley in a deep soft green. The mountains seemed to intertwine with each other, twisting around like lovers, rather than the line of rock Shelby often associated with mountain ranges. "It's staggering."

"One thing the ancients knew how to do was inspire awe," Apollo said with a grin.

They spent some time wandering the grounds as the sun sank lower in the sky. Deep orange rays hit the stones and illuminated them in a warm glow. Long shadows were cast from the few remaining columns on the large temple. Since the site wasn't open at night, there were no massive flood lights like the Parthenon's. Benny was the first to realize how dark it was getting. "Should we start heading down? Might be tricky in the dark."

Apollo shook his head. "No need." He opened his pack and pulled out two flashlights. "With the moon and these, we'll be fine. I know these hills better than the streets of Athens." He smiled and led them toward the temple of Apollo. "I'm a little partial to this one," he said pointing up the hillside.

Apollo bustled off ahead and Shelby caught Benny's arm. "Do you find it strange that he would want to be here after dark?"

Benny nodded. "Without lights, there's nothing to see. No reason to be here. He's up to something."

"My thoughts exactly."

"Can you feel anything?" Benny asked.

Shelby shook her head. "Not anymore. I felt strange on the drive all the way up here. Right up until I drank the water at the spring. Then, everything came into focus."

Apollo was stopped under the columns of the temple waiting for the two of them to catch up. "Come, come," he called down clicking on his flashlight. "There's more to see."

Shelby and Benny exchanged looks and trudged up the hill. Dusk was descending heavily into darkness and the night creatures were making noise in the hills. The air cooled, and mist rose from the hillside. Wildflowers that grew between the scattered stones dampened with dew drops and faded from cheerful color to dull silhouettes in the moonlight. As they made their way up to the platform where Apollo was, he began moving towards the center of the temple footprint. It was long, rectangular, and would have dominated the landscape in its prime. The crumbling remaining columns stood at what would have been a spectacular temple entrance. Apollo hopped along the stones towards the center, jumping deftly from one block to another, his flashlight bobbing along with him. Shelby and Benny did their best to follow in what little light there was from the moon.

"He's pretty spry for an old guy," Benny said almost missing the block he was jumping to.

Apollo and his light dropped out of sight in the center of the temple floor. "Apollo!" Shelby called. No answer. "Apollo! Are you okay?" she shouted. Nothing. With a nervous look at Benny, they picked up their pace. "Good lord, what if he's hurt? How would we get help out here?"

"He seemed to know where he was going, though. Odd," Benny said as he leaped over a large gap in the stones.

Ahead, they could see the place where Apollo dropped. In the moonlight, it was a dark space in the floor. As they got nearer to it, a light shone up from one corner of the hole, then another and another until the space was filled with warm flickering light. "What the hell?" Shelby whispered.

She and Benny came to a stop at the edge of the space in the floor of the temple. Torches burning brightly lined the inside of the space. Strange shadows danced around them as the flames threw light on the ruins above. "It must be at least two stories down," Benny said.

Shelby's hands burned painfully and sparks flew around her wrist and the bracelet. "I've seen this before," she whispered.

"Where?" Benny asked.

"Eli's journal. The map at the beginning. It was Delphi." She looked up from the hole in the ground to the semi-circle in the hillside. Then, to the columns standing behind her. "It was the temple. And everything around it. He even had this hole in the floor." Shelby tugged her backpack off, and dropped it on the stone next to her. Crouching down, she yanked open the zipper and grabbed the journal. Searing pain ripped through her hands as she touched it. She tossed it on the ground, and passed her hand over it. The pages fluttered and settled on the page with the map. "There it is," she whispered. It was crudely drawn, but it was definitely the ruins of Delphi. "Apollo?" Shelby called again into the opening below.

"I don't think our peculiar little friend is hurt," Benny said.

"I don't think so either. I just want to know what the hell is going on. Come on." Shelby looked around for a path down into the hole and began picking her way through the stones with Benny behind her. They clung to gaps in the rocks and worked their way down. Pebbles, knocked loose as they went, bounced down to the floor below. As they descended into the light toward the bottom of the opening, the walls began to shimmer and change. *No, god damn it*, Shelby thought. *Not now. Not here.* The light in the temple floor had been real enough. She wanted to know what was happening and wanted nothing to do with a memory. Her hands buzzed wildly and sparks poured from her fingertips as she gripped the stone wall. Shelby whipped her head around to look behind her and saw Benny. "Wait, if you're here-"

"I see it, too. It's changing," he answered.

The further down they went, the more the temple was transforming from dilapidated ruins to former glory. Carvings and color appeared on the walls. Stones slid heavily into place forming a floor. Running water began to flow in thin channels carved into the stones. Above their heads a roof shimmered into place held up by massive Doric columns. Then, more stones moved into place above their heads, sealing them into the sunken stone chamber.

"What the *hell is going on?*" Shelby hissed as Benny came to a stop beside her in the center of the chamber that was still reverberating with the sounds of settling stones.

A soft lilting voice answered from behind them. "Maybe I can help."

CHAPTER 20

Shelby spun around to face the owner of the voice and her mouth dropped open. "Dina!" Standing in front of her, dressed in a long toga wrapped in gold cord, was her boss. "Is this your idea of a joke?" Shelby demanded.

Dina smiled. "No, Shelby. Quite the contrary."

Benny's eyes widened as he looked at the woman standing before him. "Delphine Temple," he whispered. "The temple at Delphi."

She smiled again. "That's right. Nice to finally meet you face-to-face, Benny."

"Wait a minute, Dina," Shelby said. "You mean all this time you were controlling all of this? You *knew* what was happening to me?"

Dina moved towards them, walking with a liquid grace that seemed more ethereal than usual, even for her. "I knew. I always knew."

"How?" Shelby asked.

"It's her job to know," a familiar voice answered. The voice belonged to their guide Apollo, but the man stepping out of the shadows was not the same one. He was tall, young, and perfectly built, like a statue. Dark curls framed his face and he wore a short toga, also wrapped in gold cord. "She's my Pythia."

Dina nodded. "Shelby, I believe you've already met Apollo."

Benny stammered for a minute and finally got out, "Holy shit. She was right."

Apollo chuckled. His voice was gradually taking on a richness it didn't have before when he was the paunchy little old man. "She was right, indeed. And she knows even more than that."

Shelby thought for a minute, then realized she knew absolutely nothing at all at this point. Everything she ever thought she knew had just been turned upside down. "*You're* the Oracle of Delphi?" Dina gave a slight bow of acknowledgement. "No. That can't be right." She looked from Dina to Apollo and back again. "No. He's wrong. None of this makes any sense. I don't know anything. Nothing at all." Shelby was starting to panic and wasn't sure why. As strange as her memories were, she had come to understand them and fear them less. But this. This was a whole other level of crazy.

"Think, Shelby," Dina said softly. "Think about what you've learned. What Elijah Faircloth learned."

"Wait," Benny interjected. "You know about *him*, too?"

"Of course," Dina said. "I watched his journey in visions, like all the Travelers. He was a handsome one, too. Fair, brilliant blue eyes."

Shelby stared at her. "You've been around that long? I thought the sybils, Pythias, whatever the hell they are, were human."

Apollo walked over to Shelby. "They are. Dina's very much human, just not necessarily mortal. It's a fine line. She has the choice to stay with me or not. As long as she chooses to stay, she lives."

"And if she chooses to leave?" Benny asked.

"She will die."

Benny shook his head. "Not much of a choice, then, is it?"

"The job does have its perks," Dina said, "even if there isn't much of a retirement plan." She chuckled, then turned her attention back to the matter at hand. "What have you learned from all of this, Shelby?"

"Elijah learned about leadership in a crisis on his journey. I learned about civil savagery in leadership from Hadrian and compassion in Toledo and Paris. But how do they connect?"

"What did Seshat tell you?" Dina asked.

"That I have to find my way to the life I was meant to live. That until I did, I would watch great things happen instead of making great things happen."

"Good girl," Apollo said. "And the lessons learned are how you make great things happen."

Shelby's forehead knit as she thought. "They may be good qualities to have, but they damn sure don't tell me what I'm supposed to be doing."

Apollo shrugged as if it all made perfect sense. "You'll know when the time comes."

"But how do I find my time?"

Dina smiled at as if she were looking at a child. "You know the answer to that, too. Eli told you what you need to know."

Shelby thought back through the journal. His conversation with Thoth. "*The sages caution the Traveler. The serpent rests in the sweet breath of the god of truth and light. The Traveler follows the serpent.*"

"Serpent. Python?" Benny asked.

Apollo's chiseled face softened into a grin. "Now, we're getting somewhere."

"So, that's what all that was about at the spring," Shelby said. "And here I was thinking you were rambling."

"Not true," Apollo said. "You knew there was more to it."

He was right, of course. She had known there was something but she hadn't put anything together until just now. "What about the sages?" she asked.

Apollo walked over to the wall and casually leaned against it. "You see," he began, "long ago, there were carvings on the front of this temple. Words of wisdom, one might call them. Sages, or wise men, used them as cautions for anyone attempting to use the oracle for purposes that were less than noble. Cautions. Yet, one was specific to the Travelers. '*Know thyself.*'"

"Shelby," Dina said, "until you know yourself, you can't possibly find your destiny. That's the journey of a Traveler. When you learn what you need to learn, you will find your way back."

Shelby paced the stone room and thought. Dina and Apollo said nothing, letting her come to things in her own time. "But I didn't find my way home. You brought me here, Dina," she said at last.

"When it was time, yes. But only once you knew what you needed to for what you were meant to do."

Benny was standing in the corner absently running his finger along a crack in the stone. His eyes glistened in the torchlight. Shelby knew what he was thinking and she ached for him, but couldn't say what she wanted to. Not yet. She turned her attention to the god and the Pythia. "The sage and the serpent I get. But the instructions said the serpent rests in the 'sweet breath of the god of truth and light.' Apollo, I assume that god is you?" He nodded. Shelby ran her hand through the front of her hair, pushing it back from her face. "How the hell has my life gotten to the point that I just stand here having conversations with ancient gods like it's no big deal?"

Apollo grinned. "I wouldn't say it's no big deal."

Shelby wheeled around to face him. "Great. Another smart-ass immortal. Sorry. What does the first part mean? *'The sweet breath'* thing?"

Dina said, "I can answer that part for you." She led Shelby to a small stool with three legs in the center of the floor. "Sit down." Shelby sat tentatively. "Close your eyes. What do you notice?"

Shelby closed her eyes and sat still. From below, there came a faint sweet smell. "It's sweet."

"Good. Take a slow breath."

Shelby inhaled, filling her lungs with the vapors rising through the floor. Static images flashed into her mind. The siege of the temples in Athens. The invaders. As she breathed, the images were set in motion, slowly at first. The battle happened as if it was underwater. No, a dance. Swords rose and fell. Bodies turned and leaped. Muscles tensed. Faces cringed. Graceful. Savage.

Then, with more breaths, the pace quickened to a frenzy. Shouts, screams, blood. Athens was losing. The beauty of the temples was being looted and destroyed. Statues thrown to the ground, pottery shattered, metalwork melted down. Everything that made Athens sophisticated and civilized was being obliterated by brutality. As she watched, Shelby's hands burned with every crash of a vase or clank of sword on armor. Anger and sadness battled for the forefront of her emotions until she could take no more. Her eyes flew open and she stared wildly at Dina. "No. That can't be what happens! They can't take Athens like that! It wasn't Hadrian's doing. He didn't destroy the city. Hadrian loved Athens."

Dina knelt beside her. "Find the year. Sometimes we can narrow the place in time by what the people were wearing. How were they dressed? The Athenians?"

Shelby's eyes scanned Dina and Apollo. "Like you. They were dressed like you."

Dina and Apollo glanced at each other. "Classical Greece," Dina said to him. He nodded.

"But what year?" Shelby asked. "And how do I get there?"

Dina looked at Apollo with pleading eyes. His expression softened. "Fine," he said. "Help her find it."

Dina took Shelby's hands, pulled her to her feet, and waved Benny over to them. "Support her. Visions can take a lot out of you."

Dina took her place on the tripod stool. Apollo raised a hand and the torches dimmed. The oracle closed her eyes and began to take slow deep breaths. Dina's tensed face began to relax as she let herself slide into the effects of the vapors. Easing her head back, she let her arms fall limp at her side. After a moment, she began to rock gently side to side. If Shelby hadn't experienced the vapors herself, this would have looked like some sort of sideshow fraud.

What happened next was no fake trance. Tremors began to rock Dina's body as her skin went deathly white. Her beautiful face contorted as her head whipped from side to side, and her arms floated up from the dead hang at her side until they were straight out from her shoulders. Then, she turned her hands palms up. Almost imperceptibly, the oracle began to rise off the stool until she was suspended in thin air several feet off the ground.

The floor beneath them began to rumble and dust drifted down from the stone ceiling above. One of Dina's hands shot straight out in front of her sending the tripod stool skidding across the floor. Underneath her floating body, the stones parted revealing a hairline crack in the earth that began to widen until it was several feet across. Dina's trembling began to subside and a trickle of blood ran out of the corner of her mouth. Apollo reached out over the chasm and gathered the oracle in his arms. Tenderly, the god pushed her hair out of her face, wiped the blood away with his finger, and kissed her. When he moved back, a rush of air filled Dina's lungs and her eyes opened.

Apollo, still holding her in his arms, asked quietly, "What did you see?"

The word came hoarse and strained, but clear. "Sparta."

"God damn it, why didn't I pay more attention in school? When the hell was Sparta in Greece?" Shelby said, slamming her stinging palm flat on the stone wall and burying her head in the crook of her arm.

"I know," Benny whispered.

Shelby turned her head to look at him. His dark eyes were filled with tears and one slid down his tanned cheek. "I know when you're supposed to be."

"Benny, I-" Shelby began. A sob caught in her throat and she tried to fight back the tears, but she didn't have the strength. They came from somewhere so deep inside of her that she couldn't control them.

Benny wrapped her in his arms and held on tight. His tears dropped silently onto her dark hair as he held her close against his chest. Shelby's hands clenched his shirt as sparks jumped wildly between her and Benny. "Bella," Benny whispered, "we knew this was coming. We both knew."

Shelby shook her head. "It doesn't have to. I don't have to go." Shelby pushed back against his chest and looked up at his tear-stained face. The hard look from him wasn't what she was expecting.

"No," he said firmly. "This isn't about us anymore. This is bigger than us." He put his hands on her cheeks and wiped a tear away. "I won't be the reason you don't find your destiny." He let go of her face and took her trembling hands in his. A wash of blue sparks covered them as he turned to face the god and oracle. "404 B.C.," he said. "The end of the Peloponnesian War. Sparta defeated Athens. War and brutality took down democracy and culture."

Knowing the final piece brought the reality of it all crashing down on her. Shelby dropped to her hands and knees on the floor. Panic took over like a disease. It flooded every part of her body in a cold tremor. Her breathing became shallow and rapid. Stomach churning, she valiantly fought the urge to vomit.

Benny and Dina knelt beside her, but Apollo waved them away. "No," he said, "let her come to this on her own. Let her feel the pain, the fear, the power of it all. It must be real to her. It must consume her."

Benny stood watching Shelby suffer through the emotional punch in the gut helpless to do anything to ease the pain. Tears streamed down his face and silent sobs shook him. The torch light flickered on his tortured face. Dina stood against the wall and watched. As much as the oracle controlled her own emotions watching Shelby, a shadow of fear passed over her beautiful face. Apollo stood statuesque and silent overseeing the process of mental and emotional purging.

Sweating and exhausted, Shelby finally raised her head and looked straight at the god. "Tell me why. You owe me that much," came the hoarse demand.

Apollo tilted his head to the side as though considering her audacity for a moment, then spoke. "Because no one else could do it. It's as simple as that. This is your destiny."

"There has to be another who could do this. I'm no warrior," she insisted getting to her feet. "You need someone else if you want Athens to win that war." Shelby planted her feet in defiance against the immortal.

Apollo chuckled. "Look at yourself, Shelby. Standing your ground with a god. Courage and authority." He took her hands in his. They were strong, and warm. Somehow, she thought they would be cold and dead. "This is why it had to be you."

She looked up at him for a long moment. His eyes seemed to look through hers into a part of her even she couldn't find. Deep into the layers of lives of the past to the core of who she really was. He seemed to be pulling her deep within along with him. Glimpses of lives she had lived blended with snapshots of the raid of Athens. Lessons bled into battles. As she watched the sacking of the city, she felt it more than she had at the Parthenon. It was becoming real to her. Even more real than the memories. There was a power and a passion in the vision that she had never felt before. With a gentleness in direct contrast to the intensity of the images and sensations, Apollo pulled her back.

"Now," he whispered, "do you understand?"

Shelby let her breath out slowly. "It was always my battle. My destiny. It's part of me."

The god nodded and let her hands go. "It is."

"How do I get there?"

Benny glanced over at the two of them. His face was still twisted in emotional pain as he pieced together what had to happen. "Follow the serpent."

Apollo nodded and Dina motioned to the crack in the ground.

"Python," Shelby whispered.

"That's right," Dina said. "The temple is the gateway, and the oracle has always been the gatekeeper for the Travelers."

Shelby walked to the edge of the crevice and looked down into the blackness. The sweet vapors rose up enticing her to breathe them in, but she was wary after the last experience with them. She turned back to Benny, Dina, and Apollo. "How?"

Dina stepped forward. "We will prepare you for the journey, then the vapors will guide you."

Benny's face went white. "Down there? How do we know she'll survive that? How do we know she's not just leaping to her death?" Instinctively, he pulled Shelby back, and stood between her and the immortals.

Apollo, who had been fairly indifferent to Benny's emotional state, softened as he spoke. "I understand your wanting to protect her. You've been there for her all along and it can't be easy for you to let go now," he said.

Shelby slid her arm through Benny's and held his hand. Sparks swarmed around them. "I couldn't have done this without Benny," she said. Benny looked at the floor, embarrassed by her compliment. "If it wasn't for him, I'd have run back home a long time ago and left Athens to the Spartans. I'm not sure you understand how important he is to this succeeding."

Apollo nodded. "I understand, but this is *your* journey. You have to be willing to take this on yourself."

Shelby stood gripping Benny's arm thinking about Apollo's words. Sparks continued to swirl. Seshat said the sparks meant for her to pay attention and there was something she should be seeing here. She knew what she wanted it to be, but

Apollo was giving her nothing to go on. Not that he ever really did. For someone so interested in truth and clarity, the god was ridiculously cryptic.

"I know this has always been my journey. You showed me that. So what? What happens if I don't go?" she asked pointedly.

"Shelby-" Benny started. She held up a hand to silence him.

"Apollo," she insisted, "what happens if I don't go?"

The god looked at her for a moment, considering his words before he said, "The choice is yours. It always has been. I only ask that you consider what your choice means on a larger scale."

Shelby was becoming more brazen as she challenged the god. She paced the stone floor, all the while keeping her eyes on the god in front of her as she spoke. "I have no concept of the 'larger scale.' You've made sure of that. I've had enough of gods talking in riddles and keeping all of the information for themselves. If you want me to do something to rebalance the universe that your carelessness knocked off-kilter, then you need to do something for me."

Apollo's eyes widened as she spoke, but he said nothing. Dina leaned against the wall and crossed her arms over her chest settling in for what should be quite a performance.

Shelby continued spurred on by Apollo's silence. "You're so full of truth and light, yet you've done nothing but keep me in the dark. You lied about who you were. You had Dina lie to me. The only things you've actually told me about are your own story. Things that make you look good. I've had to guess at everything else.

"Well, I'm through playing your little game show," she said stopping her pacing in front of the dumbstruck god. "Either you start giving me something I can really use, or I don't go. Balance your own damn universe. If you even *can*."

A smile had settled on the corner of Dina's mouth as Shelby spat the last words at the god. Apollo was less amused. "And what will happen if you stay?" he countered.

"Who *cares!*" Shelby shouted. Her voice rang on the stone. "Why can't you give me a straight answer?" She looked at Apollo and laughed. "You don't know, do you? You can't answer me because *you don't know*!"

The god stared at Shelby for a long moment, then shook his head.

Angry laughter poured out of Shelby startling the others. "You call yourself a god of knowledge. The one whose oracle has controlled major events in history.

And you *have no idea* what will happen if I refuse to go back to my time! You'd just toss me down a hole without a thought!"

"She has a point, Apollo," Dina said from the corner of the room.

Apollo's angry eyes flashed at her, then turned back to Shelby. "Insolence isn't very becoming on you, Shelby," he growled.

Fear and rage made her reckless. "And what are you going to do? You can't *kill* me. You need me to fix your screw up. And if I don't go, the universe just plops me into some other time frame to find my way around until I decide to do things your way. How long has it been now? Two thousand years? How long can *you* wait? Apparently, *I* have eons."

The god and the Traveler faced-off against each other in deadlocked silence. Neither moved. Neither spoke.

"That's enough," Benny said quietly. His voice was hollow and empty.

Shelby turned slowly away from the god to Benny, showing Apollo quite clearly who was more important to her. "Benny-"

It was his turn to raise a hand to silence her. "No, no more." He went over to the edge of the crevice and looked down. The air rising from the stone below was cool and sweet. Crouching next to it, he picked up one of the pebbles that had bounced onto the floor when they climbed into the chamber. He held his hand out over the gap and let the pebble fall. As it dropped out of the light, the surface of the cavern shimmered for an instant. He stood and faced Dina. "Tell me the truth. Is it a gateway, or does it shimmer because none of this is real? The whole room shimmered into existence, but then, so do Shelby's memories and they don't really exist. Not here and now, at least. Please, I need to know the truth, Dina."

The oracle glanced warily at Apollo, then replied, "Both."

"What the hell does that mean?" Shelby lashed out.

"It *is* a gateway, and it *isn't* any more real than the memories are. Not as you understand reality. The oracle of Delphi has always stood astride two planes of existence. Your physical body exists in one, but who you really are exists in another plane. The gateway is between those planes. It connects one existence to another."

Shelby whispered, "Like Seshat's temple."

Dina nodded. "Yes. The oracle can help the Travelers cross that fine line, but they have to want to." She glided over to Shelby and took her hands. "Would it help you to see it again?"

"I don't see it changing my mind," Shelby answered darting her eyes at Benny.

"Please, Shelby. For me?" Dina asked in a whisper. Benny nodded, and Shelby walked toward the opening in the floor. The oracle placed the tripod stool a foot from the edge and motioned for Shelby to sit down. "Now, breathe. I'm right here. You haven't been prepared to go yet, so there's no danger of the vapors pulling you in if you don't want them to."

Shelby took slow measured breaths as the sweet vapors filled her lungs. Images began to flash into her mind as before. Static. Slow. Faster. Before, she had been seeing things through her own eyes, but now the lens widened out showing her more of what was going on. She wasn't in armor or leading the charge. She was carrying a cloth folded up in her hand through the Parthenon and down the back of the hillside, sliding on loose rock as she raced down. The fighting was raging around her, but she was barely noticed. No one cared about a woman. She was no soldier. She was a spy. As she ran through the thickening trees, someone fell into step beside her and handed her a sword. She turned to see who it was, and her eyes met his. It couldn't be, but there he was. Dark, deep-set brown eyes almost amused at the adventure of it all. "You've looked better," he said. She laughed and raced on, barely slowing her steps to take the head off of a Spartan caught with his pants down. In the distance, she could hear Dina's voice calling her back. She slowed her breathing, and came trembling out of the trance.

Collapsing on the floor, Shelby began to stop shaking. She looked up at Dina, who knelt beside her. "He didn't know," Shelby said amused. She got to her feet and turned to face Apollo. "The God of Truth missed something."

Apollo gave her a curious look. "What are you saying, Shelby?"

Shelby took a deep breath as she regained her strength. "In the visions, I'm not alone."

Benny's head jerked up to look at her. "What?"

Dina's eyes glistened as tears welled up in them. "Then, you saw it, too?"

Shelby's head was swimming from the vapors and she was struggling to keep focused. "Yes, but I thought at first it was just me putting what I wanted into the vision. Knowing that I never felt like I could do this anyway. Knowing I needed help." Shelby paused and looked at Apollo. "I may be the Traveler, but I'm not on this journey alone. And it doesn't *end* with me alone."

CHAPTER 21

While Apollo looked for his words, Benny found some. "What do you mean, it doesn't end with you alone?"

Shelby took his hands. Sparks leaped from her hands and curled around his. "This. Don't you see? She's been trying to tell us all along."

"Me?" Benny asked. "I don't understand."

"It was always you. Now, and then."

"Bella, you are as full of riddles as those two." Benny jerked his head at Dina and Apollo. "What the hell is going on?"

Dina stepped forward. "You're part of her destiny, Benny."

He wrinkled his brow as he let that sink in. "I-I don't understand," he said again.

Apollo strode across the floor to where the three of them gathered. "What did you see, Shelby?"

She smiled sardonically at the god before her. "Why, don't you know?" she asked sweetly.

Apollo glared at her, a muscle twitched in his jaw, but thought better of pissing off the Traveler. "No," he said quietly swallowing his immense pride. "What did you see?"

"Him," she said smiling at Benny.

Benny's mouth dropped, then snapped shut again. "I-I don't understand."

"Yes, yes," Apollo said waving an irritated hand at him. "We've established that."

Dina put her arm around Benny's shoulder and led him over to one of the walls and sat him down against it. His face had gone white and he was starting to sway.

"Sit for a minute, Benny. This is a lot to take in," she said gently. He nodded, but said nothing.

The god knelt beside the crevice looking into the gateway. He shook his head in thought, black curls shining in the torch light. "How did I miss this?" he said softly.

Dina chuckled. "Because it wasn't yours to know. Would it have changed anything you did if you knew?"

Apollo looked up at her. "No."

The Pythia shrugged. "Then, why would you need to know?"

"But you knew. The oracle only knows what I tell her. Usually." Apollo pushed his curls back from his forehead. "When did you know?" he asked the Pythia.

"Officially?" she asked. The god nodded. "Tonight. When I opened the gate. I saw him beside her just as she did. It wasn't the first time I suspected he was part of her destiny." Dina patted Benny's arm and stood. Gliding over to Shelby she continued, "I know Shelby too well. She was always independent, full of sarcasm and self-preservation. When she left Rome and Naomi told me she couldn't get Benny off her mind, I knew then there was something more to this. He wasn't a Watcher, so there was only one other thing it could be. He is a Traveler."

Shelby hissed, "Holy shit."

Benny raised his head and met Dina's eyes. "What did you say?"

"You're a Traveler, Benny. On the same journey as Shelby."

He shook his head. His hair fell into his face and he absently pushed it away. "No, it can't be. I don't have memories."

"I can answer this one," Apollo said. "There are no memories to be had. This lifetime is the first for you. Your journey wasn't about lessons. It was about finding the one you were meant to find. And you did. Well done. Most don't manage that so quickly."

Dina nodded. "That's right."

Shelby went to Benny and crouched beside him. She took his hands and grinned. "Well, you were right about one thing."

He looked confused. "What was that?"

"You won't be the reason I don't go. Unless-," she said suddenly realizing her assumption, "unless *you* don't go."

Benny got to his feet, swaying a little as he stood. "No, bella, we do this together." Shelby stood on her tiptoes and put her hands on either side of his face. Gently, her lips met his, and she melted into him. He wrapped his arms around her and lifted her off the ground. Time seemed to stand still, and with all the weirdness that surrounded them about time and space, maybe it really had.

A cough from Apollo broke the moment. "Well," he said. "That's settled, then."

Shelby's toes found the ground as Benny reluctantly set her down and let go of her. "What happens now?" she asked.

"Are you sure you're ready?" Dina asked. Shelby and Benny glanced at one another and nodded. "Now, you prepare to pass through the gateway," the oracle said. "The ceremony will cleanse away anything that doesn't need to follow you through it from this lifetime." She gave them both a warm smile and led them to the center of the room.

Apollo passed his hand over the wall behind him. Blocks of stone grated against each other and parted into a doorway. With bowed hooded heads, six priests wearing long indigo robes emerged walking in pairs, hands clasped in front of them at their waists. They formed two rows leading up to the crevice, like a processional aisle. One held a small gold bell. Their voices hummed in an eerie minor harmony, broken only by the chime of the bell in rhythmic intervals. As the priests took their places, two women glided out of the opening carrying golden bowls. Two more emerged with white cloth draped over their arms.

Apollo took his place at the head of the aisle of priests. Dina stood beside him. The god held his hands up and the humming faded to silence. The bell chimed once and the two women with the bowls came forward. In the bowl was water and a wadded cloth. A warm earthy scent of herbs came from the water. The surface glistened with drops of oil. Apollo's voice rang in the silence. "Begin the cleansing."

The priests began singing prayers Shelby and Benny couldn't understand as the women set the bowls at their feet, one in front of Shelby and the other in front of Benny. With lowered eyes, the woman attending her pulled Shelby's ponytail loose letting her long dark hair fall unchecked over her shoulders. Then, she gently took the hem of her shirt and lifted it over her head. Slowly and deliberately, the woman undressed Shelby until she stood bare before the god. The woman attending Benny had done the same. Then, the women lifted the bowls over their heads as Apollo blessed the cleansing waters. Putting their hands into the bowls and gently squeezing the liquid from the cloth, the women washed Shelby's and Benny's bodies, starting with their faces and ending with their feet. Once the cleansing was complete, the second pair of women stepped forward and draped the white cloth around them, winding gold cord around their waists.

As the cord was tied, the singing reached a crescendo, then came to an end. The echoed voices of the priests rang softly against the stone. "Step forward," Apollo said. Shelby and Benny turned to face the god, joined hands, and walked forward as they were told. Between them, their hands sparked, the blue shining brightly against the pure white cloth. The torches flickered overhead bringing the carvings along the ceiling to life, or at least it seemed that way to Shelby. The whole room began to swim around her as she neared the chasm. Sweet smells of the vapors blended with the aroma of the herbed oil in the cleansing water creating a fragrance that was intoxicating. As much as she wanted to inhale the earthy fragrance, she kept her eyes fixed on the god and her breathing shallow. The last thing she needed was to dive headlong into the chasm without knowing what the hell she was doing.

The oracle stepped forward, then went to Shelby's side. Her soft hand pushed Shelby's hair away from her ear. "These are the words from the gods. Words that will guide you," Dina said loud enough for all to hear. Then, she put her mouth to Shelby's ear and whispered words Shelby couldn't understand. How was that nonsense going to help? Shelby's brow furrowed in confusion. When the oracle finished whispering, she stepped in front of Shelby standing almost nose-to-nose with her. Dina's eyes looked into hers, through her, deep within. "When you need them, the words will be there and you will know them." Shelby nodded.

The Pythia repeated the ritual for Benny, then took her place at Apollo's side. The god came forward to stand in front of Shelby. "Traveler," he began, "your time here is ended, but the journey is only beginning." His strong face softened as he looked down at her and said quietly, "Beauty, fire, and power. You are all that Athens loved. You will serve her well." Then louder for the congregation, "Traveler, I give you passage through the gateway. May your fire give you strength" The god lifted her chin and his eyes looked into hers. Softly, he kissed her. As he did, the room began to shimmer as it had on their descent into the chamber. Apollo released her, then stepped to Benny and repeated the blessing for Benny, but changed the ending. "May your head guide your heart." The god placed his hand over Benny's forehead, then his heart.

Apollo and the oracle took their places at the edge of the crevice and motioned Shelby and Benny to join them. The priests resumed their chanting and the attending women knelt.

"Are you sure about this?" Shelby whispered to Benny.

"No," he answered, then grinned. "But, I'm Roman, so carpe diem and all that shit."

She rolled her eyes and grinned back at him. "To the past we go, then."

Apollo passed his hand over the opening as Shelby and Benny stood precariously close to the cavern below. "Breathe," the god instructed.

Shelby began the slow deep breathing she had done before. After watching her for a second, Benny did the same. Static images of Athens like before, that began to slowly move, then burst to life. Athens in the heat of battle once again. All around her fighting raged, but she stood protected from it. Standing with her, watching it all, was Benny. His eyes widened as he was seeing his destiny for the first time. He seemed unsure for a second if he wanted to go through with everything, then he set his face firmly and nodded.

"Open your eyes," Apollo said gently.

When they did, the room they were standing in was filled with blinding white light. It pulsed with electricity, but it didn't hurt. The energy was focused on the center of the floor where the light was coming from. The priests and attending women were gone. Only Apollo and the oracle remained. Over his shoulder, the god wore his quiver with shining arrows.

"It's time," Dina said. She took Shelby's stinging hands. "I'm so proud of you, Shelby." Her bright eyes were filling with tears.

Shelby nodded, smiled, and kissed Dina on her cheek. "Thank you, Dina, for everything."

Dina let Shelby's hands go and raised her own slowly out in front of her. As she raised them, Shelby's and Benny's feet left the floor. It felt like going up in a hot air balloon, leaving the ground without even realizing the earth is falling further and further away. Dina pushed her hands forward, palms out toward the crack in the ground. Shelby and Benny moved over the opening. She looked down and saw swirling colors tumbling beneath her, like an oil slick in a storm, but radiating bright sparkling light. Benny held his hand out to Shelby, who laced her fingers through his. Whatever was going to happen to them was going to happen together.

Apollo gazed up at them and nodded. "Open the gate!" he boomed. The earth shook and blue sparks shot up from the crack in the ground washing over the two figures suspended above. Gracefully, the god pulled two gleaming golden arrows from his quiver, and placed them in the bowstring. He turned the silver bow to the side, parting the arrows slightly, taking aim at the pair hovering over the chasm. Muscles tightened as he pulled the taught string back. "Now!" he cried. The oracle dropped her arms releasing her hold on Shelby and Benny as the arrows left the bow and found their targets. In a shower of golden sparks, the Travelers dropped into the abyss.

THE END

SPECIAL THANKS

Thank you first and foremost to Reagan and Black Rose Writing for helping me bring this story into the world. Your team has been incredible from the start, and I'm honored to be part of the Black Rose Writing family!

No acknowledgements section of a Nola Nash book would be complete without a special and heart-felt thanks to my dear friend and sanity-preserver author Laura Kemp. Laura, I'm so glad I have you to navigate the wild world of publishing with! Onward!

My deepest gratitude goes out to my family and friends who have been the best cheerleaders a girl could ask for. You put up with the weirdness and the ramblings of plots and research, and encourage me to keep going. I love y'all! You know I will only get weirder the longer I do this, right?

A special thanks to my mom, my toughest critic and my greatest champion. I'm grateful for her honest critiques of my writing and her support of my research. My work is so much better because of all she does in the background to support it.

And of course, thank you to my kids – the world's greatest guerilla marketing team! I love you! Go clean your rooms.

To the authors who have become great friends and huge supporters, I'm humbled to be counted among you. I'm in awe of the work you do and the generosity of your spirits. Thank you for inviting me into your midst and supporting me all long my journey.

To the readers, podcast viewers/listeners, and social media friends I've made over the years- I thank you for making me and my work part of your lives. I can write because I love it, but I'm successful because of you. Deepest, deepest thanks to each and every one of you.

ABOUT THE AUTHOR

Originally from South Louisiana, Nola Nash now makes her home in Brentwood, Tennessee, with her three children. Growing up in Baton Rouge, she spent long hours onstage or backstage in the local community theaters and devouring historical fiction and Victorian romances.

When she isn't writing, Nola is a high school instructional coach, watching British comedies, or hosting podcasts on Authors on the Air Global Radio Network. She also considers tacos and coffee major food groups.

NOTE FROM THE AUTHOR

Word-of-mouth is crucial for any author to succeed. If you enjoyed *Traveler*, please leave a review online—anywhere you are able. Even if it's just a sentence or two. It would make all the difference and would be very much appreciated.

Thanks!
Nola Nash

We hope you enjoyed reading this title from:

BLACK ROSE
writing™

www.blackrosewriting.com

Subscribe to our mailing list – *The Rosevine* – and receive **FREE** books, daily deals, and stay current with news about upcoming releases and our hottest authors.
Scan the QR code below to sign up.

Already a subscriber? Please accept a sincere thank you for being a fan of Black Rose Writing authors.

View other Black Rose Writing titles at www.blackrosewriting.com/books and use promo code **PRINT** to receive a **20% discount** when purchasing.

CPSIA information can be obtained
at www.ICGtesting.com
Printed in the USA
LVHW041541010322
712306LV00009B/762

9 781684 338962